JAILED

CAL ROGAN MYSTERIES BOOK 7

ROBERT P. FRENCH

FOREWORD

Thank you for purchasing *Jailed* the seventh Cal Rogan Mystery. At the end of the book there is information about the other books and contact information.

Enjoy and stay safe.

ACKNOWLEDGMENTS

I would like to thank Gary Botting, one of Canada's foremost criminal lawyers, for explaining some of the interesting parts of our legal system to me. Any legal errors in *Jailed* are 100% mine. Thanks also to my friend Peter Lighthall. He is even nicer than the character in the book who bears his name.

I could not have got through the publication of this book without the help and support of my Launch Team. They have dissected the book from cover to cover, finding all sorts of errors and typos and providing valuable feedback. They are, alphabetically: Alice Campbell, Alexis French, Andrew, Andrew Stewart, Andrew Tucker, Ann Downie, Barry Thomas, Bob Watson, Cathie Austen, Cindy Warrick, Daphne Osmond, Darlene Hopper, Darren Bourn, Dave McColeman , Ed Campbell, Eva Beaton, Fred M2, Gillian Romain, Ginny Sharma, Gordon Cowan, Hilary Bartlett, Holly Stolarski, Jacquie Howard, Jeff Benham, Jim Bolger, Jim Pyke, Karan K.S Cotterill, Kathryn Defranc, Kathryn Roughton, Kathy Appelblom., Kathy Green, Ken Pitman,

Korinne Tande, Leigh Higinbotham, Linda diMezza, Linda Harbour, Linda Hine, Linda Longo, Lisa Mauk, Lorraine Garant, Marie Igel, Mark Milotay, Mary Roberts, Maryclare Scully, Matt Pechey, Mel Calaby, Natoshia Avery, Neil MacDonald, Neil Watson, Pat Brooks, Patti Flanagan, Peter Lighthall, Richard Pollack, Rock Chick/Feeby13579, Rose Olea, Roz Wood, Tess Nottle, Wayne Bilow, and those who preferred to remain anonymous. If I missed anyone, I apologize.

I would like to add a very special thank you to Mary Roberts, whose command of the language unearthed some errors that no one else spotted. Although we disagree on the Oxford comma, she was amazing at spotting misuse of commas, apostrophes and other errors throughout the book.

I would also like to say a special thank you to Jacquie Howard. She found a major problem: I resurrected someone from the dead! In order to fix it, I had to go back and make changes to *Junkie*, the first book in the series, and *Cabal,* the fifth book, in order to fix the problem.

Dedication

To my wonderful wife Penny who believed in me when I had stopped believing in myself.

And In Memory of

Cynthia Gould, my amazing proofreader, who passed away in November, 2020

ALSO BY ROBERT P. FRENCH

Junkie (Cal Rogan Mysteries Book 1)

Oboe (Cal Rogan Mysteries Book 2)

Lockstep (Cal Rogan Mysteries Book 3)

Three (Cal Rogan Mysteries Book 4)

Cabal (Cal Rogan Mysteries Book 5)

Captive (Cal Rogan Mysteries Book 6)

All are available in paperback and large-print paperback from Amazon.

1

MICAH

Thursday

His stare cuts into me. The eyes look dead. They give no clue as to what's going on behind them; except that it's bad. It's worse than just bad. I can feel the fear turning my stomach to mush but I can't look away. Not just yet. Prison protocol. Not too submissive, not too aggressive.

He stands up and stretches his menacing, six-foot-six frame, never taking his eyes off me.

Beside me, a voice says, "Don't let the Giant bother you, kid."

The words give me an excuse to break eye contact. I turn towards the speaker. He's an inch shorter than me but muscled like I never could be. Blackbird is my only friend in here and has, so far, protected me from the Giant's gang who have it in for me.

Out of the corner of my eye, I can see my tormentor lumbering towards us. He stops in front of me.

I sense, rather than see, that Blackbird is tensing his muscles beside me. These two hate each other. It can only be a matter of time before violence breaks out between them and their gangs. I just pray that now is not that time.

The Giant's nose is inches from mine. Maskless, he blows in my face and leers at me, "Your boyfriend here won't be around to protect you forever." There is an intake of breath beside me. Prison honour can't let an insult like that go unpunished. I glance quickly at Blackbird. Every muscle in his body is tensed, ready to spring, and his one good eye is drilled into the Giant's face. The Giant turns towards him with a cruel smile. "Look around," he says. Blackbird doesn't move but I obey the command. None of Blackbird's gang are in the room but three of the Giant's good buddies are.

Totally outside of my control, my legs move and I take a step back from the violence about to explode. I know I can't escape it this time.

Five long seconds.

Then the Giant chuckles. "Goodbye, ladies," he says as he limps away.

For a second Blackbird and I stay frozen in our positions. I am the first to break the spell. My sigh of relief is audible.

Blackbird finally lets the tension out of his body. "Don't worry, kid," he says, "I have more friends in here than he does and he knows it. We've got your back."

"Thanks, man," I say, embarrassed by the squeak in my voice.

"Let's go," he says. "Gym time."

He leads the way out of the common room and I follow, trying to avoid eye contact with anyone else.

For the thousandth time in the twenty-three days I've been in here, I am overwhelmed with bitterness at the unfairness of it all.

I shouldn't be jailed at all.

2

CAL

Friday

I pound up the wooden steps. There are forty-three of them on this section of the trail. As I pull in more air, I luxuriate in the smell of the rainforest; there's nothing quite like it. At the top of the stairs, I run across the stones and onto the boardwalk, the last stage of my run. I accelerate and can feel my heart pounding. I check my watch. Four more minutes to go; I'm going to break my previous best time. I push a little harder.

Up ahead, I see a student sitting on a grassy patch beside the trail. Her face is red from exertion and she's gulping from a water bottle. Not one of my students but I think I've seen her around campus. Our eyes connect and, as I fly past, I see a puzzled frown wash across her face. No time to wonder what that's all about.

"Professor!" she calls at my back. No way. I've pushed really hard today and I'm not going to slow down now just because...

"Doctor Rogan!"

There is an urgency in her voice. And something else. *And* she knows my name, even if the title's wrong. Damn! As much as I don't want to, I bow to the inevitable and slow to a halt. I lean forward, hands-on-knees, and catch my breath for a moment.

I hear her footsteps on the boardwalk behind me and turn to face her. She is almost as tall as me, very blond, and stunningly beautiful. The tiny v-shaped scar on her chin somehow increases her beauty rather than detracting from it. I was wrong. I haven't seen her around campus before; I would definitely have noticed.

"I am so sorry to spoil your run, Doctor," she says with a small, hopeful smile. She pulls a mask from her pocket and puts it on.

"No prob," I lie. "And I'm not Doctor Rogan yet. I'm working on my Ph.D. and teaching a few classes on Shakespeare's relevance in the twenty-first century ."

"Sorry, I thought you were a professor," she says. She's not the first to make the mistake. Being twenty years older than the average post-grad student makes me an anomaly at Simon Fraser University. There are some full professors here with fewer grey hairs than me. "I audited one of your lectures, so I just assumed..."

"Are you studying literature?" I ask.

Her laugh is musical. "No," she says. "I'm doing an MBA in the Beedie School of Business. I'm Melanie Weston."

I can't help echoing the smile I know is there, under the mask. "So how can I help you, Melanie?"

Her smile slips away from her eyes and I think of Rosaline in Love's Labour's Lost: *my face is but a moon, and clouded too.*

She looks around and says, "Could we maybe get off the trail and sit over there on the grass?"

"Sure." I try to keep the uncertainty out of my voice as I pull my mask from my pocket. I have some time before I go pick up Ellie for the weekend. We walk off the trail and she sits. I sit two metres away from her. Not just for social distancing purposes but also because I must be innocent, *and* be seen to be innocent, of any contact with a student, especially one who looks like this.

She sits in silence, looking at her hands folded in her lap. "This is difficult," she says. I give her time to get to it. "I believe you used to be a private detective."

Her tone frames it as a question but I don't trust myself to reply; there's too much going on inside me. "Uh-huh," is all I can manage. I fight with an almost overwhelming desire just to get up and walk away.

"It's my younger brother..." there's a catch in her voice and I look at her. She's not crying but I suspect tears are not too far away.

I really don't want to ask but I do anyway. "Is he in some sort of trouble?"

"He's in prison."

"What did he do?"

"Nothing, he's innocent."

I just manage to stop myself from telling her that eighty percent of the people in jail are innocent... just ask them. But sarcasm is not what she needs right now.

"What was he convicted of?" I ask.

"Second-degree murder."

So... nothing major. Again I keep the thought to myself. Instead, I say, "Who's he accused of killing?"

"His girlfriend, Kate."

Makes sense. Most murder victims know their killers well. "And you believe he's innocent?"

"Oh, I *know* he's innocent. He was with me at the time

she was killed." There's a strong conviction in her voice. She's telling the truth... yet he was convicted.

"I'm guessing there was no third party who could verify you were together at the time of the murder?"

"No."

"What were you guys doing?" I ask.

"We were just hanging out at my apartment, planning our parents' thirtieth wedding anniversary. We were going to give them a surprise party. We'd even arranged for my mom's only sister to come out from Saskatchewan." The catch is back in her voice but she is still managing to hold back the tears.

"What did the prosecution's case hinge on?"

She gives a big sigh. "The forensic evidence. Poor Kate was beaten to death with an aluminum baseball bat in the garage of Micah's house. The police found a shirt covered in blood spatter in his washing machine. But it wasn't his. The actual killer must have put it there. The bat wasn't his either. He's never even played baseball."

She really wants her brother to be innocent but forensics just don't lie. As gently as I can, I say, "The shirt that was covered in blood spatter, it must have had his DNA on it too."

"Yes, but the police put it there."

"What do you mean?"

"When Micah was in custody, one of the detectives came into the interrogation room with the shirt. Micah told him that it wasn't his, that the size was wrong. It was way too big. The detective said it was exactly his size and made him try it on to prove it. That's how they got Micah's DNA onto the inside of the shirt. It was hot in the interrogation room and Micah was all sweaty."

"Micah may have told you that, Melanie, but I was in the

VPD and that's not something any VPD officer would do." As soon as the words are out of my mouth, I remember what my fellow officers did to me when I was back in the Department, almost five years ago now. I look up at her and a single tear is running down her cheek. It makes contact with the top of the mask and soaks in.

"Micah has never lied to me," she says. "Never."

There is a fierceness in her voice.

"Did your lawyer bring it up at the trial?"

"Yes but the cop just denied it had ever happened and the jury must have believed him."

"What was the cop's name?" I ask.

"Eric Street."

The name is like a slap in the face. He and I have a history. He's a cop whose ambition exceeds his competence by several orders of magnitude. He's the one person I know in the Department who would be OK with pulling a stunt like that.

"Did you talk to your lawyer about an appeal?"

"Yes. I saw him again this week but he said there are no grounds for one. He said we would need to either prove what Detective Street did, or find other evidence that exonerated Micah."

Despite my desire not to get drawn in, I ask, "What's your lawyer's name?"

"Jim Garry."

Another coincidence. "He's my lawyer too," I tell her.

"Yes, I know. It was Jim who gave me your name." So, not a coincidence. "He told me if anyone could find a flaw in the prosecution's case, it would be you. I recognized your name and I was going to call you this evening but then I just saw you jogging. It was like a good omen... a sign."

The hope in her eyes is palpable but I don't want to be

drawn in. I love my life right now. Doing a Ph.D. and teaching Shakespeare is wonderful. I think about what happened in Hong Kong last year and doubt that I can ever go back to having a life in my hands and failing to protect it. "I'm not a detective anymore, Melanie," I say. "I don't want to go back to that life. Let me give you the contact information for my former partner, Nick Stammo. He's a great guy and he's got a good team of people. I'm sure he can help you."

"Please Mr. Rogan, just do one thing for me." I can feel my resolve crumbling as the tears well up in her eyes. "Please just come with me to see Micah, I'm sure if you just meet him, you'll know he's innocent."

I prevaricate with, "Let me think about it."

"Thank you, thank you," she says taking a card out of her backpack. "Please think of my brother locked up in Kent Institution for a crime he never committed." I suppress a shudder, I visited Kent once when I was a cop. It is grim beyond belief. Guilty or innocent, the thought of being locked up there... I try and shake the feeling and take her card.

"I can't promise anything but I *will* think about it." I stand up. "I have to get going now. It was nice to meet you."

I step across the grass and back onto the boardwalk. I start to run and after a few paces, look back over my shoulder. She is sitting cross-legged, looking at her hands.

I should have kept running when I had the chance.

————

I NEVER KNOW WHAT TO EXPECT WHEN THIS DOOR OPENS. Every time it's just a little bit different. I take a deep breath and press the doorbell. I hear voices but cannot make out what they are saying. Then silence. Then it opens and I step inside. "Hi, Sam," I say.

My ex-wife gives a broad smile. "Hello, Cal." She's only using one crutch; her MS is not too bad today. Some days she's in her wheelchair. "El is getting some of her stuff from upstairs, she'll only be a second." She smiles awkwardly. "Coffee? Or a beer?" she asks.

"No, I'm fine thanks, Sam."

Silence.

"How's Tina?"

"She's good. Thanks."

"Good."

It's almost ten months since Sam and my daughter Ellie moved back from Toronto. Sam had suggested that we get back together but I told her it wasn't going to happen. Things have been a bit uncomfortable between us ever since.

"How's the Ph.D. going?"

"Great. I should be finished in about nine months."

"Will I have to call you Doctor Rogan?"

"Maybe," I grin.

More silence.

Then the sound of a herd of elephants coming downstairs.

"Hey, Dad," she cries, throwing herself into my arms.

"Hello, my darling girl."

I hug her so tightly she objects. "Need to breathe, Dad," she rasps.

"OK, sorry." I am grinning so broadly that my face is hurting. "We'd better get going. I'm already running late and I have to pick up Chinese food on the way home."

"Yummy."

Sam hugs El with her free hand. "Have a wonderful weekend, sweetie."

"You too, Mom."

We say our goodbyes and head down the garden path. As I open the car door for El to climb in with her backpack, I look back. Sam is standing at the door. She gives a little wave.

She looks very alone and I feel guilty.

———

ELLIE PROUDLY PULLS OUT THE KEY WE GAVE HER AND OPENS the door of the apartment. She runs to Tina and they stand in the centre of the living room and hug.

"Hello Ganesha," Tina says. Ganesha is the Hindu elephant-headed goddess of success and wisdom. She gave Ellie the nickname 'because she is Ellie-phantastic.' Ellie loves it.

"Dad and I picked up Chinese food," she says.

Tina bathes me in a broad smile and says in an even broader Indian accent, just like her mom's, "How is it that whenever it's your week to cook, you use your phone to prepare dinner?"

"I cook," I say, but even I have to laugh at the defensiveness in my tone. "Anyway, I was delayed by a student, so I didn't want to have to make you guys wait while I prepare a meal."

In minutes, we're sitting around the island in the kitchen devouring dinner.

"How was your day?" Tina asks around a mouthful of moo shu pork.

I tell them about my meeting with Melanie Weston. Ellie

is the first to respond. "You should go see him, Dad. If anyone can get him out it's you. You're a great detective."

"First, I'm not a detective anymore—"

"Once a detective always a detective," she interrupts.

"Secondly, I don't even know if he's innocent."

"Yes, but what if he is?" Tina says.

It surprises me. Tina has been very supportive of my switch to academia. Especially after what happened in Hong Kong last year. "There are a lot of people locked up in Canadian prisons wrongfully," she continues. "It's not as bad as in the US but still more than there should be. A year ago I did an article on Innocence Canada. They've done an amazing job of getting people out of jail who've been wrongly convicted. I've been thinking of doing a follow-up article. Maybe you should at least go and see him."

"Maybe I should just refer her to Nick," I say. My former partner would love something different from the missing-person and wayward-spouse cases which are the bread and butter of Stammo Rogan Investigations.

Tina chuckles. "You know Nick... He's going to say 'can she afford our fees?'" She does a pretty good impression of Nick using his grumpy voice. "I think *you* should check it out."

I can feel something growing in my gut, something I thought was dead. Something I hoped was dead. My career as a detective has somehow managed to endanger the people in my life. I never want that to happen again. Tina, Ellie and Sam are just too important to me. My life at SFU is wonderful and I love it but...

Who am I kidding? Ellie's right: once a detective, always a detective. A big part of me wanted Tina to nix the idea but now that she's supportive of it, a bigger part of me knows just how much I want to investigate Melanie Weston's story. Not just want, need.

"You guys are right," I say. "I'll do it."

Ellie laughs. "Of course we're right. I'm the goddess of wisdom after all, right Tina?"

I think of Melanie Weston, sitting on the patch of grass beside the trail, head down, looking at her hands in her lap... and I feel a little better.

Then I look up at Ellie and Tina laughing, which makes me feel better still.

3

CAL

Sunday, nine days later

The clang of the door closing behind us sends a shudder through me. But for the most amazing luck, I would be a resident here. Maybe I even *should* be a resident here. We are locked into one of the units at Kent Institution; the unit houses about a hundred high-security prisoners. The most famous inmate at Kent is Robert Picton, BC's most prolific serial killer, who had a habit of killing sex workers and feeding their remains to the pigs on his farm. He claims to have killed forty-nine women. He'll be a resident here, or somewhere in the federal prison system, until he's at least eighty-six years old.

If Micah Weston is innocent, as his sister claims, he must be living a life of hell.

The guard walks us to the next door which leads to the common area. "Remember," he says, "if you feel in danger at any time, just hit the button on that alarm and we'll be there pronto." The device he is referring to is the only thing in my pocket. All my possessions are sitting in a plastic box at the reception area. I touch the outside of my pants. I can feel the outline of the button. I want to ask him how quickly the guards can respond if I hit it, but think better of it. "The prisoner is sitting at a table in the corner," he says. He turns to Melanie. "Just ignore the things the other prisoners say, Miss." His eyes crinkle as he smiles at her under his mask. "We've never had a case of a woman visitor being physically harmed."

Her eyes return his smile. "I've been here before, I know what to expect."

He unlocks and opens the door so we can step inside.

On my previous visit to Kent, when I was still with the VPD, I met with a prisoner in a room at the main building. This is the first time I've been in a unit's common room. In some ways, it's a cliché. There are about twenty men, sporting thousands of dollars worth of tattoos, standing or sitting around, talking, laughing or watching TV. Few are wearing masks. Most of them look like their principal obsession is pumping iron. One prisoner glances in our direction and his eyes drill into Melanie. "Alright!" he says. "Hel-looooo, baby."

His exclamation draws the attention of the others and half the room erupts into a cacophony of catcalls and whistles accompanied by a not-very-inventive array of lewd gestures.

"Don't hesitate to press the button if you feel threatened," the guard repeats as he makes his exit. I hear him lock the door behind us. His assurance that they have never had a woman visitor harmed does nothing for me. All it requires is for one person to recognize me as a former cop and I'm likely to have to learn just how quickly the alarm button summons the guards. For once, I'm glad of the mask. It helps hide my identity.

"There he is," Melanie says.

I follow her gaze. Sitting at a table in a corner is a young man. He looks like he's not a day older than eighteen. He's tall and skinny, with not a tattoo in sight, and looks like he's never even stepped inside a gym in his entire life. He could not be more out of place. He gets up and he and Melanie come together in a hug. They hold on to each other like their lives depend on it and, in a way, his does.

Their embrace raises a renewed chorus from the other inmates and I scan the room until two eyes lock onto mine. Even behind the mask, which hardly covers his huge face, I recognize him. Goliath! It's my nickname for Guy Chang. Six feet six inches of malevolence, Goliath is a gangbanger and enforcer for a drug gang which I helped to put out of business. My evidence put him in here for attempted murder and weapons charges.

He hates me with a passion.

I wonder if he recognizes me behind my mask. Twice he and I have gone nose-to-nose and I've been lucky enough to come out on top both times. In here, surrounded by his buddies, he's going to be invincible. As casually as I can, I slip my hand into my pocket, take hold of the alarm unit and place my thumb on the button.

Then he does something unexpected. He slips the mask off one ear and smiles at me. But it's not a friendly smile. It's one of those creepy smiles that says, 'Gotcha!' He limps towards us. That limp is from our first encounter when I shattered his patella with my heel. I can feel myself tense up and he sees it. I glance towards Melanie and her brother. She has a concerned look but he is clearly petrified. His eyes are darting from Goliath to the other people in the common room and back.

Goliath stops, maybe five feet away from me. His mask is still dangling from his ear.

I haven't seen him in a couple of years. If anything, he's bigger and that additional weight is all muscle. And he's got more tattoos than I remember. For guys like Goliath, there's not much to do in Kent other than work out and give each other tats.

His creepy smile slides away leaving a look that I can only describe as evil. "Rogan," he says. "What a nice surprise."

I take my hand out of my pocket, still clutching the fob with the panic button, and settle on the balls of my feet. My muscles tense, ready for what's coming. I've beaten him twice before but now he has more muscle, he is way fitter than me, and almost certainly he has a fan base in here who might like to join him in beating an ex-cop to a pulp.

I sense a movement to my side and risk a quick glance. Three men have appeared beside me. Goliath's fan base I'm guessing. All three look threatening. I position my thumb on the button. The man closest to me is missing an eye. Where his eye used to be is an elaborate pattern of tattoos with odd-looking script interwoven. There is a chain around his neck, on which hangs a huge crucifix. He is small but looks very strong. Unbidden, the words fly through my consciousness. *Yond' Cassius has a lean and hungry look; He thinks too much: such men are dangerous.* And dangerous he is. I look from him to Goliath and back, assessing how to get my best shot against four men at once. Nothing computes. If they make a move, the panic button is my only hope.

Except...

I check them again.

Yes.

It's Goliath whom Cassius and his companions are

staring down. I feel my right thumb relaxing, though not the rest of my body.

Goliath's eyes slowly pan from me to Cassius. A wealth of communication passes between them without a single word being spoken.

Goliath looks at me. Everything in his face and body shows defeat, frustration and hatred. "It's not over Rogan," he says. "It's definitely not over." He turns and limps off.

I turn to Cassius. His friends wander off towards the television in the corner of the room. I nod at him. "Thanks."

He looks back at me, face neutral.

A voice says, "Hello, Mr. Rogan. Thanks for coming to see me."

Keeping Cassius in my peripheral vision I turn to Micah Weston. He and Melanie are standing side-by-side, an arm around each other's waist. There is relief in both of their eyes.

I glance briefly back to Cassius, then say, "Your sister was very persuasive."

He grins. "She is that, isn't she?" He turns to Cassius. "This is my friend Blackbird," he says. "He's really the only friend I have in here. Blackbird, this is Cal Rogan, he's the private detective I told you about and he's going to help get me out of here."

"Pleased to meet you," I say.

With zero change of expression, he nods at me and walks off.

I turn to Micah. "What's the story with those guys?"

Fear takes a walk across his face. "The big guy hates me for some reason. I think it might have been something I said on my first day in here. I don't really remember what it was I said. I was pretty freaked the whole time. It was during what passes for lunch here. He grabbed me and was about to hit me when Blackbird intervened. Blackbird and the big guy—his name's Guy by the way but his buddies call him Giant—they're in rival gangs here. Blackbird and his people have protected me ever since."

"You don't know how lucky you are," I say. "I know Guy Chang; I'm the reason he's in here. He is one bad dude. Your buddy Blackbird must really hate him. Normally one gang will only interfere in another gang's fight if one of their own is involved. I'm surprised they didn't just sit back and watch Guy Chang beat the snot out of you."

"I was surprised too, Mr. Rogan. I talked to Blackbird afterwards and he told me that when he came here he found the Lord and that he is doing the Lord's work in protecting me."

I nod but I don't buy it. Members of gangs are not in the habit of doing favours for anyone without there being strings attached, though what they might want from Micah eludes me.

"Anyway, let's sit down and talk about your case," I say.

We sit down at the corner table. Melanie sits beside her brother and places a supportive hand over his.

I look Micah in the eye and say, "Last week, while I was waiting for the Correctional Service to approve me as a visitor, I talked to Jim Garry. He told me to tell you that our conversation is not privileged and to remember that anything you say that is overheard by a third party can be reported to the authorities."

He smiles. "Mr. Garry is such a good guy," he says. "I was sure he was going to get me acquitted but when that cop lied on the stand, there was nothing he could do."

"I know Eric Street," I tell him. "He's a dirty cop and, believe me, I know first hand what he's capable of. But that said, it's going to be difficult to disprove." I look at Melanie.

"Even if I'm able to find evidence that throws doubt on Micah's conviction, the appeal process will take at least two years and—"

"I can't stay in here that long," Micah says. There is terror in his voice. "Sooner or later Guy Chang or one of his guys are going to get me and hurt me; maybe even kill me. I don't know how I've survived in here for the last thirty-three days, Mr. Rogan. I'll never survive two years."

Melanie squeezes his hand. "Let Mr. Rogan finish, Micah," she says.

"First thing," I say, "please, both of you, call me Cal. Second thing, Jim Garry also said that if I can get proof that a key piece of evidence is faulty or that there are other strong suspects—especially if I could get a confession from someone—then he can probably get you released on bail while an appeal goes forward. That's what I'm thinking we should aim for."

"How long will it take?" There is pleading in his voice.

"I can't give you an answer to that, but believe me, I'll do everything I can to find the truth." As I say it, I can feel the old rush. This kid should not be in here. I want this case. I need this case. "What I *can* tell you is that it won't be cheap. The legal costs of an appeal are substantial and my firm's fees are not small."

"The cost is the least of our worries," Melanie says. "Our parents have given me an unlimited budget to get Micah exonerated."

I don't think I'll have much difficulty in getting Nick to agree to take on this case when he hears there's an unlimited budget.

"OK, good," I say. "Now, let's talk about the case." I lean forward. "I want you to tell me everything, starting with when you first met Kate."

There is an uncertain look in his eyes. "We met at UBC, she was in the same chemistry class as me. It was love at first sight..." he gets a faraway look now, "well, for me anyway. She was a bit distant at first but when we got to work on a project together, we both realized how we felt."

I can see he's fighting to hold back tears. Crying is never a good thing to do in a prison. I need to divert his thinking. "Was chemistry your major?" I ask.

"No. I'm in—" He pauses. "I *was* in engineering but we had some mandatory pure-science subjects. Kate was doing chem and she was a genius at it."

He seems to have recovered his composure, so I continue with, "Jim told me her body was found in the garage of your house. Did you guys live together?"

"Not officially. She was in residence but she was at my place most of the time."

"Where is your place?" I ask.

"It's not actually my house," he says. "It's owned by my parents. They let me live there because it's on campus. It's on Newton Wynd."

His parents must be loaded. There's not a house on that street worth less than three million bucks. The view alone is worth a million. I turn to Melanie. "I'll need to look at the crime scene, do you have a key?" She nods. I turn back to her brother, "Your sister tells me that you were with her when Kate was killed."

"Yes, I was at Mel's place. It was a Saturday and we were planning our parents' wedding anniversary. When I got home, I opened the garage door and Kate was there lying in a pool of blood. I ran to her and knelt down to see if she was breathing. That's how I got blood on my clothes. The bat they used to kill her was lying across her chest. I took it off her, that's how I got my prints all over it."

"You said 'they.' Do you have any idea who might have killed her?"

"No. No idea. Why would anyone want to kill Kate? She didn't have an enemy in the world."

He reaches into his pocket and pulls out a small laminated picture. He doesn't hand it to me but holds it so that I can see. A beautiful girl smiles out at me. She looks like a younger version of Tina. "She's beautiful," I say. "Is she Indian?"

"No. Lebanese. And yes, she is, or was, beautiful. But she was so much more."

"So when you realized she was dead, you called the police?" I ask.

"I can hardly remember, I was completely in shock. It was like I couldn't think what I should do, so I called Mel, although I have no memory of doing it."

"That's right," Melanie adds. "After we'd finished planning the anniversary party, Micah went home and I drove over to Kits to do some shopping on Fourth Avenue. When he called, I drove straight over to his place and found him kneeling beside her. It was me who called the police."

"That morning, when you left to go over to your sister's place," I ask, "was Kate at your place?"

"No," he says. "She'd stayed over the previous night but when I left to go over to Mel's she left to go visit her parents in Burnaby."

"Did you both leave at the same time?" I ask.

"No, I left first. I offered to drive her to her parents' house, or drop her off near where they lived, but she said she had some things she had to do first and that she would take the ninety-nine bus and the Sky Train."

"She didn't have a car?"

"No."

"Do you know whether she ever got to her parents' house?"

"She must have. Her brother testified at the trial that she had come over to their house in tears; he said that Kate told him we'd had a big fight. But it wasn't true. We never fought. Plus her parents didn't even know we were together. She wouldn't tell them because they wouldn't have approved of her dating someone who wasn't part of their faith."

I mull it over for a moment. "Do you know how she got back to your place?"

"Almost certainly the Sky Train and the bus. She wouldn't have had her parents or her brother drive her to my house." He thinks for a second. "They might have driven her back to her residence at UBC. She could have walked from there to my house in about half an hour. Though she wasn't much of a walker."

"Which residence was she in?"

"Totem."

"Did she have a roommate?"

"No. Students in Totem each have their own rooms."

"Did she have any close friends there?"

"Not really."

I can feel a nagging tug. I really want to know everything that happened from the time Kate left Micah's house until she returned there to be killed.

"And you can't think of any reason why anyone would want to kill her?"

They both shake their heads.

Yet someone did have a reason.

And I really want to find out who that someone is.

———

THE CAR DOOR CLOSES BEHIND ME WITH A CLICK AND SHE immediately asks, "What do you think, Mr. Rogan?" I don't answer straight away. I really want to know who killed Kate but, if I accept this assignment, there will be no going back. And if I accept this one, will I accept the one after? With a twinge, I can see my new life vanish with a pop. I squirm around so that I can look over my shoulder at the ugly buildings of the Kent Institution. I think of that poor kid in there. Blackbird might be his friend now but I wouldn't trust any gangbanger further than I could throw him, which is not too far. If he withdraws his protection for a second, young Micah will be in big trouble, probably dead.

"I'll have to talk to my partner first to get his agreement," I say, to avoid making the decision now.

"What do you think he'll say?" she asks, her voice begging. I look into her eyes and try to ignore the desperation I find there.

Good luck with that.

I capitulate. "I think he'll agree to take the case."

She launches herself across the console of her SUV and envelops me in a hug. "Oh thank you, thank you, thank you."

So much for social distancing.

But it feels good.

She lets go and sits up straight in the driver's seat. "Sorry," she says. "It's just that my brother is so vulnerable in there. Those prisoners are terrifying. I'm relieved he's befriended Blackbird. I don't know what would happen to Micah if it weren't for him." She starts the SUV and pulls out of the parking lot and onto Cemetery Road. I've always found it ironic that Kent Institution, which houses so many murderers, has its address on Cemetery Road.

"I am so worried about Micah in there with that monster," Melanie sighs.

"Full disclosure," I say. "I've had some run-ins with Mr. Guy Chang over the last five years and I'm one of the reasons he's in Kent Institution. He was a member of a drug gang that tried to assassinate the MP Larry Corliss a couple of years ago. I was the one who took him down. The fact that he knows I am helping Micah makes it even more dangerous for your brother." As I say it, I think about my recent encounter with Goliath. When he slipped off his mask and smiled at me, that smile made my blood run cold.

"Every day, I pray that Blackbird will be able to protect him."

"Let's hope so," I say. I don't tell her how I really feel. I don't buy the religious conversion for a nanosecond. Gang members often claim that they believe but their actions are not what anyone could call godly. That giant cross around his neck could be used for a weapon as readily as for its symbol of his devotion. My guess is that at some point Blackbird is going to require repayment and I hate to think what form that might take. Maybe...

"You mentioned that your family are wealthy," I say. "Has Blackbird asked for any money in return for his services?"

"No. In fact, at one point Micah suggested it to him. Blackbird was insulted and said he would never take money for doing what was right."

I still don't buy it but I keep my peace.

As if she can read my thought, Melanie says, "The Lord works in mysterious ways Mr. Rogan, uh Cal." She says it like a true believer. "Apparently Blackbird went to a church service on the first Sunday he was in Kent and had a vision, a Damascus Road experience of his very own.

Micah and I were brought up in a very religious family and my brother is sure of the genuineness of Blackbird's belief."

Maybe I've become too cynical. I guess there's a time for me to push my own biases to one side and accept that people can indeed change. "I'm glad he's there to help Micah."

She pulls onto Highway 7 and heads west.

"Tell me about Kate," I say, glad to turn my thought away from Kent and its denizens.

She chuckles. "It was a Romeo and Juliet thing," she says. "Micah was totally besotted by her. But they were star-crossed; is that the right expression?"

"*A pair of star-cross'd lovers,*" I quote. "How so?"

"Kate's actual name was Kitana Ajram. Her family are devout Muslims. Our parents are devout Baptists. Neither set of parents would have approved. Hers certainly didn't. At the trial, they denied there was any consensual relationship between them."

Something in her voice prompts my next question. "How did *you* feel?"

"I was worried that Micah would get hurt. I guess I was right, but not in the way I expected."

"Did you like Kate?"

"Kate was nice," she says it like a question and the phrase 'damning with faint praise' springs into my mind.

"But...?" I prompt her.

Melanie is silent for a moment. I give her time. The seconds tick by. Finally, she replies. "I was brought up never to speak ill of the dead. That's one of my mother's favourite phrases. I liked Kate but there was something... I don't know... something off about her."

"In what way?"

"I dunno. I guess I felt like she was using Micah in some way. He was totally in love with her and couldn't see it."

I look over at her. "Using him for what?"

She shrugs. "Maybe as a way to get away from her parents. She'd lived in Canada since she was two and found her parent's religion and their old-world attitudes stifling." She sighs. "Maybe it was something else."

I need to dig more into the victim's background if I'm going to help Micah. "Your brother said he didn't know any of her friends. Did you?" I ask.

"Not really. Kate and I didn't spend much time together. We had lunch once but really didn't have anything in common."

She turns her head towards me and I can see she's smiling behind the mask. "Thank you for agreeing to help my brother. This is the best I've felt in a very long while. He calls me every Tuesday, Thursday and Saturday. I can't wait to tell him you're going to take the case." She turns her large, blue eyes back onto the highway.

Micah must feel like he's in hell locked up there in Kent. But this girl is in a different kind of hell and I need to do this as much for her as for him.

4

CAL

Monday

"Who the hell are you?" I ask. He's the only person in the office and I've never seen him before. Not only that, but he's sitting at my desk, rifling through the drawers. Lucy must have forgotten to lock the front door when she went out for lunch. I feel myself tense up.

"I work here," he shoots back. Quick thinking on his part.

"Nice try, but I don't think so."

He stands up and looks me in the eye. I'm between him and the main door to the office so it's going to be fight rather than flight. Except that his look is more puzzled than aggressive. He looks hard at me.

"Are you Cal Rogan?" he asks.

"Yeah."

He smiles. "Sure, I've seen your picture on the company website. I just didn't recognize you behind the mask. I'm Zeke Stone. I work here. Nick hired me about six months ago."

The name rings a bell. I remember Nick being keen on hiring someone to deal with the rapidly-growing workload. Is it really six months since I quit after the Hong Kong case? No. It's eight months. With a twinge of guilt, I realize that the only contact I have had with Nick and the gang is that I signed some documents, as a director of the firm, relating to the twenty-twenty year-end.

"Sorry," I say. "I didn't know. It's just when I saw you going through my desk, I thought..." Another twinge. "I guess it's your desk now."

"Yeah," he nods. "But if you want it back, I can—"

"No. No prob. You keep it."

We lapse into an uncomfortable silence. He picks up a mask and slips it on, then clears his throat.

"Where is everyone?" I ask.

"Lucy's at lunch and Nick and Adry are meeting with a possible new client."

I nod. More uncomfortable silence.

"So... are you coming back to work here?" There is concern in his voice.

"No. Well, maybe. There's this case that's fallen into my lap and I wanted to talk to Nick about it."

He sits back down at my... at *his* desk. "What sort of case?"

I sit on the guest chair at Adry's desk. "There's this kid in prison for a murder I'm pretty sure he didn't commit. Micah Weston."

"I remember that case. Killed his girlfriend, right? We were chatting about it here. Nick knows the detective who arrested him."

"Eric Street," I say and he nods.

"I thought the case against him was solid. The DNA evidence was the kicker."

"My client—" I stop myself. He's not a client yet but I'm thinking of him that way. "He says Street faked the DNA. I met him up in Kent yesterday."

"That's a bit hard to swallow, though I must admit Nick didn't think much of Detective Street."

"He's as dirty as they come. I know firsthand what Eric Street is capable of. Faking DNA evidence is not a stretch for him."

"Proving it," he says. "That's a whole other thing."

I hear laughter and the front door opens.

"We got it!" I hear Nick whoop from the reception area.

I swivel in the chair and see him wheel into the office. "They want us to—" He sees me and stops. Adry follows him and bumps into the back of his wheelchair.

"Rogan?"

"Cal?"

The tones of their voices could not be more different.

Adry takes a step towards me and stops herself short. "I'd give you a big hug but... you know, the damn virus!" There's laughter in her voice.

"I know." I stand up. "It's great to see you."

"It's great to see you too. Are you coming back to work?"

I look from her to Nick. There is hostility in his eyes.

"We need to talk." He spins his chair around and wheels towards the conference room.

Adry shrugs and gives me a crooked smile. She moves to one side so that I can follow Nick.

This does not bode well for my getting help on the Micah Weston case.

5

NICK

"What the fuck, Rogan," I say as he sits down at the other end of the conference table. The room is so damn small it's difficult to keep a decent distance. "None of us hear a word from you for what, eight months now, and you come waltzing in here without letting me know first."

He takes a deep breath.

"I know Nick. I'm sorry. I should have called. It's just that..."

He leaves it hanging but I'm damned if I'm gonna let him off the hook by speaking first. He takes another deep breath and I'll bet money that behind his mask he's biting his bottom lip. He always does that when he feels guilty about something. I doubt he even knows he does it. It's one of his tells. Damn masks! They make this job a hundred times more difficult. It's so much harder to know who's telling the truth and who isn't.

"It's just that what happened in Hong Kong, what happened to that poor girl and Tina damn near dying... It was all my fault. I just didn't want to have the responsibility for another person's life in my hands again. I couldn't face the idea of another case. I just wanted to make a clean break."

If anything, him baring his soul makes me angrier. "So why didn't you call and tell me? We could have worked something out. In eight months you haven't taken any of my calls or answered any of my emails." I can feel the volume of my voice rising. I dial it down a notch. "It took the accountant two tries to get you to sign off on the financial statements."

"I know, Nick. I'm sorry. It was completely irresponsible of me. It was just that every time I thought about getting in touch, I thought of that girl and…"

Above the mask. I can see a tear forming in his eye. Shit! Only another cop understands the bond you have with some victims. I don't know how many times it's happened to me. I remember a case years back. It was the rape and murder of a young boy. I never solved it. I failed that poor kid. When I left the VPD to start this firm, I thought I'd left all that behind. Fat chance. I know *exactly* how Rogan feels. I let out a long, silent sigh as my anger deflates.

I push the ever-present box of tissues across the table. He takes one.

"It's good to see you," I concede.

"You too."

"So what made you decide to come in today."

He tells me about Micah Weston and I gotta say I'm interested, even if the kid is more likely to be as guilty as hell.

He tells me about Melanie Weston's budget and I'm hooked.

———

"OK GUYS, LISTEN UP. CAL'S GOT A NEW CASE HE WANTS US TO consider." I wheel over to my desk and leave the floor to Rogan. As he tells the story again, I watch the others. Adry is taking it all in and I sense she is on board. She's got a real strong sense of fairness. A wrongly convicted person case would be something she'd want to help with. Zeke is harder to read. He's an ex-cop from Victoria PD. Like me, he was invalided out from the force, except that he can still walk. He was a rising star there and he's done some good work with us but I sense he misses the excitement of real police work. When Rogan finishes, he's the first to ask a question.

"How convinced are you that Micah didn't kill her. Every prisoner is innocent, just ask them. Maybe he's just trying to con you."

Rogan shakes his head. "I thought about that. But our lawyer, Jim Garry, is also Micah's lawyer and he believes Micah's story. Plus the key piece of evidence is the DNA. Nick and I know Eric Street. He's the sort of cop who would fake that."

Zeke glances at me. I wonder if he's spotted the flaw in Micah's claim about Eric Street making him try on the bloodied shirt in the interview room.

He looks back at Cal. "What about the chain of custody?" He asks. Good lad!

"What do you mean?" Adry asks.

"Cal said the shirt covered in Kate's blood was found in a washing machine at Micah's house," Zeke explains. "The crime-scene guys would have tagged it and bagged it and it would have been sent for DNA analysis. If Micah's DNA was on it Eric Street would have had no need to make him put it on in the interview room. If it came back that Micah's DNA *wasn't* on it, how would Street retrieve the shirt, get Micah to put it on and then have it re-tested."

Rogan frowns. "Good question," he says. Damn right it is. I can't help smiling at his discomfort. Good job he can't see my mouth under the mask.

I throw my ten cents in. "If there had been a chain of custody issue, Jim Garry would have spotted it, brought it out in court and Micah would be at home right now. Zeke's right. It doesn't make sense."

"But if it was Micah's shirt, why would he leave it in the washing machine for the crime-scene guys to find."

"I dunno," Zeke says. "Maybe he panicked? After he killed Kate, maybe he just threw it in there, meaning to wash it later, but when his sister showed up and called the police, he forgot about it. He wouldn't be the first criminal to do something that stupid and, thank God, he won't be the last. And remember as criminals go, he's an amateur."

Rogan's frown deepens.

"Zeke makes some good points there Cal," I say. "Maybe he is guilty."

He thinks about it. "Nevertheless, I believe the kid," he says.

"Are you sure you're not letting your feelings about Eric Street cloud your judgement?" I ask. "This kid feels guilty as hell to me." I see Zeke nodding his head.

Rogan thinks this over. Adry looks at me. She looks like she's about to say something but I give her a shake of my head. After a while Rogan says, "You make good points. It's just that I can't believe I read him wrongly. I'm still sure he's innocent." He looks at me. "Does this mean that you're not prepared to take the case?"

"Oh, we're taking the case."

"Why?" Adry and Zeke say in unison with different tones of voice.

"Because I trust Rogan's gut feel. He's been right before when everyone else thought he was crazy."

"Thanks, Nick, I appreciate it," says Rogan.

"It's great to have you back," says Adry.

"It'll be good working with you," says Zeke.

I chuckle. "Besides, didn't you say the kid's parents are loaded and the sister has an unlimited budget?"

I don't want Rogan to think it's all about his famous gut feel.

6

CAL

The offices of great lawyers are usually palatial. Over the years, I have been overawed by many of them. Jim Garry's are the exception. He is a brilliant lawyer with two Ph.D.s and the author of several legal textbooks, yet his office is in his house. He doesn't look like your average lawyer either. His grey hair is tied back in a ponytail and he always has a jovial expression. In the courtroom he is formidable.

"Micah gave me permission to discuss any element of his case with you, Cal," he says. "So fire away."

"First thing, could you send me a transcript of the trial?"

"Sure. You'll find it interesting."

"Do you think he's innocent?" I ask.

"My job isn't to consider the guilt or innocence of my clients; my job is to give them the absolutely best defence I can."

"I know, but indulge me."

He smiles. "Yes, I do believe he's innocent."

"Me too. However, at the office, we've been talking about

the chain of custody of the bloody shirt and it doesn't make sense. Can you shed some light on it?"

"Ah, yes. I thought this might be an area of interest for you. Let me start with Detective Street. I usually like it when he's involved in my clients' cases. He's sloppy and he tries to cover up his mistakes but he's very smooth on the witness stand. Juries seem to like him. Twice I've had clients found not guilty because of him taking shortcuts. Both times I took him apart on the stand and convinced the jury. I think it's safe to say Detective Street is not a fan. I'm surprised VPD didn't fire his ass years ago."

"But how was he able to frame Micah? What was the chain of custody of the shirt?"

"Like everything with Street, it was not completely standard. He read Micah his rights and sent him off in a cruiser to be processed. He stayed at the crime scene and it was he who found the bloody shirt in the washer. He called a crime scene tech over to bag it and tag it. Then he told the tech he wanted to keep custody of it so that he could use it in Micah's interrogation, confront him with it and maybe get a quick confession.

"After they'd processed Micah, they took him to an interrogation room and Eric Street turns up with the shirt. According to Micah, Street tricked him into putting on the shirt."

"Yeah, but what did the video show?" I ask.

"Nothing. According to the VPD, there was a failure of the recording equipment."

"You're not serious."

"Oh yes, I am. About ten minutes into the interrogation, Street's boss went into the adjacent room to observe, discovered that the equipment wasn't working, stopped the interrogation and had them move to another room."

"Ten minutes is enough time to get Micah to put on the shirt." I think about the implications of what Jim has said. "But the jury didn't buy it?"

"No. I suggested that Street had disabled the recording equipment so that he could trick Micah into putting on the shirt but a senior communications officer testified that they had been having troubles with the recording equipment in that specific room for several weeks."

"But Street would have known about the faulty equipment and he could have used that room on purpose."

Jim sighs. "That was what I argued. I had one of my assistants interview the officers on duty at the time but no one could remember why Micah was taken to that specific room."

"Closing ranks?"

He shrugs. "Possibly."

"Couldn't you create reasonable doubt about what might have happened in that ten-minute window?"

"I tried but there were two strikes against us. The first strike was that the manager of the forensic lab swore that the seal on the bag containing the shirt was intact. The second strike was the Crown Prosecutor's argument, which I think is what swayed the jury. He asked why would a detective, with an open-and-shut case, risk everything by disabling an interrogation room's recording equipment just to ensure that the accused's DNA was on the shirt.

"I tried to make the case that Detective Eric Street was a screw-up and needed to win this case at all costs. I interrogated him on the witness stand and brought up his previous mistakes. I argued that he was desperate to keep his job and that he had to make sure there was enough DNA on the shirt to get his conviction. Unfortunately, the jury didn't agree."

I chew over his words for a while and it hits me.

"There is another possible explanation as to why he'd make Micah put it on," I say.

He looks at me with a smile. "Go on."

"What if Detective Street knew in advance that Micah's DNA *wasn't* on that shirt."

The smile slips from his face as the implication sinks in.

―――――

I HOLD THE SECURITY GATE OPEN FOR MY NEIGHBOUR AND HER greyhound. "Hi Martha," I say cheerily. I reach down and fondle her dog. "Hey, Biscuit. Who's a good girl then?"

Her smile is its usual, frosty self. "Cal," she says neutrally. Martha doesn't like us very much. Maybe the fact that Tina and I are a mixed-race couple doesn't fit with her image of the townhouse complex we live in.

She's about to say something when my phone beeps. I take it out of my pocket. Martha sniffs and walks off. It's a text from Nick. *She emailed the retainer, it's a go.* I breathe a silent sigh of relief. I don't think Nick's one-hundred percent convinced of Micah's innocence but with a healthy budget, he'll give it the good old college try.

I hear laughter as I open the door. Today is an Ellie day. She was with Sam over the weekend and Tina picked her up from school today.

After the hugs and kisses, I ask, "What were you guys laughing at?"

"I was telling Tina about Ethan." Ellie spent a while living in Toronto with Sam; Ethan was her best friend from school. He's an all-around great kid with a big smile and a sense of humour to match.

"He's *so* talented," Tina says. "Ellie showed me a video of him playing the guitar and singing *Stairway to Heaven*."

"How is he?" I ask.

"Good," Ellie says. I manage to stop myself from pointing out her grammatical error. "I miss him."

"I'm sure he misses you too, sweetie," I say.

She sighs. "He does. A lot." There is a wistfulness in her voice. Tina and I exchange a glance; she smiles. "Can I ask you guys something?" Ellie asks.

"Sure," I say.

She takes a deep breath. "I know I'm only just over eleven-and-a-half, but how old do you have to be to start dating?"

Tina and I reply at the same instant with "Sixteen" and "Twenty-five" respectively.

"Sixteen?" Ellie says, dismissing my reply. "That's four and a half years. Why do I have to wait that long?"

Where do I start? "Because firstly you're—"

Tina rests a finger gently on my lips. "Let me tell you a story," she says. "Your Dad already knows this; we talked about it when we first started dating." She reaches over and squeezes my hand. "We were sitting in a car on a cold winter night outside the house of a Canadian Army general in Ottawa." She collects her thoughts. "You know my parents immigrated here from India when I was about your age. We lived in Belleville, Ontario. My parents followed the old traditions and arranged for me to marry someone from the old country. He was fourteen at the time."

"You got married when you were my age?" Ellie gasps.

"No, no no," Tina chuckles. "We didn't get married but our parents agreed that we would marry when I was sixteen."

"Didn't you get to choose?"

"No."

"Wow!"

"At the time, I didn't mind. Balvir's family lived near us and I liked him a lot. He was cute and very funny, like your friend Ethan. And his parents were very rich too. But as he got older, he started to change. He got involved with some pretty sketchy kids at his high school. When I moved there from elementary school, he was pretty mean to me when we were together at school. When our families got together, he would be all nice and attentive and friendly. But at school, he would mostly ignore me and if I tried to speak to him, he would tell me to shut up. One day he told me that if I didn't do as he said, when we got married, he would beat me until I obeyed him."

"What did you do?"

"When I got home, I told my parents. I told them that I didn't love him and that I wouldn't marry him. My dad just said, 'That is not your choice.'" Tina does a pretty good impression of her father's accent. "'When you are sixteen,' he said, 'both families are going to India and you are getting married there. That's final.' I was devastated."

"That is like so harsh," Ellie breathes. "But you didn't marry him, right?"

"No. I thought to myself, 'This is Canada. No one can force me to go to India and marry someone I don't love.' So I did some research and discovered that I could apply to the courts for emancipation from my parents."

"What does emancipation mean?" Ellie asks and I suppress a horrible image of a future where Ellie emancipates herself from Sam and me.

"It means that a sixteen-year-old can apply to the court to manage her own affairs and that they don't have to do what their parents tell them."

"Cool. Is that what you did?"

"I started the process although I knew that my parents would be very upset with me. But I didn't want to be married to someone who would abuse me."

"What did your parents do?"

"Nothing. They never knew about the emancipation procedure because I got lucky. I told you that Bal got involved with some pretty bad dudes at school. Well, he and a couple of his friends beat up a kid they didn't like. The kid nearly died; he was in the hospital for almost four weeks. To avoid him having to stand trial for assault, Bal's parents packed him off to India.

"My father was brought up as a strictly non-violent Hindu. Non-violence was more important to him than the sanctity of a marriage arrangement, so he told Bal's parents that the marriage was off. They were furious but Daddy stood his ground. The families never spoke again."

"So you didn't have to marry him?"

"No. But the point here is that when I was your age, I thought that Balvir was wonderful. It wasn't until I was sixteen that I was able to see through him. That's why I don't think it's a good idea to date until you are older." She looks at me and grins. "Not twenty-five, but sixteen feels about right. Especially for a girl as wise as you, Ganesha."

Ellie glows. Tina handled that way better than I would have done.

"How did it go today?" she asks me.

Ellie chimes in, "Yes, how was Uncle Nick?"

"How did—"

"Tina told me about your visit to the prison yesterday and that you were going to see Uncle Nick this afternoon. Did he agree to take the case?"

I look from one to the other. There is expectation in both faces.

I smile. "He did."

"Sick!" Ellie says.

Tina is more circumspect. "So you guys are good?" she asks.

"He was mad at me at first but I think we're OK," I say and she nods. "They hired a new guy," I add. "Zeke Stone."

"Cool name," Ellie laughs.

But Tina catches the tone in my voice. "And..." she says.

"Too early to tell," is all I say.

But something inside doesn't feel quite right.

7

ADRY

Thursday

"I wonder if you could help me please?" I feel awkward approaching the student leaving the Totem residence at the University of British Columbia, but this is important. I'm excited that Nick put me on this case with Cal. My lovely Jason is a bit of a crusader for people in the downtown eastside who have been wrongly accused by the police and I'd love to be able to prove that Micah is innocent even if he is a rich kid. But this is a long shot. Cal wants to know what happened to Kate from when she left her parents' house until she was found dead at Micah's.

She smiles. "If I can," she says.

I hand her a business card. "I'm Adry Locke, I'm a private investigator looking into the death of a student here, Kate Ajram."

She frowns. "Wasn't she the one who was killed by her boyfriend?"

"Yes, except there may be a question as to whether it was he who killed her."

"Wow. Didn't he go to jail for it?"

"Yes. Were you a friend of Kate?" I ask.

"Not really, she was in chem and I'm in psych."

"I need to know what she did on the day she was killed. Was she friendly with anyone in residence?"

"She would often hang out with one of the other science geeks, Sarah I think her name is. She might know."

"Could I ask a huge favour?" I say. "Would you check if Sarah is in and, if she is, ask her if she would come down and talk to me for a few minutes?"

She checks her watch. "I'm a bit late for a lab, plus I don't know how to contact Sarah," she says.

"I understand. Could you just let me into the building? If you could tell me Sarah's room number, I could just go chat with her for a minute."

Above the mask, her eyes narrow. "I'm sorry. You seem nice and all, but we're not allowed to let strangers into the building." Before I can say anything she turns and hurries away.

I look towards the entrance and, through the glass, I see another couple of students come to the door. As they reach it from the inside, I reach it from the outside. One of them pushes it open. I grab the handle and smile. "Hi, I'm looking for Sarah, I'm in one of her chem classes. Do you know which room she's in?" Although I feel a bit old to be a student, they don't seem suspicious.

One says "Don't know her," but the other says, "Yes, second floor next to the stairwell. I don't know if she's in though."

I go inside and find my way to Sarah's room. I knock at the door, step back two meters and remove my mask so that she can see I'm not threatening.

The door opens. She is tall, slim, young and very pretty with long hair and glasses. I'm jealous. "Can I help you?" she asks.

"Hi, yes." I introduce myself and slip my mask back on so I can take a step forward and hand her my card.

"I believe you were friends with Kate Ajram,"

"Yes," she says. "What did you want to know?"

"Were you and she good friends?"

"Yes... I guess. Why?"

"We have reason to think that her boyfriend Micah may not have been the person who killed her."

Her eyes go wide. "Really?"

"Do you know him?"

"I saw him in class, but I only spoke to him a couple of times. He seemed nice."

"I need to know what she did on the day she was killed. She'd been at her parents' house but she was killed at Micah's house. Do you have any idea what happened in between?"

"No, I didn't see her that day."

"Did she have any other friends who might have seen her?"

She screws up her face. "I don't really think so. She was a super-brain and was totally into her studies, so she didn't spend much time socializing."

"She was ambitious?"

"Completely. More than anything, she wanted to be independent and not have to live with her family after graduation. She wanted to go to graduate school in the States and get her Ph.D. She had her heart set on Harvard but her parents couldn't afford that plus there was no way they would let her move to the States. But Kitana was a very determined person. Having a lot of money was a huge issue with her."

"Sounds like she didn't get on too well with her family," I say.

"She loved them but she felt stifled by them. They were like soooo religious. They made her wear a headscarf all the time."

"A hijab?"

"Yeah, that's it. She always removed it in residence but she was scared to not wear it outside."

"Why?"

"In case anyone who knew her family saw her without it and told them. They were very strict. Her brother especially. If *he'd* known about Kitana's relationship with Mikey, he'd have killed—" She puts her hand to her mouth and looks mortified. "I didn't mean it literally. It was just an expression. I am so, so sorry."

I smile what I hope is reassuringly. "No prob," I say. She half-smiles. "You called him Mikey," I say.

Her smile broadens. "Yes, Kitana went by her Lebanese name but he always westernized it to Kate. She loved him so she thought it was cute but insisted on calling him Mikey in return."

I grin. "So they had a good relationship?"

She returns the grin, "Because of her parents, she'd never had a boyfriend. Micah was her first and she was totally in love with him."

"Was he in love with her too?" I ask.

"I only saw them together once but I could tell he definitely felt the same way about her. Also, when she talked about the little things he did for her, it was really cute."

"Like what?"

"He had a lot of money so he often bought her nice things but it was the little things she loved. They met on a Wednesday, so every Wednesday he would give her a single red rose. And he liked to cook for her. He even took a course on Lebanese cooking so that he could make her favourite dishes."

"So they basically had the perfect relationship."

She gives a quirky grin. "Pretty much. I gotta say I was a tiny bit jealous." She thinks for a second or two. "When he was charged with her murder, I had a lot of difficulty believing it," she says.

"On the day she was killed, you didn't see her, or talk, or text with her?" I ask.

"No. In fact, I hadn't seen her for a few days before. She missed one of the classes we were both in, which was totally not like her."

"And you can't think of anyone else who might have seen her on that day?"

She shakes her head. "No, sorry."

With a sinking feeling I realize that if I'm going to find out what Kate, or rather Kitana, did on the day of her death, I now need to put plan B into action, something I definitely don't *want* to do but Cal definitely *cannot* do.

I thank Sarah and leave.

———

AS I WALK UP TO THE FRONT DOOR, MY PHONE RINGS. IT'S AN unknown number. Probably a spam call to tell me the Canada Revenue Agency has a warrant for my arrest; all I need to do is send them money. I decline the call and put my phone back in my purse before I press the doorbell.

While I wait, I rehearse in my mind the story I'm going

to tell. I don't like it but it was the best Nick and I could come up with.

The woman who opens the door looks flustered. She has a scarf loosely thrown over her head and is holding one end of it across her lower face.

"Yes?" she says.

"Mrs. Ajram?"

"Yes."

"I'm Jane Cameron. I'm with Correctional Service Canada." With a big twinge of guilt, I hand her the phoney business card Nick made with Photoshop. For once I'm glad of the mask.

She looks at the card and back at me. "What do you want with me?" she asks.

"Could we talk inside?"

She looks past me at the street for a moment, then steps back and opens the door wide. Something she wouldn't have done for Cal.

I walk into the hallway.

She closes the door and drops the end of her scarf so that I can see her face. Another thing she wouldn't have done for Cal. She leads me into the living room and we sit.

What I'm about to do makes me feel dirty, but if we are going to find out who really killed her daughter, it's got to be done.

"It's about Micah Weston," I say.

Her face is impassive.

"His lawyer has requested he be moved to a medium-security facility." I'm hoping she doesn't know enough about Canadian law to know this is complete BS.

"What?!" she says. "He gets a mere twenty years for killing my daughter and now he wants to be moved."

"Yes. We have opposed the move but if it goes to court we might need you to make a victim impact statement like you did at the sentencing. Would you be prepared to do that?"

"Yes, definitely. I would do anything to keep him in there."

I take out my notebook. "I apologize because I know you have been asked these questions before, but could I just go through some of the details with you?"

"Yes."

I ask the questions Nick and I devised that we guessed would be the basis of a victim impact statement. After she has answered them all, I get to the real agenda. I ask, "Can you tell me about the day of the murder?"

"What is it you want to know?"

Before I can answer her, a man's voice says, "Who are you and what do you want?"

He looks to be in his late teens or early twenties and has a scowl on his face that feels to me like it's a permanent fixture. He is bearded and wearing a white, knitted skull cap. His clothes are black and he is wearing a baggy teeshirt over a long-sleeved cotton shirt. The teeshirt has white, Arabic script on the front.

"Please Haasim." She glances down at my phony business card. "Ms. Cameron is our guest. She is here to make sure that your sister's killer doesn't get moved to a less secure prison."

"He shouldn't be in prison at all," he snorts.

What?! Her brother thinks Micah is innocent.

"Why do you say that?" I ask.

"He should have been beheaded but the stupid Canadian system doesn't 'believe' in that." He says it with scare quotes. So much for him thinking Micah is innocent.

"We live in Canada now, Haasim," his mother says gently. "Canada's laws are our laws."

He looks at her and I suppress a shudder at the hatred in his eyes. "*Allah's* laws are our laws." He holds her gaze for a long moment then without another word, stalks out of the room.

"Excuse my son Ms. Cameron. His sister's murder has shaken him up. I think he feels responsible."

"Responsible? Why?" I ask.

"The morning of the day she was killed, Kitana came here to see us. She seemed very worried about something but she wouldn't say what it was. It was not like her at all. She was never a worrier. After lunch, she said she had to go back to the university. Haasim drove her but they had an argument in the car. Haasim got so angry with her, he made her get out and take the bus. He keeps telling himself that if he had taken her back to her residence instead of dropping her off, she wouldn't have been killed."

Survivor's guilt? Perhaps.

I just say, "It must be difficult for him."

She nods several times.

"You were her mother," I say as gently as I can. "Before she was killed, did you know about her relationship with Micah Weston?"

She shoots a glance at the door, then looks at me, puts her finger to her lips and nods.

"Did your husband or your son?" I whisper.

"My husband, no. He had no idea. But my son found out that day. She told him in the car when he was driving her to UBC. That was what they argued about."

"Thank you for speaking with me, Mrs. Ajram. I'm sorry if my visit has been painful for you."

She tries to smile. "Just make sure that he stays in that jail."

She walks me to the door and opens it for me. As I walk to my car, I look back at the house and catch the movement of a curtain in an upstairs window. I see a face. A young man, late teens to early twenties, is staring at me. But it isn't Haasim Ajram.

8

CAL

Nick savours the lemon chicken. It's his favourite dish from his favourite Chinese restaurant. I took a detour to pick it up because I need him in a good mood. He puts down his chopsticks. "I know it's not morning anymore but let's do morning prayers." 'Morning prayers' is his name for the daily morning meetings at Stammo Rogan Investigations. "Zeke's on the Hillside case in Surrey today so he'll have to miss out." He takes another piece of chicken. "Right. First the Wendell divorce case. Lucy," he turns to our Office Manager and general factotum and, incidentally, his daughter, "you were looking into the husband's social media posts."

As Lucy reports on her progress, Adry looks at me and winks. We both know Nick's punishing me by leaving the Micah Weston case to last. He wants to remind me I've been absent from the office for eight months and so he's going to treat me like a rookie. No amount of lemon chicken is going to buy me out of that punishment.

I listen with half an ear while Adry, Lucy and Nick report on their progress, or lack thereof, on their cases over the last twenty-seven hours since yesterday's morning prayers. There are quite a few cases. I see now why Nick hired Zeke Stone; business is booming.

"Finally, the Micah Weston case," he says. "What did you find out this morning, Adry?"

She opens her notebook and tells us about her meetings with Kate's friend Sarah and with Kate's mother and brother.

"You said you found the brother a bit creepy?" Nick asks her.

"More scary than creepy. He came over as the fundamentalist type."

"What if he knew about her relationship with Micah," Nick says. "Do you think he's capable of punishing her for it?"

"What? A so-called honour killing?" She mulls it over. "It's possible. He learned about the affair that day. But an honour killing? I don't know. They're pretty rare in Canada."

"If he drove her home, he was the last one to see her alive. Maybe the story about dropping her off at the bus stop is a crock." Nick warms to his theme. "Maybe he took her to Micah's house to have a showdown with him. When they get there, Micah's not home so he kills her in the garage and leaves his shirt in the laundry to implicate Micah."

"I like the theory, Nick," I say. "Jim Garry said we need to have one or more plausible alternative killers. Adry's description of the brother would certainly make him a suspect. The problem is, if it happened like you say, they would have found the brother's DNA on the shirt and made a familial match with Kate's DNA."

"But Micah told you that Eric Street tricked him into putting on the shirt to get *his* DNA on it," Nick says.

"True, but that wouldn't eliminate the brother's DNA,"

Adry says. "Both of their skin cells would be there. And I still don't buy the brother as the killer. He was unpleasant, yes, and probably some sort of fundamentalist but I'm just not buying the honour killing."

Nick shakes his head. He's not ready to let it go. "DNA labs are always backed up. There are always more cases than they can handle. When the lab got the shirt, the first thing they'd do is get the DNA from the blood. Then they'd go for the DNA of the wearer. The obvious place to check is under the armpits; that's where you find sweat and hair. They find Micah's DNA, match it with their prime suspect and stop looking."

"Aren't they more thorough than that?" Adry asks.

"They're supposed to be but who knows."

"Easy way to find out," I say, "is to ask Jim Garry to get a court order for the shirt and have an independent lab do a thorough analysis of every square inch of it."

"Great idea!" Nick says, "I'll call him right after the meeting." He scribbles on a Post-it and sticks it on his laptop's screen.

As he's writing, Lucy says, "Why don't I do a scan of the brother's social media. See if he posts anything about honour killings."

"Another great idea!" Nick says. "What a team eh, Rogan."

I can't resist a chuckle. "There's something else," I say. I tell them about my meeting with Jim Garry yesterday afternoon.

When I finish, Nick looks off into infinity for a moment.

Adry's phone pings. She looks at it, gets up and leaves the room.

Nick says, "So what you're saying is that so-called Detective Eric Street tricked Micah into putting on the shirt because he knew that Micah's DNA *wasn't* on it?"

"I'm just saying, why would Street risk everything to make sure that Micah's DNA *was* on the shirt?"

Nick takes another bite of lemon chicken and chews on it while he chews over my words. "You know what? Our former colleague Steve Waters made Inspector while you were AWOL. He's Street's boss. When I phoned to congratulate him, we talked about getting together for a beer. Maybe now's a good time to do that."

Before I can react, Adry strides back in. She's talking on her phone. "Can I put you on speaker, so my colleagues can hear?" she says. She listens, nods, taps on the phone and puts it on Nick's desk. "Guys, this is Sarah, Kitana's friend. She has some additional information for us. Go ahead, Sarah."

"Hi," Sarah says.

"Tell them what you just told me, Sarah," Adry encourages her.

"I don't know if it's important but the last time I saw Kitana, she was worried about something."

"Do you know what it was?" I ask.

"A couple of days before she died, we had a class together but we didn't sit together. Normally we would, but she arrived a few minutes late and had to sit at the back of the room. After the class, she came over to me and asked if I could talk. I told her I had to rush off to another class and could we talk later. She said it was important and she'd talk to me about it that evening. I'm sorry I didn't mention it this morning but I'd kind of forgotten it. I had the same class this morning and it reminded me."

I go to speak but Adry stops me with a gesture. "Thank you so much Sarah," she says. "This might be very important. Do you have any idea what she was worried about?"

"Not really." Her voice sounds uncertain.

"Do you think it might have been something to do with her relationship with Micah?"

"I don't think so. I don't think she'd discuss that sort of problem with anyone. She was very private about that."

"What about her family?" Adry asks.

There's a pause. *"Maybe, but I got the impression that it was to do with her studies but that didn't really make sense because she was so smart. She was acing all her courses."*

"And she didn't give you any clue as to what it was?" Adry persists.

"No, sorry. Maybe it was nothing."

There's another pause, longer this time. Adry fills the silence. "I think it *was* important Sarah and I really appreciate you letting us know. If you think of anything else, please reach out again." They say their goodbyes and hang up.

"Probably nothing," Nick says. "Students are always worrying about something or other."

"I don't think so," Adry replies, "I forgot to tell you guys this. I was so focused on the creepiness of the brother that I didn't mention Kitana's mother said that she seemed worried about something and she said it was unusual for her to worry about stuff. I wonder what it was."

"Maybe Micah can shed some light on it," I say.

"Were you planning to go visit him in Kent again?" Nick asks.

I suppress a shudder. "I'm planning never to set foot inside that place again; not for the rest of my life."

"Well, you can't just phone into the jail and ask to speak to him."

"Doesn't mean I can't speak to him," I say with a big

smile. Slowly, the smile turns into a grin and I can tell it's getting to him.

"WTF, Rogan," he says. "You fancy yourself as a psychic or something?"

My grin gets bigger. I use one of his favourite phrases. "Watch and learn," I say as I pick up my phone.

———

THE VIEW IS STUNNING. THE APARTMENT LOOKS ACROSS FALSE Creek at Yaletown, with the backdrop of the north shore mountains behind. It's a beautiful sunny day and it feels like I could reach out and touch the top of Grouse Mountain. I can't contain the "Wow" escaping my lips. The building is exclusive with a uniformed doorman/front desk person. He called ahead to announce my arrival and get Melanie's approval.

"This is a beautiful place, " I say.

"Thank you," she says. "My parents bought it when the building was under construction; in the original plans it was three apartments but they had it built as one unit."

I am at a loss for words. A rare event.

"Your timing's perfect. My brother always calls as close to three o'clock as he can."

"I remembered when we were driving back from Kent, you said that he called every Tuesday, Thursday and Saturday afternoon."

"When you called me, you said that Kate was worried about something and you wanted to know if Micah could throw any light on it. Is that right?"

"Yes, we've heard it from two sources now. It might be relevant to who really killed her."

"I am so grateful that you and your partner agreed to take Micah's case."

"No prob. I can't stand the thought of anyone being locked up in Kent, especially someone who's innocent."

She gestures to a couch and we sit.

"You teach at SFU, right?" she asks.

"Yes." She knows this already.

"So you've had the vaccine?"

"Yes, both jabs."

"That's great. So have I. We can dispense with these." She takes off her mask and drops it on a side table.

"How did you get it? Are you in a high-risk category?" Ooops, too personal a question. "Sorry, I shouldn't have asked that," I add hastily, taking off my mask and slipping it into my pocket.

She laughs and, for the first time since we met on campus almost two weeks ago, I see again how beautiful she is. "Don't worry," she says. "And, yes, I am."

My embarrassment is saved by the ringing of her phone. She picks it up, nods at me and answers. "Hi Micah," she says. "It's lovely to hear your voice. Mr. Rogan's here, he's agreed to take your case." She pauses and smiles at what he's saying. "Yes, it *is* great news," she says. "He wants to ask you something." She puts it on speaker and drops it on the couch between us.

"Hey, Mr. Rogan. Thank you so, so much for agreeing to take my case. What is it you need?"

"Hi, Micah. We've heard that a few days before her death, Kitana was worried about something, do you recall that?"

"Yes, I do. It wasn't like her. The only time Kate ever worried was when she thought of her family finding out about us."

"So it wasn't about her family?"

"Not that time. I think it was something to do with her work."

"She worked? I didn't know she worked."

"Yes. Kate was very driven and very independent. She wanted to earn a lot of money so that when she graduated she would be able to go to Harvard and to live in her own place. I asked her to live with me but she said she wasn't ready for that."

"How did she fit in her work with her studies?"

"She worked part-time in the evenings, three or four times a week."

I'm seeing a whole new side of Kitana. "Do you know where she worked?" I ask.

"Not really. It was in some sort of lab. She didn't really want to talk about it for some reason. I think it was all part of her independence thing." There's pain in his voice. *"I felt like she wanted to keep it a secret from me."*

"You don't know the name of the lab, or where it was?" I ask.

"Not the name, but I remember her saying something about it being near the Port of Vancouver. Sorry I can't be more helpful."

"If you think of anything, I want you to call me as soon as you can. It may not be relevant to her murder but you never know." I give him my cell number.

"Sure," he says. *"Is there anything else?"*

"Not that I can think of." I get up from the couch. "I'll leave you guys to have your phone call."

Melanie also stands. "Hang on, bro," she says. "I'm just going to see Mr. Rogan out." She walks me to the door. "Thank you again," she says. "If anyone can get to the truth of who killed Kate it's you, Cal." Unexpectedly, she reaches up and kisses me on the cheek. I don't recognize her perfume but it's spectacular, very subtle and probably very expensive. "Thank you," she repeats. She hugs me and I feel the soft curves of her body pressing against mine. I don't want her to stop and, for several long and delicious seconds, she doesn't. When she finally lets go, I am swept by a strong and guilty desire to hug her back, knowing that I'll regret it if I do... and if I don't.

But I don't.

As I walk to my car, I pull out my phone and give Adry a couple of tasks. One very easy, the other, not so much.

9

NICK

A s I wheel across the floor I see my target. I don't have a lot of time before Steve notices that I haven't shown up at his office door. I head over to the desk. "Hey, Eric. How's it going?" He swivels round in his chair and looks at me in surprise. He and I have never been buddies, especially after what he and his cronies did to Rogan when we were still in the department.

"Hi Nick, I'm good. You?"

I just nod. "I wanted to say congratulations."

"For what?" he asks. "I haven't made sergeant yet."

And hopefully, you never will. I don't let the thought show on my eyes or in my voice. "I heard that it was you who busted that Micah Weston guy, the one who killed his girlfriend."

I can see him swell up a bit. "Yeah, thanks be to—" He cuts himself off in mid-sentence; he probably knows I'm not religious. I'm surprised he is. "What a slime, killing that nice kid."

I smile at him. "You done good. I just wanted to tell you that."

"Thanks, Nick." He's all smiles now, relaxed and feeling good. Time to strike.

I start to turn away. Then stop. "Just one thing, why did you interrogate him in a room where you knew that the camera was faulty?" I hold him in my gaze and I see it flash across his face. Guilt. Just like I've seen it in the eyes of the hundreds of lowlifes I've interrogated over the years.

"What the fuck are you talking about?" he starts to object. But I'm already wheeling away. I've got the first thing I came here to get. Now to work on the second. I roll across the floor to Steve's office and knock.

———

LEMON CHICKEN TWICE IN ONE DAY. STEWART HATES CHINESE food so we never have it at home. This restaurant is the best one that's not too far from Steve's office. The food's good and they have a well-stocked bar. It's been good to catch up on all the goings-on at the VPD.

"One thing's a real problem these days," Steve says. "There's been a ton of crystal meth on the streets recently. Over the last couple of months, it's eased off for some reason, but we're worried it's gonna come flooding back."

"Better than heroin and fentanyl, I guess. Less likely to have people OD-ing all over the city," I say. "But meth can be bad news too."

"Oh, we've still got the opioid problem. The meth is just an add-on. And it's high-quality stuff too. We don't know where it's coming from. What we figure is that a couple of the big gangs were warring over who was going to do the distribution. There were a couple of gang shootings and an innocent kid was caught in the crossfire of one of them. His dad was driving the family Prius along Hastings just as a couple of gangbangers opened fire on each other. A stray bullet went through the window and killed the kid in the back seat. One of them must have come out on top because when the shooting stopped, the meth started flooding the streets."

I shake my head. "I've talked to Rogan quite a few times about it and I'm starting to come to the conclusion that the only way to deal with the gangs is to take 'em out of the picture by making the stuff legal. Have it controlled, just like booze and cigarettes, and manufactured by legal, licensed companies."

"I dunno, Nick." He shakes his head.

"If it's all properly manufactured all the hinky stuff like fentanyl, and lacing weed with cocaine or heroin, and meth labs making dangerous product, that all goes away."

"You're starting to sound like your Member of Parliament, Larry Corliss," he says.

He's talking about our former client. He's a crusader for drug legalization and Rogan saved his life when a drug gang tried to take him out. "My point exactly. Corliss wants to legalize drugs, so the drug gangs wanted to kill him. They know that legal drugs is the end of their business model."

He shakes his head again. "I still don't buy it," he says.

We lapse into silence and I catch up on my lemon chicken and chow mein.

"What you working on these days Nick?" he asks.

"Well you know, the usual. Divorce investigations, the occasional missing person, some corporate stuff."

"Don't you miss investigating real crime?" he asks. He's looking at me intently, like it's an interrogation.

What's he getting at? "Little bit," I say casually. "But I sure as hell don't miss the politics you have to put up with every day." He gives a grim little grin. "Why do you ask?"

He leans forward. "The new Mayor of Vancouver has increased our budget but we're having difficulty hiring good people. So the senior brass has this idea of hiring experienced, retired cops to come back into the Department as case managers. You'd still get your pension and you'd be paid a good rate on contract. The job would be to manage cases and make sure the more junior guys do the job right. I was wondering if you'd be interested?"

A thousand thoughts and questions whirl around in my head and I gotta admit my heart's beating hard at the thought of being in the Department again. But one big idea comes to the fore. I just need to approach it the right way. "So, I'd be keeping guys like Eric Street on the straight and narrow?"

He chuckles. "Yeah. Think you could handle it?"

I smile. "Maybe." I wait a beat and see that he's looking at me eagerly. "It's a big job. I heard he took some serious shortcuts on the Micah Weston case."

His smile slips away. "Where'd you hear that?"

"You know, stuff gets around. Didn't you guys look into the brother? My sources say he's a good candidate for her murder."

"We thought about it but he had an alibi. Anyway, the DNA evidence nailed Weston as the killer."

"Funny coincidence: Weston's lawyer is me and Rogan's lawyer too. He claims Street tricked Weston into putting on the bloody teeshirt in the interrogation room, the room with the faulty camera."

Steve's eyes narrow. "Where are you going with this Nick?"

"Just saying. If there's stuff like that going on, managing guys like Street is a helluva big job."

He relaxes a bit. "It *is* a big job but you'd be well

compensated. And Street's the exception rather than the rule. If I had my way we'd fire his ass but you know what that's like... human relations department, the union..." he sighs.

"Do *you* think he made the kid put on the teeshirt?"

"No." He shakes his head but his eyes say that maybe there's something he's not saying. "Anyway," he says. "What d'you think about coming back to work?"

I try and hold in my excitement. "I'll have to think about it and get back to you." It's a no-brainer but I'm not going to tell him that.

Always leave room for negotiation.

Wednesday

I feel guilty about being here. I managed to get another Ph.D. candidate to take my class but I'm also going to miss a meeting with my thesis advisor. I console myself with the fact that if I were out at SFU teaching my class, I'd feel a thousand times more guilty. I'm sure Shakespeare would have had something to say on the subject but I just can't think what. Maybe it's a sign.

Nick and Zeke are droning on about the Hillside case, one of the corporate cases Zeke's working on and I'm waiting impatiently to get onto my case. Nick frowns at the sound of the main door to the office opening. Lucy hurries into the room, stopping him in mid-sentence. He scowls. Lateness and being interrupted are two things he hates, even when his own daughter is the guilty party.

"I found something," she says. "It's the brother. I'm sure he killed her."

"We're talking about the Hillside case," Nick objects.

"You need to look at what I found. I spent most of last night working on it."

"OK," Nick grumps. "Tell us what you've got."

She sits down and pulls her laptop from her backpack. "First thing I did was to try and find him on social media. First, I scoured through Kitana's Instagram and the only thing I found was a selfie of her and her mother at home with her brother in the background at least I assume it's her brother." She opens her laptop and shows it to Adry.

"Yeah, that's him," Adry says.

Lucy gives a big smile. "What was odd was that as I went through her Instagram, there was no reference to her brother, no comments by him, no likes, no dislikes, nothing. Just that one picture. So I tried to find him on social media. I tried Facebook, Twitter, Instagram, Reddit, Pinterest, TikTok. Nothing again. I found quite a few Haasim Ajrams but he wasn't one of them, they didn't look even a little bit like him. It was odd. I mean everyone has *some* social media presence." She giggles. "Except my Dad." Nick just grunts. "Anyway, it made me suspicious, so I did some digging, a lot of digging, and this is what I got." She taps her mousepad and turns it around so we can all see.

It's a website. It looks like a very professional news site. It even reminds me of the dailynewshound.com, the site Tina writes for. The thought of her brings a smile to my lips, which immediately vanishes as I read. The site's banner is in dark blue Arabic script on a yellow background. Under the script are the words 'The news and the Prophet's teachings.' But it's the headline of the article that gets my attention. It reads, ADULTERESS KILLED BY HER LOVER. Under the headline is a picture of Kitana Ajram. It is not a flattering picture. She looks angry.

The article is a hate-filled, religious diatribe, the gist of which is that Allah's justice was served by Kitana's death at the hands of her infidel lover. One sentence captures my eye. 'Her lover's decision to kill her, robbed her family of the right to punish her as she should be punished—being stoned or beaten to death by her male relatives—a punishment they were eager to give her.'

Nick is the first to finish reading. "Man, that's ugly," he says.

"Why do you think this implicates the brother, Luce?" Adry asks.

"Well it's not exactly evidence but how did this news site know that Kitana's family was eager to punish her like that? They must have talked to them and most likely to her brother. He couldn't admit to them that he'd killed her but must have said that he wanted to."

"He may have wanted to," Zeke weighs in, "but you can't convict for thought crimes; we're not quite in *Minority Report* yet."

Lucy looks a bit deflated. "You did well, Luce," I say quickly. "I think you're moving in the right direction. Find out everything you can about this so-called news site and keep digging into the brother. If we can build any sort of case that there are other credible suspects, it's going to help to get Micah out of jail." She looks a lot happier. I turn to my partner. "You said the VPD cleared him, Nick?"

"Yeah. Steve said he had an alibi."

"What?" Adry's voice is the definition of incredulity. "There's no way he had an alibi. His mother told me that Haasim drove Kitana part of the way to UBC and then dropped her off at a bus stop. What was his alibi?"

"Steve never said and I didn't think to ask." Nick looks embarrassed as he says the words.

"Call him and ask him," Adry says.

Nick just bites his lip.

"You didn't tell Steve about us trying to clear Micah?" I ask.

"Of course not," he says. "I'd never breach client confidentiality like that. Plus, they're not going to be too helpful if they know we're trying to overturn one of their cases. If I go back and ask Steve about Haasim's alibi, he'll want to know why I'm asking."

I ignore the feeling I get that Nick isn't telling us everything. "I don't think it matters," I say. "Eric Street was the lead investigator. He would be the one who told Steve that Hassim had an alibi. We all know that Street is lazy and incompetent at best, and dirty at worst. Maybe he fabricated the alibi so as not to muddy the waters with his prime suspect, Micah."

Another silence envelops us as we all mull over the implications.

Zeke is the first to speak. He says, "I missed yesterday's meeting but Nick briefed me on it first thing this morning. Cal, didn't you have a hypothesis that Eric Street may have tricked Micah into putting on the bloody teeshirt because he knew Micah's DNA wasn't already on it." I just nod. "If you're right about that, it means that Eric Street is somehow implicated in the murder. If he also fabricated an alibi for Haasim..." He leaves the sentence hanging.

———

WHEN I TELL HIM ABOUT LUCY'S DISCOVERY OF 'THE NEWS and the Prophet's teachings' website, Jim Garry gives a big smile. "You guys are amazing," he says. "If we can find the brother's DNA on that shirt and show a judge this website, I can get Micah out of Kent within a day."

"Can you speed up the process?" I ask. "I'm sure Melanie Weston would be happy to pay a premium for an expedited test."

Jim sighs. "I wish it were that easy," he says. "I've requested the evidence but it will take time before it's delivered to the independant lab I use. No one's motivated to give us that shirt quickly. It's a lot of paperwork and procedures to get hold of the evidence from a closed case. I doubt we'll have it until this time next week."

"There's another problem," I say. "Nick says the VPD claims Haasim has an alibi for the time of his sister's murder. But according to Mrs. Ajram, Haasim started to drive Kitana to UBC then dropped her off at a bus stop. So we need to know the alibi to see how good it is and to see if we can break it. The problem is, Nick doesn't want VPD to know we're working on the case. Can you find out what it was?"

"Sure." Jim grabs his phone and dials. "The Crown Prosecutor on the case is a friend of mine," he tells me. "I'm sure he'll let me know. He's a good guy, not one of those win-at-all-cost types." He holds up a finger and speaks into the phone. He listens for a while and hangs up. "He said he'll get back to me asap. That probably means tomorrow. Hopefully, the alibi is someone unreliable, like a family member."

We slip into silence. What if he has a rock-solid alibi? If he does, the best way to help refute it would be the DNA evidence on the shirt.

"Is there anything you can do to get the bloody shirt to the lab faster?" I ask.

"Speed up government?" he sighs. "Now there's a concept." He thinks about it for a while. "I feel good about the theory that the brother is the actual murderer but it might help if we could find other possibilities in case there turns out to be a weakness in the case against Haasim. Do you have any other leads?"

"Not really. There is one thing: Micah, one of Kitana's friends at UBC and even her mother say that she was worried about something. If she had any idea what her brother was into, that would scare her silly. Though Micah thought it might be something to do with her work."

"Huh," he says. "I didn't know she worked." He thinks for a moment. "Anything else?"

I start to shake my head and then remember. "It's not so much a lead as an anomaly," I say. "Everyone says that Kate was totally focused on her studies. But Micah told us her job was at a lab. I asked one of my colleagues to look into it but I don't know if she did." I shrug. "It's probably nothing, most students have jobs."

Jim rubs his fingertips through his beard. "Hmm," he says. "When Kitana's mother was giving her victim-impact statement at the sentencing, she said her daughter loved her studies and that the family completely supported her so she wouldn't have to work and could focus a hundred percent of her time on her UBC work."

I call Adry and put her on speakerphone.

"When I called you yesterday afternoon, after I'd spoken to Micah and Melanie, did you get a chance to look into where Kitana may have been working?"

"No, sorry Cal, I didn't."

"It may be nothing but if you get a chance, could you check it out."

"Sure, but it'll probably be tomorrow if that's OK."

"No prob. It's probably not important."

I hang up.

But my feelings belie my words.

What was Kitana's job?

Another random thought.

Haasim? I wonder if he has a job too?

———

I SEE MELANIE IN HER SUV IN THE LARGE CURVED DRIVEWAY. I pull up behind her and she gets out. "I love your car," she says. "What is it?"

"A nineteen-sixty-one Austin Healey three thousand," I grin proudly. "A mark four," I add, not that it will mean anything to her.

"It is *so* cute. You must take me for a ride in it sometime soon."

"Sure."

She takes a deep breath and as she looks towards the house, the smile rolls off her face.

She doesn't move. I know why. This is her brother's house. The place where Kitana was murdered. The crime scene I need to see.

"I haven't been here since the day Kate..." She leaves the sentence hanging. "I had specialist cleaners do a thorough cleaning after the police released it and I have someone come in once a week to keep it clean. My parents wanted to sell it but Micah wouldn't let them. He really believes in our justice system and that he'll be out soon, living back here and going to UBC again."

"I might have some good news on that front," I say.

Her eyes light up.

"One of our people found an extremist website. It had news of Micah's conviction and said that a woman who commits adultery should be beaten to death by her male relatives. It also said that the family were deprived of the opportunity to execute her by beating her to death."

"So you think her brother killed her?"

"It's a distinct possibility. I should know more later."

She sways unsteadily and grabs my arm. "So this nightmare could be over soon," she whispers.

"Don't get your hopes too high," I say. "It's just circumstantial at this point."

She keeps hold of my arm and takes a few deep breaths.

"Oh my Lord. I can't thank you enough."

I don't say anything. I'm not sure if she's thanking me or God.

After a moment she seems to regain her composure. She lets go of my arm.

"So why do you want to look at the crime scene?" she asks.

"I don't know. It's just something I always do. I might see something relevant that the crime-scene guys missed. They were looking for evidence of Micah's guilt. They may have missed, or worse, ignored something that's evidence of his innocence."

"OK, good."

She clicks a fob on her key ring and the garage door slides open. It's a three-car garage but there is just one vehicle inside. It's a purple Lamborghini Aventador. Not just any Aventador but an SVJ. This family must be rolling in cash to buy their son a car worth close to a million bucks Canadian.

"This is where I found Micah and Kate." She has walked into the garage and is standing at the back wall. I take three steps towards her. The concrete floor shows no sign of the bloodstains which must have been part of the scene. I look around. Except for the car, the garage is completely bare. No storage lockers, no tools or workbench, not even a hose. But I guess if you're that rich, you don't use a hose to wash your own car, you have it professionally detailed.

Melanie points to the floor. "Micah was crouched here, cradling Kate's body." I can see from her face that she's reliving the horror of that day.

"Where was the murder weapon?" I ask.

She points to the car.

"It was under the car?"

"No, the car was outside. Micah had come home, opened the garage door and saw Kate lying inside, covered in blood. He just jumped out of the car and ran into the garage. When I arrived the car engine was still running."

"Makes sense." I nod. "Show me where they found the shirt."

She unlocks the door leading into the house. "Follow me," she says.

The house is as spectacular inside as out. It is minimally but expensively furnished. There are some wonderful African wood carvings and some oil paintings which look, to my untutored eye, like originals. "The laundry room is upstairs," she says, leading the way. I follow her up the curved staircase and try to focus on the art covering the wall rather than on the sway of her hips. At the top of the stairs, there is a large semi-circular foyer with rooms leading off. She opens the door to a laundry room. It's bigger than Ellie's bedroom at home.

She points to a Miele washer. "It was there."

"In the washer?" I walk over and open the door.

"Do you think Kate's brother left it there, after he'd killed her?" she asks.

"No. It doesn't make sense. He'd never been here before, he wouldn't know where the laundry room was. If he'd just killed his sister, he wouldn't go searching through the house to find somewhere to put the bloody shirt."

"So who put it here?"

It's a good question and I have a good answer to it.

"I'm thinking Detective Eric Street. The guy who supposedly found it."

———

"What's the celebration?" I ask as Tina hands me the foaming flute.

"Because you inspired me," she says and clinks her glass against mine.

Ellie gets in on the glass-clinking action. She sees the question on my face. "Sparkling apple juice, Dad," she giggles.

I take a drink. I'm not a connoisseur, not of champagne anyway, but I can tell this comes from an expensive bottle.

"Inspired you to what?" I ask.

"To do a follow up to my piece on Innocence Canada. I thought I'd make the Micah Weston case the focus of the article. I'm already three-quarters of the way through it. After dinner, I want to interview you about it."

A number of conflicting questions flash through my consciousness. Will a news article on Micah help or hinder my attempts to prove his innocence? If Haasim Ajram killed his sister will Tina's article put her in any danger? If Goliath thinks that my client may soon be released from Kent, will he intensify his efforts to injure or even kill Micah? By telling Tina in the first place, have I breached client privacy? Should I feel this happy that the woman I love says I've inspired her?

"Wow!" is all I can think to say.

Ellie says, "I know! It's great isn't it Dad," but Tina can read my tone of voice better than my daughter.

"But..." she says, looking askance at me.

I consider the options and choose the one that concerns me the most. "I'm worried you will alert the real killer and maybe put yourself at risk."

"Every time I write a controversial article, I'm putting myself at risk," she says dismissively. "I'm used to it."

"Even so," I say, "remember what happened in—" She stops me by putting an index finger gently on my lips.

"You worry too much," she says and kisses me on the cheek. "It's one of the reasons I love you."

I kiss her back, on the lips, and feel a wave of emotion wash over me. I really love this wonderful person who has come into my life and the words *will you marry me* pop into my consciousness. But before I can say anything, Ellie chimes in with, "Dad and Tina, sitting up a tree, k-i-s-s-i-n-g."

"Watch it, young lady," I say, trying to decide whether I am relieved or upset that she interrupted.

"Watch it or what?" Ellie chuckles.

"Watch it or there will be a consequence," I say.

That just makes her chuckle some more. "Hmmm," she says. "Maybe I'll have to try that emancipation thing Tina was talking about the other day."

"You are an evil child," I say through the laughter that bubbles up. I grab her and start to tickle her ribs. "Thank heavens you'll be with your mother for the next few evenings."

Tina joins in the laughter and the tickling. "That's right," she says. "And I'm going to take your Dad out for dinner tomorrow and I'm not even going to tell you where we're going because you would be soooo jealous."

We collapse in a laughing heap on the sofa.

Life doesn't get much better than this.

———

We float in the warm afterglow of our lovemaking. "I hope Ellie didn't hear us," Tina whispers. The thought feels spiky in my gut. Our townhouse is tall and narrow so Ellie's bedroom is on the floor below ours. I'm hoping the floor will insulate us.

"Tomorrow night," I whisper back, "after dinner, we can be as noisy as we like. Sam's house is two kilometres away. El probably won't be able to hear us over that distance."

"Probably. But our nosy neighbour, Martha, will be reporting it in full detail to her little cadre." She chuckles and I join in.

I think again about the question that bubbled up into my consciousness earlier. I want to ask her but something holds me back. Is it because this is not the right time and place? or should I talk to Ellie first? I'm pretty sure she'd be OK with it but I can't be sure. Is it Sam? Or is it that I'm just plain scared to ask her? As I wrestle with a maelstrom of emotions, Tina asks, "Are you OK?"

"Yeah, sure. I'm more than OK." I smile at her.

"You remember where we met?" she asks.

"Of course." I remember it well. It was eighteen months ago. Devastated about what happened with Em, who was my lover for a brief period, I had disappeared into a vortex of heroin. I met Tina, a former coke addict, at an NA meeting. She helped me out of the cycle of using and we fell in love in the process.

I wonder where she's going with this question.

"You haven't been to a meeting in a while," she says.

Ah! She's right and my mind floods with a whole bunch of rationalizations and excuses but I have been an addict long enough to know they are all BS. I just take a breath and say, "I know."

"How about on our way to dinner tomorrow, we stop off at a meeting together. It'll be like old times." Her smile bathes me in warmth... but I still can't say the four words I really want to say.

Thursday

As alibis go it's a pretty good one. But I'm here to break it. Jim Garry's call this morning put a damper on our enthusiasm for the theory that Haasim Ajram killed his sister. Haasim's alibi is that he was at a café with friends at around the time his sister was killed. His car was parked outside the café and he even had a parking ticket to prove it. But a parking ticket just proves his car was there, not that *he* was.

The Hamra Café has a rundown look. It's on East Broadway, next door to a halal butcher's shop near the corner of Fraser Street and right opposite a ninety-nine bus stop. That alone gives me pause. According to Adry, Mrs. Ajram said her son and daughter had an argument on the way back to UBC and that he dropped her at a ninety-nine bus stop. But then again, all the best false alibis have elements of truth in them.

I push open the door of the Hamra. It has one of those

old-fashioned bells on a spring that jingles when the door is opened or closed. There is the tinny sound of middle-eastern music coming from a cheap speaker. As my eyes adjust to the dark interior, I see several pairs of eyes lasered in on me. The eyes are not welcoming. I am the only person in the place wearing a mask and the only person in the place without a beard. It smells of coffee, smoke and disrepair.

I walk over to the counter. There is an assortment of snacks laid out on uncovered plates, in complete contravention of city hygiene regulations. Behind the counter is a gleaming espresso machine but there is no one to operate it. To the left is an open doorway leading to what looks like a kitchen.

I wait.

Nothing.

I cough politely, but loudly enough to be heard by anyone in the kitchen.

Nothing.

I wait some more.

I turn to the sound of a chair scraping across the floor.

The man rising from the chair is tall and bulky and is wearing an apron. The apron is clean and pressed, completely at odds with the rest of the place. He walks over but does not go behind the counter to serve me; he just stands in front of me and says, "Yes?"

"A double-shot espresso please." I give him my friendliest smile. Mr. Charming, that's me. Then remember he can't actually see it behind the mask.

"We're closed."

I let my gaze roll across the customers sitting at the tables. They all have cups and plates in front of them, although no one is eating or drinking at this very moment; they are far too busy watching me.

"Really?" I say.

"Really," he growls.

"At nine-thirty in the morning?"

He shrugs.

Mr. Uncooperative.

I take a shot in the dark.

"You told my colleagues that Haasim Ajram was here at the time his sister was murdered."

That was a hit. I wouldn't have spotted it if he'd been wearing a mask: a slight twitch of jaw muscle and a tiny nostril flare to match the confusion in his eyes.

I just hope he doesn't ask me for ID.

He doesn't.

Maybe I still look like a cop.

I watch his brain ticking over for about five seconds. "That's right," he says.

"But that wasn't true was it?"

"Yes it was," he says. He's Mr. Defensive now. "We all saw him." He gestures at the assembled patrons but now all the pairs of eyes are minutely examining their food and drink. All except for one. One dead-looking pair of eyes is staring at me from out of a hard, teenage face. He's sitting at the table with the chair pushed back from it. He looks like a smaller version of the man standing in front of me. Probably his son. But the familial similarity is not what is striking. It's the hatred on such a young face. It sends a cold worm crawling through my gut.

But I got what I came for.

I'm now ninety-nine percent sure Haasim Ajram's alibi is BS.

I turn and walk out, hearing the jangle of the bell behind me as the door closes.

I cross Broadway and walk to my car, parked outside a bank, just past the bus stop.

It is warm and sunny and, after my visit, I crave fresh air. I unlock the Healey, take the convertible roof down, pull off my mask and throw it on the front seat. A drive with the wind on my face and in my hair is just what the doctor ordered.

As I pull away from the curb, I take a last look at the Hamra Café. The sixteen-year-old kid with the hard face is standing outside, his phone camera pointing straight at me. As I accelerate down Broadway, I check the mirror. He is still pointing the camera in my direction.

I've been ID'd.

Nothing good can come of that.

———

"Yeah, that's good but how are you gonna prove he actually killed his sister?" Nick asks. "Your gut feeling that his alibi is BS isn't going to get our client out of jail."

"If Haasim's DNA is on the bloody teeshirt, we've got him," I say.

"But if it's not, we're hooped. Plus I'm guessing we're gonna have to wait a while before the cops get round to handing over the shirt to Jim's independent lab."

"What about good, old-fashioned fingerprints?" Zeke says. "If Haasim killed her, his fingerprints should be at the scene."

"It's a good thought," Nick says. "Except that his fingerprints weren't on the baseball bat, so if he was there, he was probably wearing gloves."

"Good point," Zeke concedes, "but that could work in our favour."

"How?"

"We know Micah wasn't wearing gloves because his prints were on the bat. So if Micah touched anything he would have left bloody fingerprints. But if the brother killed her and he *was* wearing gloves, he must have touched something. He would have left a bloody smudge with no sign of a fingerprint in it. If there were bloody smudges at the crime scene, they would indicate someone wearing a glove made them, meaning someone was there, in addition to Micah."

"Oh... my... God." Lucy's voice says from the reception desk. There is a pause and then she gives a little victory whoop. "No way!"

Before I can ask her what's up, she rushes into the main office, laptop in hand. "You guys have got to see this," she says. She puts her computer on Nick's desk and Zeke, Adry and I gather round in a semicircle behind Nick's wheelchair.

It's a website and it's all too familiar. Lots of sites, looking just like this one, have appeared on news broadcasts all over the globe. The header is a picture of a group of five young men standing together with stern expressions and holding weapons. They are in front of a flag with white Arabic script on a black field. Lucy points to one of the men. "That's Haasim Ajram, Kate's brother," Lucy says. "You should hear the stuff they say on this site. One thing—"

"OMG, show me that." The urgency in Adry's voice stops Lucy in her tracks. She leans forward, squints at the screen for a moment, then points to another face in the picture. "You see that guy?" she says. "He's the guy I told you about. When I left the Ajram's house on Tuesday, I looked back and he was standing at an upstairs window. I'm sure it's the same guy."

I can't stop myself from breaking into laughter. "There goes Haasim's alibi."

"What'ja mean?" Nick asks.

"I saw him this morning."

"Who?"

"The guy Adry's pointing to. He was at the Hamra Café this morning. He followed me out and even took a photo of me driving off. He was sitting at the table with the owner of the café and I assumed they were father and son. Haasim's alibi that he was at the Hamra at the time of the murder isn't worth a damn if the son of the owner is in the same radical group as Haasim.

I look at the site. Although the writing on the flag is in Arabic, the text is in English. The caption of the picture says, 'The Rasul Brigade brings the truth to Canada.' I read the first paragraph of the text out loud. It is a diatribe on the evils of modern western society.

"Holy crap," I say. "They're pretty extreme."

Lucy grins and breaks into song. "You ain't seen nothing yet," she sings. Nick has schooled her well on Canadian rock groups of the seventies. She scrolls down and says, "Here's a list of laws this Rasul Brigade wants to have enacted in Canada. The fifth law is…" she pauses for effect. "Adultery is punishable by death. The offending woman shall be stoned or beaten to death by her male relatives."

A stunned silence settles on us. Finally, Nick speaks. "Well done Luce." She glows. "How did you find this website?"

She grins. "It was really bugging me that I couldn't find any social media accounts for Haasim. So I spoke to Connor about it."

"Who's Connor?" I ask.

Her grin widens. "He's my boyfriend, we met while you were in Hong Kong. He told me about all this facial recognition software you can use to search the web. So I used that pic from Kitana's Instagram; the one with Haasim in the background. I cropped the photo so it was just him and used it to do an image search on the internet. This website was what I came up with."

"Smart kid, eh Rogan?" Nick crows. "Must run in the family."

We all laugh.

All except Zeke. He's still drilled in on Lucy's laptop. Without looking up, he says, "I think I know why Detective Eric Street accepted Haasim's alibi so quickly."

Nick chuckles. "Are you saying red-haired, blue-eyed Eric Street is part of this Rasul Brigade. You have got to be joking."

"Actually Nick," Zeke says, "in the history of terrorism the vast majority of terrorists have been white. Also it's not exactly unheard of for white men to join radical Islamic groups."

It's a crazy idea, but not completely crazy.

"Just look at this." He has his finger on the screen. He's pointing to one of the young men in the header photo. Unlike the other four, he's wearing headgear and has a bandana across his face. Only his eyes are visible. And they are blue. "Could that be Eric Street?" he asks.

Nick and I almost bang heads as we lean in to look more closely.

"No way to tell," he says, "but it could be."

"I agree," I say.

A sense of frustration infuses my gut. "If that were Street, then the whole case against Micah would be null and void. The lead detective on the case being in an Islamic terror group with the victim's brother would be cause to get the case dismissed. Especially when that group mandates killing women who commit 'adultery'. But like Nick says, there's no way to know."

Lucy chimes in. "I wouldn't say there's *no* way to know."

We all turn towards her. She does one of her dramatic pauses and just as I sense that Nick is about to explode, she says, "Connor taught me a lot about all this facial recognition stuff. Everyone's eyes are different. The picture on that website is quite high resolution. If I can get a hi-res photo of Eric Street's face, it might be possible to do a detailed comparison of the two images. It may not be conclusive, but it sure could be a strong indication that it's Eric Street behind the mask."

Adry gives Lucy a big hug. "You are amazing," she says.

Nick is so proud he's almost in tears and even Zeke seems impressed.

Lucy grabs her laptop. "I'll get on it right away," she says.

"One thing's clear," I add. "We need to know more about this Rasul Brigade. And I know exactly who can give us that information."

With a big grin, I grab my phone and scroll through my contacts.

"Who you gonna call?" Lucy and Zeke ask in unison.

Nick and Adry exchange glances and grin.

"It sure as hell ain't Ghostbusters," Nick laughs.

———

NO SOONER HAD I FINISHED MY CALL—AS NICK RIGHTLY SAID, not to Ghostbusters—I got the call that summoned me here.

I pull into the driveway and get out of the Healey. The view is spectacular. I can look over English Bay to West Vancouver and to the left, I can see across the Strait of Georgia to the mountains on Vancouver Island. It's a picture-perfect day. I turn around and face the house that overlooks this magnificent vista. Not in my wildest dreams —and my dreams can get pretty wild—could I ever afford a house like this. Micah Weston's parents must be worth a fortune if they can afford to buy this house for their son; not to mention that Melanie's apartment on False Creek must also be valued in the millions. I ring the doorbell.

The door opens almost instantly. "Cal! Thank you so much for coming. Come in, please."

I step inside and enjoy the intoxicating scent of Melanie's perfume.

"I found something," she says breathlessly, "and I wanted you to see it first hand. It might be evidence and I didn't want to disturb it, in case I do something wrong. Come with me." She leads me through the living room to a room at the side of the house. It's a study with two expensive-looking desks, set facing each other. The room is spectacular. The desks are clearly antiques. There is a grandfather clock quietly ticking in a corner and there are two large wing-back leather chairs which remind me of those gentlemen's clubs you see in old British movies. This doesn't look like the sort of furniture a young man would choose. I'm betting it was picked out and purchased by the parents.

"This is where Micah and Kate studied," she says. "This was Kate's desk." She pushes the chair away from the desk. "After we came here yesterday, I thought I'd come back and clear out Kate's things. My plan was to pack everything in a box and send it to her parents; they would probably appreciate having all her things. However, when I looked to see what was in the drawers, I found this."

She slides open the top right-hand drawer. Instead of the pencils, pens, stapler and other office bric-a-brac usually found in top right-hand desk drawers the world over, there is just one item. A two-tone grey Beretta APX pistol, a gun favoured by women because it's small enough to fit in a purse.

The word 'evidence' is screaming in my head. Reflexively, I reach into my jacket pocket but, having not practiced my profession for eight months, there are no gloves there.

"You wouldn't have any latex gloves in the house by any chance?" I ask.

"No, I don't think so. There are probably some rubber kitchen gloves. Would they do?"

"Sure." As she turns to go, I add, "And if there are any large Ziploc bags bring those too please."

She leaves to get them and I check out the rest of the desk. Using a handkerchief, I open the other drawers on each side of Kitana's desk. They have the same contents as any other desk, in any other office, anywhere. This desk has a shallow, lockable, centre drawer. I pull the handle. It's not locked and it slides open. Inside is a bulky red manila folder.

Melanie comes back in with a box of Ziploc bags and a pair of yellow kitchen gloves. They are a small size and I struggle to get my hands into them.

I take the Beretta first, check the safety and I smell it. "It's not been fired recently." I get Melanie to open a baggie and I drop it in.

I fully open the middle drawer and take hold of the red folder with both hands. It contains more than just paper. I place it on the desk in front of me and open it. On top is a hand-written list, headed 'For 1830 Powell.' It's an address on the east side of Vancouver and it's vaguely familiar. More interestingly, it's near the Port of Vancouver. Micah said Kitana worked in a lab close to the Port. The list is of equipment you would find in a lab. I don't recognize the names of most of the items but beakers, pipettes and flasks are all items I remember from High School chemistry classes. It goes on for three pages.

Underneath the third page is a phone. It's not a smartphone. It has a manual keypad and a small, two-inch screen. A burner. Why would Kitana have a burner phone? I press the on button and nothing happens. The battery must be dead. I pop it into another Ziploc.

The remaining pages are chemical equations. Chem was never my long suit but I remember enough to know that these equations describe organic chemical reactions and some of the molecules described are pretty complex.

I close the folder and slide it into a Ziplock. It's too large, so I grab a second bag and as I manoeuvre the other end of the folder into it, a key drops out onto the desk. It's a standard Yale style with a thin strip of red ribbon knotted into the hole at the top. I drop it into a different bag and seal it.

Just to be on the safe side, I check all the other drawers but find nothing of interest.

"It's OK with you if I take these?" I ask.

"Please do," she says. "Especially the gun. I hate guns."

"Are there any other places in the house where she may have kept things?" I ask.

"Only the bedroom, but I've already taken her stuff— just clothes and makeup and a few pieces of jewellery—and put it in the box for her parents."

"Good. But if you do find anything of hers that's out of

the ordinary, let me know." I struggle out of the too-small kitchen gloves and grab the evidence bags. "I'd better get these back to the office."

She walks with me to the door. As she opens it, she puts her hand on my forearm and says, "Thank you so much for what you are doing for Micah. I really appreciate it; my parents do too. They asked me to tell you that if you needed to increase the retainer, it will be no problem."

"Tomorrow's the last day of the month," I say. "You'll get an invoice for the work done to date. When we close the case, we apply the retainer to the last bill and if there are any funds left over, we return them to you."

"Perfect," she says. "I'll pay it as soon as you email it to me." That'll be music to Nick's ears when I tell him.

I turn and walk to my car. As I drop the evidence bags in the trunk, a small Mercedes pulls into the driveway. I close and lock the trunk. It's a useless exercise because anyone who really wants to get into the trunk of a Healey can do it in about thirty seconds. As I open the driver's door, the occupant of the Mercedes gets out of his car. He is a man in his sixties with a kind face and a broad smile. "Nice car," he says.

"Thanks, I love it, especially when the weather's like this." I look more closely at his tanned face and play a long shot. "Are you Melanie and Micah's dad?"

"No." He gives a little laugh. "I'm Peter Lighthall." He extends his hand, then remembers Covid and gives a little wave.

"Cal Rogan," I say.

"Peter, it's so nice to see you," Melanie has joined us. "Please, come in." She takes his arm and I wonder if he's a boyfriend, albeit an older one. I cannot suppress a little bite of jealousy at the thought. Then I feel a little bite of guilt about that little bite of jealousy.

"Nice to meet you, Cal," he says as she leads him away.

"You too, Peter," I reply.

I drive down Newton Wynd, right onto Westbrook and then right onto northwest Marine Drive. Maybe a sunny drive along the beach, with the wind in my hair, will clear my mind of the thoughts I keep having about my client.

To entertain the time with thoughts of love,
Which time and thoughts so sweetly doth deceive.

———

"She had a freakin' Beretta in her desk drawer?" Nick is aghast. "Why would a twenty-year-old chemistry student have a handgun?"

"Maybe she was scared of her brother," Adry suggests. "Maybe she knew about his website and was worried that he and his friends would come after her. It's a shame she didn't have it on her when he beat her to death."

"I wonder if it was registered in her name," Zeke says.

"Good question," Nick says. "And here's another good question: what are we going to do with it?"

"We'll have to turn it into VPD," I say. "They'll test to see if it's been used in any crimes and hopefully reward us for being upstanding citizens by letting us know the details."

"Yeah, I suppose," Nick says. "I'll take it in and give it to Steve."

Zeke takes a pair of gloves and a huge-assed magnifying glass out of his desk drawer. "Let me have a look at it first," he says. I hand it over. He checks the safety then takes it out of the Ziploc by inserting an unsharpened pencil into the barrel.

He examines the Beretta with the magnifying glass, turning it and looking at it from all angles. "Hmmm." He switches on the light on his desk and angles it towards the gun for another detailed examination which lasts as long as the first. Finally, he slides the gun back into its bag. "That's odd. Maybe forensics could find one but, as far as I can see, there's not a single fingerprint on it. It looks like it's been wiped clean."

"Second mystery," Nick grunts. "Why would she wipe it clean of fingerprints?"

"If she kept it in a desk drawer at Micah's house," Adry says, "surely he would have known she had it."

I check the time and grab my phone. She picks up on the first ring. "Hi, Melanie. You said you talk to Micah every Tuesday, Thursday and Saturday around three o'clock. When he calls in half an hour, would you conference me in please?" She agrees and I hang up without giving her an explanation.

"We'll ask him," I say. "There are some other questions I have too." I show them the baggie with the burner phone in it. "She also had this. The battery's dead, do we have a charger that would work with it?"

"Definitely," Nick says. He grabs the phone and wheels over to our stationery cabinet. Apart from the usual office stuff, Nick has a bunch of electronic gizmos and parts. He rummages around for a moment and wheels back with a charger in his lap. He hands it to Adry and she plugs it into the power bar on her desk. She opens the Ziploc bag an inch so that she can plug the other end of the cable into the phone. "Give it half an hour or so," she says.

I walk over to the stationery cabinet and grab a handful of nitrile gloves. I put one pair on and stuff the rest in the pocket of my jacket, which is hanging on the back of my chair. I sit down and slide the red folder out of its Ziploc and spread the papers out on my desk. "The phone and a key were also in the folder," I tell them.

Adry and Zeke get up and stand behind me, one looking over each shoulder. Nick wheels his chair up to my desk for a better view. They scan the papers and Adry is the first to speak. "That address, 1830 Powell, is familiar."

"That's what I thought," I say. "I think it might be the lab she was working at. Micah said he thought it was some-where near the Port. Powell runs right beside it."

She grabs her phone. After a couple of taps she says, "I thought so. That's the Doan Brewery. Jason and I love that place; or we did pre-covid."

Ahh. Pre-covid. When you could just drop into a brewery and have a pint or two.

"Doan's had amazing beer," I say. "But they left that loca-tion a couple of years ago to work out of some brewery collective. I'm not sure they survived covid. I thought their Powell Street building was empty."

"Maybe someone took it over and turned it into a lab," she says. "Do you want me to check it out?"

"Definitely!" Nick says. "I still think the brother killed her but there's obviously more to her than meets the eye. Why would she have a gun and why would she have a job that she didn't tell her parents about? We need to know a lot more about Kitana Ajram." He's really fired up about this case. "If we can maybe find some other possible suspects, it's gonna be easier to get that poor kid Micah out of jail. Rogan, give me a pair of those gloves you stuffed in your pocket." I hand them over. He puts them on and starts sorting through the papers in the file. He riffles through the pages of chem-ical formulas. "Huh. Bunch of gobbledegook. Anyone know anything about this stuff?"

Everyone shakes their head. "All I know is that it's

organic chemistry," I say. "But I can find out, I know one of the assistant profs in the Chemistry department. I have to go up to SFU this afternoon so I'll give him this stuff and see what he says."

"OK. Good," Nick says. "Here's the plan: I'll take this gun into Steve, I wanna talk to him anyway; Rogan, copy those formulas and that list of chemical equipment and show 'em to your professor buddy; Adry, go check out that lab, see what they do and see if Kitana worked there and what she did."

Nice to know Nick and I are on the same page. It feels good to be on this team again.

"Sounds like a plan," I say. I take the last Ziploc bag. "Adry, this key was in the folder with all the chemical equations. Take it, see if it's the key to 1830 Powell."

"Will do," she says.

Nick has already taken the gun and is wheeling out. "Hey Nick, say hi to Steve for me."

"Sure," he says as he pushes his way through the front door. He seems like he's in a hurry. I wonder what was the other thing he wants to speak to Steve about.

———

Magnus Ahlström is a very bright guy. There are not a lot of twenty-five-year-old assistant professors but he's one. He and I met on the SFU Loop, the trail where I first met Melanie. We discovered that in addition to running, we both love craft beer and when he learned I used to be a cop, he confided in me that he's working on a crime novel. He and I have spent quite a few happy hours drinking beer at the excellent Dagoraad brewery, just down the hill from the university.

I hand him the papers I got from Kitana's desk at Micah's house.

He scans the list of equipment and drops it on his desk. As he examines the pages of chemical formulae a frown wrinkles his brow. He runs his hand through his blond hair. He glances up at me for a second and then returns his attention to the papers. When he gets to the last page he grunts. "Huh."

"What?" I ask.

He shakes his head and picks up the equipment list, which he examines much more carefully this time. He spreads out the papers so that he can look at the equations and the list at the same time. I watch his eyes flip back and forth between the two. I can't quite read his expression. It goes from puzzlement to concern to something unfathomable.

Finally, he drills his blue eyes into mine. "Where did you get this?" he asks, his Swedish accent more noticeable than usual.

"From a student," I say.

"A student? No way."

I just nod.

"Who?" he asks. "A student here at SFU?"

"No, UBC."

"Unbelievable. The kid's a genius. He's come up with an incredibly clever manufacturing process." I'm thinking the unfathomable look was admiration or maybe even jealousy.

"He's a she," I tell him. "Or was."

"She's dead?"

"Yes. Murdered."

"Wow."

"This manufacturing process, what was the end product?" I ask.

"C ten H fifteen N."

"Gee thanks, Magnus. I've just got one tiny, clarifying question: what the heck is C ten H fifteen N?"

He tells me.

My mind goes into overdrive.

12

ADRY

The little brick building still has the sign for the Doan's Brewing Company. Surely if there were a lab here, they would have changed the signage. There are faded flyers pasted on the inside of the window and the place has an abandoned look. I peer through the window but can't see much at all. The door is locked. I knock, wait, and knock again. No response. Just to be on the safe side, I take my keys and rap on the glass pane in the door. Still nothing.

I put my keys back in my purse and take out the key that Cal found in the red folder he took from Kitana's desk. My hand is trembling slightly from the excitement of breaking into someone's property, but the key slides in smoothly. It turns and the door opens.

I step inside and close the door behind me. No beeping of an alarm. Good.

I'm standing in what used to be the tasting room. Everything is gone except the bar. It feels deserted and a bit eerie. I glance over at the spot where Jason and I would usually sit and wish he was here for backup. I step over to the bar. There is a thin layer of dust on it. It hasn't been used in a while. I pass the bar and walk through the door that used to lead to the brewing room. I've been in here before. Evan Doan, the brewmaster, loved to show customers his domain. The brewing equipment is gone except that there is one large, gleaming, stainless-steel vessel that resembles a brewing kettle. There are several workbenches with nothing on them. I run my finger across one and it comes back clean.

There is a slight smell in the air. A kind of hospital smell.

This definitely looks like a lab but I don't see any of the equipment that was on Kitana's equipment list. To my left, there is a slide-up door, like you would see in a garage, and beside the door is a cupboard. It has a lock but the key is in it. I open it but it's empty. On the shelves, there are discoloured rings that look as if wet glasses had been placed there. They are different sizes and I can imagine they may have been left by recently washed flasks and beakers.

I start to close the cupboard but it's not completely empty. On one of the shelves are some glass shards that look like they've come from a beaker and on the very bottom shelf are some other bits of glass, except they're not evenly shaped. They look more like small shards of clear ice. I pull a nitrile glove out of my purse, put it on and pick one of them up. It's too light to be glass but it doesn't feel like plastic.

A little tingling in my tummy tells me that this is important. I take another glove out of my purse—it'll work fine as an evidence bag—and drop a couple of the shards inside.

I don't know what they are but I plan to find out.

———

THIS FEELS SO DECADENT. I FELT GUILTY ABOUT NOT GOING back to the office after my visit to the former brewery but Jason's call was just too intriguing. When I got home, he was in the bedroom with a bottle of champagne in an ice bucket, a plate of tiny gourmet snacks from Meinhardt's, and wearing nothing but a big grin.

In the glow of the champagne and our lovemaking, I say, "I still can't believe it."

"I know," he says, giving me a little squeeze. "When Bob left I had no idea they would make me Executive Director. When the Chairman of the Board asked me to lunch today and offered me the job, I was floored. I didn't know *what* to say."

"I hope you said yes."

He laughs. "I don't really remember but I'm pretty sure I did."

"Good! To hell with cooking, dinner's on me tonight, Mr. Executive Director of Insite, one of the world's first safe injections sites."

"You're on," he says and gives me a lovely, tender kiss. "How was your day?"

"Not as exciting as yours but pretty good. I was working on Micah Weston's case."

"Anything to exonerate him yet?"

"We're pretty sure Kitana's brother killed her," I say, "but Cal found out she owned a gun. *And* she worked secretly in a lab. Her parents and her best friend at UBC didn't know. She'd mentioned it to Micah but he didn't know where it was. Well... I went there today. Guess where it was?" I answer before he can say anything. "In the old Doan Brewery."

"Wow! I loved that place. What sort of lab was it?"

"That's the thing," I say. "It felt like it had recently been abandoned. There was nothing there, except for something odd." Suddenly feeling energized, I hop out of bed and go get a Ziploc bag from the kitchen, pull the nitrile glove out of my purse and empty the contents into the baggie. I hold it out to Jason. "It might not be anything, but I just get a gut feel it's important. Any ideas what it might be?"

He leans over the baggie and takes a sniff. His eyes widen. "Oh, I have every idea what that might be."

My pulse quickens. "What is it?" I ask.

"Cotton candy."

"What?"

"Dunk. Gak. Scooby snax."

He chuckles at my look of confusion.

"It's more precisely known as C ten H fifteen N."

13

CAL

Normally, I wouldn't have seen them. Normally, I would have just driven into the underground parking. But nothing's been normal today. Two men sitting in a car parked on the street is not normal; not in my world anyway. It screams surveillance. They are in a Toyota Camry positioned so that they can see both the entrance to the parking garage and the security gate into the townhouse complex.

The plan was for me to park outside our townhouse and text Tina, so we could go straight to dinner. I'm parked on the opposite side of the road, within their line of sight, but they are studiously avoiding looking in my direction. Amateurs. They remind me of the customers in the Hamra Café this morning. The hard-faced kid took a picture of me leaving in the Healey; the kid who's on the Rasul Brigade website. If he had a friend in the VPD, a friend like Eric Street, for example, it would be a snap to get my address from my licence plate and send a couple of goons to my house.

I can feel the anger starting to burn. Too often my job

has spilled over into my private life. The fact that they're here at my home, the home I share with Tina and Ellie—both of whom have been victims of criminals I've been tracking in the past—stokes the flames. The anger is made doubly bad by the guilt overlaying it, guilt that I agreed to take on this case in the first place, instead of just continuing my nice, quiet, normal, safe life at SFU.

I get out of my car and head towards them. They drop the subterfuge and look straight at me. The driver starts the engine, just as I get to his door. I yank it open before the car starts to move and activates the door locks. I grab the front of his jacket with both hands, yank him bodily out of his seat and slam him onto the pavement. Up close, I can't tell if he is one of the customers I saw in the Hamra Café this morning but I don't care. I kneel on him and look him in the eye. "Who sent you to spy on me?" I snarl, pulling back a fist.

"Back off, man!"

I look towards the voice.

The car passenger is pointing a Glock through the open driver's door and right at my chest. There is not the slightest tremble in his hand. Maybe not such an amateur after all. Also not one of the men from the Hamra, I would have recognized him from the jagged scar on his cheek.

I let go of the driver and stand up. The Glock follows me, never wavering.

The driver gets to his feet and reclaims his seat behind the wheel. He slams his foot down and the car leaps away, the momentum slamming his door closed. They accelerate down the street and hang a right at the corner.

But not before I memorized their licence plate.

Two can play that game.

Friday

I recognize her even behind the mask. I think it's her tailored suit and purposeful stride. The man walking beside her is my height and has slicked-back, black hair— try saying that three times fast. They both have carry-on bags and walk past the carousel in my direction. Definitely not the Ghostbusters.

"Hi Cal," she says. "Good to see you. I'd give you a hug but... you know..."

"I know. Great to see you, Jen."

"This is my boss's boss at CSIS, Jim Sharkey." Jen Halley had a big promotion as a result of our last encounter, so Jim must be high up in Canada's Security Intelligence Service.

My hand comes up to shake his until I remember. Damn Covid!

He gives a little wave. "Nice to meet you, Cal," he says. "We have a car waiting. Would you be OK coming with us so we can talk on the way into town?"

"No problem for me, I've been vaccinated, both jabs."

"I can have someone drive your car home too."

"Not necessary. I came here on the Sky Train. It's the quickest way from downtown."

As we walk out of the terminal, a clean-cut young woman in a suit approaches us. She has RCMP written all over her. Canada's federal police force hires a lot of smart young people like her.

"Mr. Sharkey, I'm Constable Malone, I'll be driving you." She leads us to a black stretched limo.

As soon as we are settled inside, Jim says, "Your call to Jen yesterday has set a lot of wheels in motion."

I gesture at the inside of the limo. "So I see."

"First I have to thank you and your firm. We've been trying to find out who the people are in the Rasul Brigade for about a year now. There are a ton of wannabe terrorist websites on the internet but we think the Rasul Brigades's the real deal. We think they're aligned with the Syrian Ahfad al-Rasul Brigades.

"Do you remember the murder of a Jewish businessman in Vancouver last year?" I nod. Who could forget it? The poor guy was beheaded. "We got some images from a gas station CCTV camera and one of the people who killed him was a facial recognition match for one of the guys on the Rasul website. There are other incidences connected to them but we were never able to put names to any of the people on the site. We used software to scan Facebook and Instagram to try and find a match for the faces on the website but came up with zip. So as you can imagine, your call to say that you had the name and address of one of them got our attention. How did you do it?"

I tell them about Lucy's night-long search through

radical websites using the photo of Haasim in the background of one of Kitana's Instagram posts.

"We should hire her," Jim says.

"Over my partner's dead body," I chuckle.

"I'm looking forward to seeing Nick, Lucy and Adry," Jen says.

"Where are we going now?" I ask.

"We have two Emergency Response Teams assembling. One for the Ajram residence the other for the Hamra Café. I'm going to meet up with my RCMP colleagues and we're hopefully going to arrest Haasim this afternoon. We thought you might like to come along."

This was what Jim Garry was worried about.

"I appreciate it but here's the thing. As I told Jen on the phone this morning, we believe Haasim Ajram murdered his sister but our client is in jail for it. To prove our client innocent, we need Haasim's DNA and something to refute his alibi." I tell them about the bloody shirt, the sloppy investigation of Kitana's murder and our concerns about Detective Eric Street. I conclude with, "I'm worried that when you arrest Haasim Ajram, the possibility that he killed her will be overlooked in the investigation of his terrorist activities."

Jim Sharkey nods and looks out of the car window at the Vancouver cityscape. I know not to interrupt his train of thought.

Finally, he looks back at me. "We owe you and your firm, Cal. Not only will I make Ajram's DNA available to you. I'll have the RCMP officially make a request for the quick release of the bloody shirt and have them do a thorough DNA analysis. If Ajram's DNA is on that shirt, the Mounties will find it."

"Thank you so much, I can't tell you how grateful I am."

He gives a little grunt and I suspect he's smiling behind the mask. "There's also a little bit of self-interest too," he admits. "It may be difficult to prove Ajram was involved in the killing of that businessman last year but, if we can get him convicted for his sister's murder, that will put him behind bars. It will also give us some leverage. Maybe we can get him to name other members of the Rasul Brigade and other affiliated groups."

He takes a deep breath and leans forward in his seat. "Now," he says, "tell me about this Detective Eric Street."

I tell them everything I know about Street, including that his involvement in the Rasul Brigade would explain how they were able to get my home address and put surveillance on me last night. I tell them the whole story.

"Give me the licence plate and I'll find out who they are. Maybe we can have the Mounties pick them up too." She taps the plate number into her phone. "Not so easy," she says. "It was a rental car." She turns her phone towards me and shows me the details. "I'll send someone to the rental company to check them out," she adds.

"Let me do that," I say. "Coming to my home... That makes it personal."

"I dunno, Cal." She looks towards her boss and he gives an almost imperceptible shrug. "OK. But keep us in the loop."

"Thanks, I appreciate it."

"How did Tina take it?" Jen asks.

I squirm a bit in my seat.

"I didn't exactly tell her."

ADRY STARTS SPEAKING BEFORE I'M EVEN HALFWAY THROUGH the door. "Cal, you will never guess what I found in that lab on Powell Street. I'm not a hundred percent sure, so I sent it out to another lab to confirm it, but I'm pretty sure it was—"

"Crystal meth," I say and then regret it as I see her face fall.

"How did you know?" she asks.

"My chemistry guy at SFU looked at all those equations and said Kitana must have been a *bona fide* genius. She came up with a really efficient way to manufacture large quantities of meth safely."

"What?" Nick almost shouts it. "When I had dinner with Steve on Tuesday evening, he was saying that there was a flood of very high-quality meth on the streets up until a couple of months ago. He said that a couple of the big street gangs had been fighting over distribution."

I process this for a moment. "That explains something else," I say. "You remember Goliath, the big guy from George Walsh's gang?"

"Sure. Guy Chang. He tried to kill Larry Corliss a couple of years back but you stopped him."

"He's in Kent and he's got it in for Micah but I couldn't figure out why. If Kitana was manufacturing meth for Goliath's gang, the supply would dry up when she died. Like the rest of the world, Goliath thinks Micah killed her. That's why he wants to get to Micah. The only thing stopping Goliath from killing Micah is a guy called Blackbird. He's the one protecting Micah. Maybe he's from the rival gang."

"It fits the logic these guys operate under," Nick says, "but I've still got a problem believing that a smart, young woman like Kitana Ajram would get involved in manufacturing crystal meth for a street gang."

Adry pitches in. "Her friend Sarah said that she was very ambitious and wanted to make a heap of money so she could be independent of her family and go do a Ph.D. at Harvard."

"Micah said she was very ambitious too," I add.

Nick nods. "Manufacturing meth would generate enough cash to go to Harvard, that's for sure."

I pivot.

"What did Steve say about the Beretta?" I ask.

"There was nothing on the serial number in Canada. He said he'd check to see if it had been used in a crime in the US."

"Isn't there some gun database in the US?" Adry asks.

"Only on TV," Nick grunts.

We lapse into silence.

But not for long.

"You know," Nick says. "Maybe we're thinking too much like cops here."

"What do you mean, Nick?" Adry asks.

"Cops are trained to try and prove a crime beyond a reasonable doubt. But what we're doing here is trying to *show* reasonable doubt. If we can prove that the brother knew about Kitana's relationship with Micah and that his warped belief system meant he had to kill her for it, then that's reasonable doubt. We can also show there's a good case to be made that Kitana was mixed up with rival drug gangs and that one of those gangs had a good reason to kill her. That's reasonable doubt too."

"You're right," I say. "Jen and her boss have invited me to watch them pick up Haasim Ajram this afternoon. They're going to interrogate him about her murder. Maybe we'll get lucky and he'll admit it. But even if he doesn't admit it, his alibi that he was at the Hamra Café won't be worth anything, because they're going to raid that place too."

"Yeah," Nick says. "And if they can prove that slime ball Eric Street is the blue-eyed terrorist on the Rasul Brigade website, then the evidence he gave at Micah's trial won't be worth a damn and Micah will be out of jail in no time."

"Let's see how things pan out this afternoon but I'm feeling pretty good about our chances of exonerating our client without needing to get to the bottom of this crystal meth thing."

There is a noise at the front door and Lucy comes into the office struggling with some shopping bags. I get up and help by grabbing two of the bags. One has about two dozen beers in it and the other has four bottles of wine. "Planning a party, Luce?" I say.

"No," she says. "It's our new thing at the office. Every Friday, we stop work at four-thirty and have a few drinks and snacks and chat about the week. Sometimes we even invite clients. I picked up some nice craft beer for you Cal."

"Hopefully I'll be back in time from seeing Haasim's arrest. Maybe we'll have something special to celebrate."

That'd be good," Lucy says, "because one of my ideas didn't work out."

"Which one," I ask.

"The white guy on the Rasul website. I tried to get a picture of Detective Eric Street to try and see if I could get a match with his eyes. The only pictures I could find of him were on Instagram and Facebook and I couldn't find an image with high enough resolution to make a comparison."

"Shame," Nick says. "Good try, Luce."

"Thanks, Dad." Lucy turns to Adry. "I'm dying to know. What was on that burner phone Kitana had? Were you able to charge it up OK?"

"OMG," Adry says, "I completely forgot about that." She shuffles some papers around on her desk and pulls the phone out from underneath them. It's still in its Ziploc bag. She powers it up. "It's working," she says. She taps some buttons. "There's only one number in the call log. Looks like she only used it to talk to one person." She pauses a moment. "Should we call it?" she asks.

"And what would we say?" Lucy adds.

We kick ideas around for about fifteen minutes before coming up with a solid plan. "You do it, Rogan," Nick says. "If anyone can talk to a drug dealer, it's you." Nick opens his desk drawer and pulls out a burner phone. We always keep a few on hand. He slides it across his desk and I take it and dial the number. I put it on speakerphone and Nick turns on the digital recorder on his desk.

"*Who's this?*" a deep male voice says.

"My name's Vince," I say. "I'm a friend of Kitana Ajram."

"*Never heard of her.*"

"Then how'd you know it's a her?" I'm betting he's not enough of an expert in middle-eastern first names to give me the obvious answer.

A pause.

"*What d'you want?*"

I use the words we carefully crafted. "She was helping you with a certain product," I say. "Now that she's dead, I can maybe take her place."

"*How'd you get my number?*"

"She gave it to me. Said I should contact you if something happened."

Another pause. Longer this time.

"*She's been dead for months. Why now?*"

"I've been... away. Just got back into town and heard about her." I see Adry crossing her fingers.

An even longer pause.

"Same quantities and same quality?" he asks. Adry and Luce make cheerleader gestures.

"Absolutely."

"Yeah. OK. What's it gonna cost me?"

"I'll be in touch," I say and hang up.

Nick turns off the recorder. "Son of a bitch!" he sighs. "I gotta admit I had my doubts that Kitana Ajram was involved in this whole crystal meth thing until I heard that guy." He shakes his head. "I'm losing my faith in human nature." He takes a deep breath. "I'll call Steve, get him to track down that guy's cell."

"Are you sure Steve's going to do that for you?" I say.

"Yeah, I told you; I got some leverage with him right now."

Nick sounds pretty confident but he won't say what that leverage is and it gives me an uneasy feeling.

———

EVERYONE'S WEARING MASKS BUT THERE ARE SO MANY OF US cramped in the command vehicle that our social distancing can only be measured in inches. Then again, it's almost certain that everyone in here has been vaccinated.

I have been watching two of the screens intently. One shows an image of the Ajram residence and the other is the Hamra Café. A City of Vancouver public works truck is parked outside the café. I watch as two men in neon jackets and hard hats haul out orange and black striped barriers and use them to block off the sidewalk. They start directing pedestrians to the other side of the street.

The senior RCMP officer—the Crown and pip on his epaulettes mark him as a Superintendent—gives the command and the members of the ERT pour out of the truck and burst into the Hamra. On the other screen, a team takes down the door of the Ajram residence and rushes inside. A cacophony of sound fills the command vehicle as the ERT members bark their commands and the occupants of the two premises react with screamed questions and objections. The images on the body cams of the team leaders don't show much, they are moving too fast.

It's over in less than sixty seconds.

"Let's go," the Super says and opens the back doors of the command vehicle. He leads the way with Jim Sharkey. Jen and I follow. We trot half a block, watching as a bunch of RCMP vehicles appear as if from nowhere, then we turn on to the Ajrams' street and walk onto the front lawn of the third house along. Four people are kneeling, handcuffed on the grass. There is an older couple who I assume are the parents. The others are Haasim Ajram and the hard-faced kid from the Hamra.

Just as we get there the ERT team leader comes out of the house and strides over to the Superintendent. "No other occupants, sir. It's clear."

The Super nods, "Good work." He pats the team leader on the shoulder then turns and waves at one of the trucks. Five people in crime-scene clothing spill out of the vehicle and lug their equipment into the house. Four uniformed constables from another vehicle hustle Haasim and the kid into separate police cars, which take them away. A corporal and a female constable help Mr. and Mrs. Ajram to their feet and the constable talks to them in what sounds to me like Arabic. Mr. Ajram is protesting volubly. They are gently led to another cruiser.

An odd silence descends.

I turn to Jen. "You and your boss have been busy. You

arrived in Vancouver less than six hours ago and got all this organized."

She smiles. "Oh, we started organizing this about one hour after we got your call yesterday morning. You guys did amazing work linking these guys to the Rasul Brigade."

The Super has gone off to organize his people but Jim Sharkey is still standing with Jen and me. "I agree with Jen," he says, "but I have some less-than-great news for you. We have been examining video from the bank machines opposite the Hamra Café. Fortunately, the bank archives them. We had one of our guys check out the videos for the day of Kitana Ajram's murder. The bank is right by the bus stop. We were able to see Haasim drop her off at the stop. He was clearly very angry; it looked like he was shouting at her. He then did a U-turn and parked at a meter outside the Hamra, left his car without feeding the meter and went into the café. A few minutes later a ninety-nine bus came along and she got on board. But her brother didn't come out of the café. He stayed there for hours. Didn't come out until seven-fourteen, which is well after her time of death. It looks like his alibi is good."

After the initial hit of disappointment, I take a deep breath and mentally recreate the scene he's just described. I realize he's not looking at it with cop's eyes. "Doesn't mean his alibi's solid," I say. "That section of Broadway is busy. There's a constant stream of trucks and buses going along there and there's a traffic light too. I know that bank. Its ATM cameras are right opposite the café but I'll bet that almost half the time, the line of sight from the cameras is obscured by passing trucks and busses either driving by or stopped at the lights. Haasim could have easily left the café, maybe with a friend, and taken a vehicle to UBC." I remember Stammo saying we just need reasonable doubt and warm to my theme. "The Rasul Brigade are not idiots. They would almost certainly know about the ATM cameras opposite their hangout. Haasim could have left through the café's back door and taken a friend's car to UBC, killed his sister and returned. Then he timed his exit from the Hamra when there were no trucks or busses to obscure a clear line of sight from the bank's cameras."

Before Jen and Jim can comment on my hypothesis, the RCMP Superintendent marches over to us. "The operation at the Hamra Café went perfectly," he says. "We picked up seven people; two of them were on the Rasul Brigade's website." He holds his phone so we can see it and swipes through the photos. I think I recognize a couple of the faces from the visit I made to the Hamra, but I don't see the faces I'm looking for.

"There are others," I say. I tell them about the two guys in the Toyota outside my townhouse last night.

"Would you recognize them again?" the Super asks.

"For sure, I got up close and personal."

"Good. Give me your card and I'll get you to come have a look at some mugshots of known and suspected terrorists. See if you can find a match."

He turns and marches off. Clearly a busy guy.

————

IT'S GOING TO BE A WHILE BEFORE THEY GET TO INTERROGATE Haasim Ajram. It's time I can put to good use. The Tuxedo Rent-a-Car location, at the foot of Granville Street just beside the Arthur Lang Bridge to the airport, has a parking lot full of vehicles. I walk into the office. There are five stations, one bored-looking employee and no customers.

Full parking lot and empty office: I guess the car rental business is also suffering from Covid.

"How can I help you, sir?" he asks as I approach his station.

I introduce myself, slide a business card under the plexiglass screen and check his name badge. "I wonder if you could answer a few questions for me, Hamid?"

He half-smiles. "If I can," he says cautiously.

I give him the licence plate number for the Toyota Camry which was parked outside my home last night. "I believe this is one of yours," I say.

He taps at his keyboard. His eyebrows flicker up. "Yes, it is."

"Can you tell me who's renting it at the moment?"

"No one. It was returned this morning."

I silently curse. All rental cars have GPS trackers. I was hoping to get him to tell me where I could find the car and hopefully the two guys who were in it last night.

"Who was it rented to?" I ask.

He looks at me for a moment. "How do I know you're really a PI?" he says.

It's a question I'm rarely asked. I guess he's just being careful. I take my BC Security Worker Licence out of my wallet and show it to him through the plexiglass. "Because the government says I am," I say.

He looks at the licence, then at my face and then back to the licence. I can tell by the confusion on his face that, in common with most of the population, he had no idea the BC government issues licences to people in any aspect of the security industry. Mine clearly says Private Investigator.

But there is more than just confusion on his face. "I still don't have to answer your questions," he says.

"That's right, you don't," I tell him. "But you should

know I'm working with CSIS and the RCMP on a terrorism case." I pull out my phone. "One call and you'll be asked the same question by a couple of Mounties." I look into his dark brown eyes and, with a strong feeling of shame, I play the race card. "They'll want to know why *you* didn't want to cooperate on a terrorism investigation."

The colour of his face reddens and there is a flash of contempt in his eyes. "I'm happy to answer any questions..." he says and pauses, "...to a *real* policeman."

Knowing I deserve his disapprobation, I say, "Listen, I'm really sorry. I shouldn't have—"

He interjects, "Is there anything else I can help you with sir?"

I've blown it.

"No, thank you," I say and slink out.

As I climb into the car my phone rings.

Even the good news I receive does nothing to assuage the guilt.

I feel like Lady Macbeth.

All the perfumes of Arabia will not sweeten this little hand.

───────

"SO, STEVE CAME THROUGH FOR YOU," I SAY AND RUFFLE Nick's hair. He hates that.

"Cut it out, Rogan," he says, smoothing his hair back. "And yeah. I told you he would." He hands me a slip of paper. "They got Telus to triangulate the location of the phone you called from Kitana's burner phone." Scribbled on the paper in Nick's spidery handwriting is an address on Gore Street, right in the heart of the downtown east side. "If you go there, be careful."

"Yeah, Cal," Adry says. "We've got the voice recording, isn't that enough."

"Unfortunately not. I talked to Jim Garry about it. He said we need to get a positive identification of who the person is on the recording. The more solid the evidence the better. So I'm going to do what we planned."

"How about I give you back up," Zeke says.

"Good idea," Nick chimes in before I have a chance to react. I have a gut feel about this new guy that just won't go away. And it's not good... But maybe I just need to get to know him better.

"Sure," I say. "That'd be great."

Lucy comes in from the reception area. "Everyone's here and it's four-thirty. Party time."

Zeke stands up. "Good," he says. "Let's crack a couple of beers and work out the details."

I think about the idea of sitting for hours on a stakeout with Zeke, waiting for the owner of that phone to show up at the address on Gore Street. I don't like long stakeouts at the best of times. Then I think of something Nick did a year ago in order to avoid a stakeout and a smile spreads across my face. I pull out my phone and make the necessary arrangements. When I tell him the fee, the words, "Fuckin' A!" ring in my ear.

As I hang up, Lucy presents me with an empty glass and a can of Cyclhops. "I remembered this is one of your favourite IPAs, Cal," she says.

I look longingly at the bright green beer can with the crazy design. "Sorry Luce, I've gotta pass. Jen Halley's boss said he's going to see if the RCMP guys are OK with me being part of the interrogation of Haasim Ajram. They could call me at any time. I can't show up with beer on my breath; they won't let me near him."

"In that case, here's another thing I can help you with," Zeke says with a lopsided grin. He takes the can from Lucy but not the glass. "Cheers," he toasts me and downs half of it.

It's another thing not to like about him. A good beer should be drunk from a glass. That way you get the full taste and smell and you can enjoy the carbonation properly. Hmm... am I becoming like one of those annoying wine snobs you meet all too often at dinner parties? Yeah, I probably am.

"Not bad," he says, taking another deep swig.

Before I can tell him that it's way more than just 'not bad', Nick wheels over, his glass of Jack Daniels balanced on his lap. "Got a minute Rogan?"

"Sure."

He nods his head and wheels out of the main office. I follow him to our tiny conference room. He makes sure the door is closed. "It's been a week, eh?" he says as I sit down.

I grunt my assent and watch him take a long sip of his Jack. He clears his throat and looks at me. I can't read his expression. Is it embarrassment? Not like him. Not much embarrasses Nick. I use that powerful interrogation trick: silence. After a second he realizes what I'm doing and smiles.

"Y'know Rogan," he says, "on Monday when you waltzed in here, I had mixed feelings about taking this case and, to be honest, about the idea of having you back in the firm."

He pauses and I nod.

"I got some decisions to make and I need to know if you're gonna be coming back permanently or if this is just a one-off case?"

I knew this question was going to arise sooner or later. I was kind of hoping that it wouldn't come up until after we'd got Micah out of Kent Institution because I just don't know the answer. I was enjoying my life in the world of academia. It was good to know that what I was doing wasn't endangering the lives of my family or myself. This new case has plunged me back into the world of crime and I am not at all happy about those guys in the Toyota hanging around outside my home last night. It makes so much sense to get Micah released and then return fully to my new life at SFU. It makes sense, but... As I mentally review the events of the past week, I have to admit to myself that I have felt ten times more alive than at any time in the last eight months.

I look at Nick and he's watching me like a hawk. "I've gotta be honest," I say. "I just don't know. Can you give me a few days to think it over?"

"Sure," he says. "But just a few days, OK?"

"Definitely," I say. Then the obvious question comes to mind. "You said you had some decisions to make. What specifically were you thinking?"

He takes a deep breath but before he can say anything my phone pings at me. I sneak a peek at the screen. It's a text. The one I wanted to get. But there's one thing about it that I don't like at all.

"Hold that thought," I say. "I've gotta go. Right now."

———

HE LOOKS UP AS WE WALK INTO THE ROOM. THE BLANK LOOK slides away. We are new faces to him. I stand by the door and watch the discomfort in his body as Jen walks over to the table to which he is chained. She doesn't sit on either of the chairs opposite him. She stands and looks down at him with a sneer on her face. "Good evening, Mr. Ajram," she says. "We're here to ask you some more questions." I can't know what's going on in his mind but if the content of his Rasul Brigade website is anything to go by, he will not be happy with being interrogated by a woman. Following our plan for this interrogation, Jen places her fists down on the table in front of him. She's tall and has to lean forward, bringing her breasts just inches from his eyes.

He squirms.

"You don't think very highly of women do you Haasim?" I say.

His eyes flick to my face, back to Jen's breasts for an instant, and then down to the shackles on his wrists.

"You believe that a woman is only half the value of a man, isn't that so Haasim?" Jen says.

I can see his masseter muscle undulate as he clenches and releases his jaw. The provocation is working.

"Where did you get such a *silly* idea as that?" I ask. He looks up at me and sees the supercilious smile on my face

"It's in the Hadith," he snarls at me.

Anger. Good. I didn't expect such a quick reaction.

"Oh... the Hadith," I say dismissively. "Then it *must* be right." I laugh.

"It is the teaching of the Prophet, peace be upon him," he shouts at me.

I look into his eyes. "So what did you think about your sister, Kitana?"

Confusion overlays the anger. Not a question he was expecting.

"How did you feel about her relationship with Micah Weston?"

His eyes are blazing now as his anger ramps up again.

"Did you lie in bed at night thinking about them?" I ask.

His jaw starts working again.

"I'll bet you did," I say. "Did you think about him fucking

her? I spoke to Micah you know. He told me she *really* liked it. He said she liked to—"

"She was a whore!" he screams. We're getting closer.

"No, no, no," I say, shaking my head. "She was just a nice young woman expressing her love for a nice young boy."

"She was a whore. She deserved to die!" he rages.

"So that's why you killed her?"

Rage and shock struggle across his face and he is panting, trying to control himself. I just need to push him over the edge.

"You killed her because it was Allah's will, right?"

He starts to bang his manacled wrists on the table in front of him. He is banging over and over. Almost there. I wait through three more bangs. "It was your duty to kill her, wasn't it?" I say in my most reasonable voice.

"YES!" he screams. "IT WAS MY DUTY!" Each word is emphasized with a bang.

He stops and his head flops down onto his chest. He draws in a deep breath and exhales, "It... was... my... duty."

Jen glances at me and I nod. She takes one of the chairs and carries it to a corner of the room and sits down. I walk over to the table and sit on the remaining chair.

"I want to apologize," I say. "I didn't mean to seem dismissive about the Hadith. I respect everyone's religious views and I will always defend everyone's right to practice their religion." He still sits with his head down. "I understand that it went against your beliefs that Kitana was seeing someone who was not of your religion but can you explain to me why you had to kill her?"

"She brought shame on my family, by committing adultery and squandering her virginity on a kuffar." This is good. The more you can get a suspect to justify an action, the easier it becomes for them to admit to it.

"I understand that," I say. "It's a terrible thing that she brought shame on your family but it's not against the law."

He pulls his head off his chest and looks me in the eye. "Not against your laws perhaps but the Sharia is the law of Allah and must be obeyed at all times." More justification. Good.

"So you felt she had to be punished by death?"

"Yes."

I pause for a second.

"Can you tell me how you killed her?"

"It is not relevant," he says. "She has been punished and she is dead—Allah have mercy on her—and the kuffar who violated her is in jail."

"Did any of your brothers in the Rasul Brigade help you with Kitana's punishment?" I ask.

"No."

"Your car was parked outside the Hamra Café during the time of her murder. Who drove you to Micah's house that afternoon?"

"None of this matters," he says. "Allah's will has been done. Why should I help you?"

"If you cooperate with us, you'll get a lighter sentence."

He thinks about this for a moment and I can feel myself holding my breath. His next words are going to exonerate my client. As he thinks, he nods his head as he works out what he is going to say. Just as I feel I am going to explode with the tension of waiting for him to confess, he gives a mirthless laugh.

"If I admit to you that I killed my sister," he says, "what will you do?"

"Firstly," I start to say, but he cuts me off.

"What you'll do is use my confession to get Micah Weston out of jail. The kuffar who seduced an innocent girl would be set free. I don't think so. No. It may have been my duty to punish my sister for her adultery but it wasn't me or any of my brothers who carried out the law." He smiles. "The real murderer is in jail and I hope he rots in there for the rest of his life."

15

CAL

Saturday

Zeke's car is a Ford Focus. We agreed that it's a lot less conspicuous than an Austin Healy three thousand and also a lot drier on a day like today. We are parked outside the address on Gore Street. Private investigators spend a lot of time on stakeouts. We may be here for a while but it will be a chance for me to get to know Zeke and find out if my initial dislike for him is warranted. Last night, Tina asked me, only half-jokingly I suspect, whether I was jealous of the fact that, during my absence from the firm, Zeke had become the *de facto* number two at Stammo Rogan Investigations. I rejected the idea out of hand, only half-truthfully I suspect. I have just finished telling him about yesterday evening's interrogation of Haasim Ajram.

"What did the lawyer say," he asks.

"I called Jim Garry after I left the interrogation. He said that the video of Ajram would do a lot to cast reasonable doubt on Micah's conviction. But, because Ajram didn't outright confess to killing his sister, it alone wouldn't be enough."

"What about this dirty cop Eric Street?" Zeke says. "Did you get a chance to ask if he was the white guy on the Rasul Brigade website?"

I give a frustrated sigh. "No. When they told me I was cleared to interrogate Ajram, they said that it was on condition I didn't mention anything about Street. They want to investigate that themselves."

"That sucks the big one."

"That's what Jim Garry said, but in more lawyerly terms. If we could prove that Street had any connection with Haasim Ajram, it would invalidate all the evidence he gave at Micah's trial and Micah would be out of Kent in twenty-four hours."

"Maybe your CSIS buddies will come up with something," he says.

"Maybe. But even if they don't, Jim said if we could get a positive ID on this gangbanger it would add another reasonable doubt." I pat the camera with the telephoto lens that's sitting in my lap.

The building we are parked opposite has an abandoned clothing store on the ground floor—probably a victim of COVID—with two shabby-looking apartments above. The rain makes it look even bleaker than it already is.

"Do you ever think the world has gone crazy?" Zeke asks. "How is it that a brilliant, young student, like Kitana Ajram, with her whole life ahead of her, decides she's going to go into the drug business? How does she even know how to hook up with a gangbanger like this guy?" He inclines his head towards the building.

That's a hell of a good question. "I don't know the answer to your second question but the lure of easy cash drives people to do strange things. Kitana wanted to go to Harvard. That's sixty grand a year US plus the cost of living, which has got to be another thirty. To go there for a Ph.D., you're looking at close to a quarter of a million Canadian. I doubt the parents could afford it and, even if they could, I get the feeling they wouldn't have approved of her going anyway. However, if she was smart enough to work out a process for making large quantities of meth, a quarter of a million bucks is well within reach."

Zeke mulls it over for a moment. "That gives us two possible motives for her murder. She was selling the drugs to one gang; maybe the rival gang murdered her to cut off the supply. But the other possibility is that she had made the cash she needed for Harvard and told the gang she wasn't going to manufacture any more meth for them. They suspect she's struck a better deal with the rival gang and so they kill her."

"Motive for two gangs to want to kill her is better than just one, I guess. It doubles the reasonable doubt that Micah did it," I say. Something doesn't feel quite right about what he's saying but I can't work out what it is.

"Are these your guys?" Zeke asks.

I follow his line of sight and sure enough, I see them, ambling down the road. "That's them," I say. "Ghost and Tommy. I've known them for years, from back when I was living on the streets. They're both alcoholics, both homeless. I've tried to help them get off the streets but they're too used to the life."

"You trust them," he asks.

"Sure," I say. "As long as I can put them to work in the morning before they start drinking, they're a hundred percent reliable."

Ghost is checking the street numbers on the buildings

and when he gets to the one we're surveilling, he nudges Tommy and says something. Zeke grabs the burner phone we brought with us and dials the number; his thumb hovers above the green button. I crack open the window a couple of inches and bring Nick's expensive Canon, with the even more expensive telephoto lens, up to my eye. I point it through the window so that the pictures I take will not be distorted by the rain on the car's windshield.

"Whodja think yer pushin'" Tommy's voice comes to me from across the street. He grabs Ghost and pushes him into the window of the shop, I can hear the bang as elbow meets glass.

Ghost shouts the expletive that makes me cringe, grabs Tommy and sends him crashing into the faded-green wooden door beside the window. As Tommy pushes himself off the door, he pushes his hand onto the doorbell like he's trying to regain his balance.

"We should nominate these guys for an Academy Award," Zeke says. He chuckles. "The homeless are yet another minority underrepresented by the Academy."

They get louder and keep pushing each other into the door and the window, all the while shouting obscenities at the tops of their voices. Less than a minute of this has the desired effect. The door crashes open and two men step out. I focus on the faces and press the record button on the Canon.

"It's ringing," Zeke says.

One of the new arrivals shouts, "What the fuck..." but Ghost and Tommy are doing a fairly decent impression of the Roadrunner and Wile E. Coyote. In seconds, they disappear around the corner onto East Hastings.

The second man pulls a phone out of his right-hand pocket, looks at it and stuffs it back in. His other hand goes into the left pocket and pulls out a second phone. I aim the telephoto lens at his face and increase the magnification.

"Who's this?" I see his lips move and hear his deep voice coming from the phone in Zeke's hand. It's the same voice that recognized Kitana's name. I take six pictures in two seconds. Now we have the face of the drug dealer she was selling to. If VPD cooperates, we'll soon have his name.

———

"HOW LONG YER KNOWN ROCKY?" GHOST EXTENDS A HAND that hasn't seen soap in a while and shakes with Zeke.

The latter looks confused. "My street name," I tell him.

He nods. "Cal, uh, Rocky and I met on Monday," he says.

Tommy gives a big grin as he takes his turn shaking hands. He has even fewer teeth than the last time I saw him, about eighteen months ago.

"Yer can take yer masks off," he says. "We both had our shots. Both jabs."

"It's good to be in a country where folk like us got health care," Ghost adds. "Not like them poor buggers down south."

The waiter comes over to our table.

"See," Ghost says to him with a big grin. "I told'ja someone was coming to buy us breakfast."

The Ovaltine Café is in the heart of the downtown east-side and has been a fixture here since 1942. The decor dates back to its opening. It is the oldest continuously-running restaurant in the city. But it's clean, with good food, served in big portions, and is probably the only place in Vancouver where you can still get a good, filling breakfast, any time of day, for less than ten bucks.

The waiter pours coffee all round and takes our orders. We all choose the corn beef hash. It's the best in the city.

"So didja get the pictures OK?" Ghost asks.

I pull the camera out of its bag and show him the screen. They peer at the pictures. "I know that guy," Tommy says. "Seen him around here a lot. Gang guy. I seen him talking to the street dealers. Acts like he's the boss."

"Do you know his name?" I ask.

He shakes his head. "Nah," he says. "Sorry." He thinks for a bit. "I think he's got a foreign accent."

"Hispanic?" Zeke asks. There are a few Guatemalan dealers. They used to dominate one block on Hastings, just west of where we are now.

"Dunno," Tommy says. "If yer like, Ghost and me'll try and find out his name."

"Don't put yourself at risk guys. We'll probably get his name by showing his ugly mug to the drug squad."

Ghost pitches in. "We don't mind... a little extra money..." He leaves the sentence hanging.

I take my cue and pull out my wallet. Ten twenty-dollar bills slide across the table, get split evenly and vanish into deep pockets.

"Thanks, Rocky," Ghost says.

"You're welcome guys," I say.

"Let me see that picture again." I hand him the camera. He looks at the screen and pulls a smartphone out of his jacket. It's old but it works. He lines it up and takes a picture of the Canon's screen. He looks at the resulting picture and nods, satisfied. "We'll get a name for yer Rock. You'll see."

The waiter brings a huge tray and puts it on the adjacent table. He places a large, steaming plate of hash in front of each of us. Tommy rubs his hands together in anticipation. Ghost gives a big grin and uses his signature expression.

"Fuckin' A!"

———

NICK'S PHONE RINGS AND ALL THREE OF US JUMP. NICK JABS the speakerphone button. "Stammo," he says.

"Hi, Nick. It's Domenic Dixon from the drug unit, Steve said to call you."

"Hey Dom, good to hear your voice. It's been a while. I'm sitting here with my partner Cal Rogan and another one of our guys Zeke Stone. It was them who got the photograph and we're kinda hoping you can put a name to it."

"That's what Steve told me." He pauses. *"Do you want the good news or the bad news?"*

Simultaneously, I say, "Good." and Nick says, "Bad." We're nothing if not predictable.

My voice must have been louder because he says, *"The good news is that he is almost certainly a major drug dealer. We've got a bunch of other photos of him in the company of known dealers. The bad news is he's fairly new in town and we don't have a name for him yet. When I saw the picture, I was hoping you'd be able to ID him."*

"No such luck," Nick says. "If we find out anything, I'll let you know." They exchange pleasantries for a minute or two and hang up.

"That sucks," Zeke says.

"Maybe Ghost and Tommy will come up with something?" I say.

"What are they gonna do?" Nick asks. "Walk up to dealers on the street and say, 'Is this guy one of yours? If so, what's his name?'"

"Street-level dealers may not even know his name," Zeke says.

I look at him and nod. "And we can't exactly go to one of the gang leaders and ask…"

My voice trails off and they look at me. I can feel the smile spreading across my face.

"What?" Nick says.

"*We* can't go to one of the gang leaders," I say. "But I know someone who can."

I check my watch. Ten forty-five. With a bit of juggling, I just have time.

———

THE CALL GOES TO VOICEMAIL. "HI, SWEETIE," I SAY. "IT'S ME. Something's come up. Can you phone Bridges and change our reservation to one o'clock? Seeing as the rain's stopped and it's warm and sunny, maybe we could get a table on the dock. I'll meet you there, then. Love you."

A week ago today, Tina and I planned for this weekend to be a romantic stay-cation weekend. That was before my visit to Kent Institution on Sunday. When I told her that I had to work this morning, I promised to make up for it by taking her to lunch at Bridges. It's a much-loved Vancouver restaurant that has been on Granville Island for over forty years. It gets its name from the fact that it's between the Burrard and Granville bridges. I just hope she checks her voicemail. I wouldn't want her to show up an hour before me. Definitely not the stuff of romance.

I pull off Chancellor Boulevard, onto Westbrook Crescent and then Newton Wynd.

Melanie opens the door five seconds after I ring the bell. She is wearing shorts and a loose teeshirt with nothing under it. Her hair looks less than lustrous but she is still stunning.

"Do you have some good news?" she asks. Her eyes are sparkling with hope. She takes my arm and leads me into the living room.

"We're getting there," I tell her. "I emailed you about the interrogation of Kitana's brother last night. He didn't come out and admit that he killed her but he looks good for it. He actually said that it was his duty to kill her. But that's not what I wanted to talk to you about."

"Is it about the things we found in Kate's desk?" she asks.

I nod. "The chemical formulae in that red file were descriptions of a process for manufacturing crystal meth."

Her eyes do a fairly good imitation of saucers. "Crystal meth?" she echoes. "She was manufacturing drugs? Are you sure?"

I tell her about Adry's trip to the former brewery.

"Unbelievable," she says.

"You remember the burner phone that was in her desk?" She nods. "It had the number of a drug dealer. We think she was selling him the meth. However, to make a case that he or a rival gang may have killed her, we need a positive identification of who he is."

"How are you going to do that?"

"When you visit Micah tomorrow, I want you to give him this picture." I hand her an envelope with an eight-by-ten print of the photo I took this morning. "Get him to show it to his friend Blackbird. See if he can come up with a name. With a picture, a name and the recording I made of him, together with the recording of Haasim's interrogation, maybe Jim Garry can make a case for Micah's release."

She looks at me and tears start to well in her eyes. Before I can say anything, she throws her arms around me and hugs me. "Thank you, thank you, thank you," she says softly. Her breath in my ear sends a shudder through me. She holds me tight and I can feel the warm pressure of her breasts through the teeshirt. I feel my body react. So does she. But she doesn't let go.

She looks up at me and I feel an overwhelming desire to kiss the v-shaped scar on her chin. I see her lips part a fraction and I start to lean in. I feel her rising up onto her toes and she rubs herself against me. Our lips are inches apart. I feel my arms moving up to slide around her waist and know that unless I stop now...

I take a quarter step back.

She takes her arms from around my shoulders and puts her feet flat on the floor.

"Oh, Cal. I'm sorry. I didn't mean to... I just felt overcome with gratitude... I'm really sorry."

I manage to pull myself together. "No problem," I say. "I understand. Really."

We stand twelve inches apart, looking at each other. For a second, I think we are going to fly into each other's arms again and if we do, there will be no going back. She stands still, waiting. Waiting for me to make the decision. And I know she is mine if I choose.

"I'd better go," I say. "I have to..."

"Yes, of course," she says awkwardly. She still has the envelope in her hand. "I'll get Micah to show this to Blackbird."

I turn and step out of the living room and across the hall.

As I reach to open the front door, I hear her voice. "Cal. Wait."

I turn back.

She walks out of the living room. She has taken the picture out of the envelope. "I know this man," she says. "Well, not exactly know him but I've seen him before. I told you that when Micah first started to date Kate, she and I met for lunch." I nod and she continues. "As we were leaving the restaurant, this man came up to her and said he needed to talk. She seemed kind of embarrassed. She didn't actually introduce us but she said he was one of her professors. Then she said a very quick goodbye to me and went off with him. I thought it was kind of odd at the time but I didn't think anything more about it until I saw this photo."

"Do you remember anything else about him?" I ask.

"Not really, except that he had a very deep voice."

It's definitely the same guy. "Tomorrow, see if Micah's friend Blackbird can put a name to the face and call me as soon as you can."

"I will, for sure," she says.

She opens the front door to let me out.

———

Granville Island isn't actually an island. It's a thirty-five-acre peninsula. It was built in 1916 out of material dredged from False Creek and was an industrial area for sixty years until the federal government repurposed it. Now it's a vibrant tourist and shopping area and is home to some of Vancouver's best restaurants.

I finally find a parking spot, which is never an easy task on the weekend. It's at the far end of the island from Bridges restaurant but beggars can't be choosers. I get no reply from Tina's phone which means she's probably driving here or, more likely, scouring the island for her parking spot. She is a stickler for not using her phone when she drives; she won't even use the Bluetooth connection in her car to take a call. A wave of guilt passes through me as I think of my meeting with Melanie Weston. It was pretty obvious how she felt and I can't believe how close I came to responding. Even now I think... I shake my head. There's no way I could do that to Tina.

The walk to the other end of the island will give me time to clear my head of those thoughts and also to make another call. We have two pillars of reasonable doubt so far. The first is that Haasim Ajram killed his sister. The second is that someone from a drug gang killed her. But a third pillar, which would trump the other two, is that Detective Eric Street is the blue-eyed caucasian on the Rasul Brigade website. If he is, that alone would be reason enough for an appeal of Micah's conviction. Jen Halley answers on the third ring.

After the usual pleasantries, I ask, "Have you moved on Eric Street?"

There is a pause. *"We haven't talked to him yet."*

I wait for more but she doesn't elaborate. "Did you get a pattern match on his eyes? Is he the blue-eyed guy on the website?" I ask.

Another pause. *"We, uh, don't have a high-enough-resolution picture of his face to do the pattern matching."*

"So why not pick him up, take a close-up picture and interrogate him?" I can hear the impatience in my voice.

"We don't exactly have probable cause, Cal," she says. *"Just because you think he might have fabricated the DNA evidence on Micah's shirt, it doesn't in any way connect him to an extremist website."* She drops her voice. *"Listen, I'm as frustrated as you but we can't just arrest him."*

"Jen, he's a cop. If he doesn't already know about the arrest of Haasim, he will soon. If he's the one on the website, he'll disappear before we can question him."

"I get that," she says. I hear voices in the background. *"Sorry Cal, I have to go."*

Before I can push her some more, she hangs up.

As frustrated as I feel, I can't refute the logic. The idea that a red-haired, blue-eyed detective is part of a radical group is a bit far-fetched, to say the least. When I think of it like that, even I have my doubts. But just because it's logical, doesn't make it right. Something stirring in my gut tells me I can't let this go. But how do I get enough evidence to support probable cause? Maybe I should—

"Excuse me, could y'all help."

The voice snaps me out of my thoughts.

The speaker is a kind-looking, older man in a check shirt, shorts, long socks and sandals. He is standing in front of the Granville Island Public Market with a similarly dressed woman. "Could y'all take a picture of us?"

We Vancouverites pride ourselves on our hospitality, most of us anyway. "Sure," I say. "I'd be happy to. Where are you folks from?"

He hands me his phone. "Richmond. The one in Kentucky, not Virginia."

"I've never been there. But we have a suburb called Richmond." I take a picture, step back and take another.

I hand him the phone and he checks the pictures I've taken. "Why, thank you, son. Those are just about perfect," he says. He shows them to his wife.

As we say our goodbyes, it hits me. In the last fifty metres to Bridges, I call Nick, update him on the conversation with Jen and tell him my idea. He's all over it like white on rice.

I take a deep breath and let it out slowly. With everything under control, I can have a nice brunch with Tina. I look over Bridges' deck and see an empty table with an umbrella and an uninterrupted view along False Creek and out into English Bay.

I give the hostess a big smile. "I have a reservation for

two people at one o'clock. It's either in the name of Johal or Rogan and I'd really like *that* table." I point out the one with the view.

She returns the smile and then some. "I'll see what I can do," she says and consults her list, while I muse that the names Johal and Rogan sound good together.

The deck at Bridges is a pretty romantic setting. I wonder if I should—

"I just have a reservation for twelve. I called the number for the reservation but just got voicemail. I had to let the table go at twelve-fifteen. I'm so sorry."

Tina must have missed my earlier call.

"How long would I need to wait for a table for two to come free?" I ask.

She runs her finger down the list. "I can put you down for one-thirty," she says.

I confirm and watch her write our names on the list. They look good written down too.

I call Tina.

Voicemail.

16

NICK

Rogan's right. It's completely bat-shit crazy to think that Street is a terrorist, that he's the white guy on the Rasul Brigade website. Crazy... but not impossible. Talking of impossible, I thought it would be impossible to find these two jokers sober at two in the afternoon, especially after Rogan gave them a hundred bucks each this morning, but hey, sometimes miracles *do* happen.

I'm sitting in my truck kitty-corner from Street's apartment building in Burnaby. It's a while since I've done a stakeout. For some reason, it gives me a craving for a smoke, but if Rogan can stay away from the heroin, I can stay away from the smokes.

It's an older building. One of those where it rests on pillars and the ground floor is completely taken up with an open parking area. It makes things easy for our purposes and lets Ghost and Tommy use a trick they've used before. We go over the details one more time before they get out of my truck. They seem to be clear on it.

Tommy's Indigenous Canadian and insists *he* should

wear the cowboy hat. He said he thought it would be ironic. Rogan would like his choice of words.

"Remember guys," I say. "Do this right and there's another hundred bucks each for you."

"We won't let yer down Mr. Stammo," says Tommy.

"You and Rocky can always trust us," says Ghost.

They wander across the road and into the building's parking lot. I remember from when I was back in the department that Street has a white Dodge Challenger with a blue racing stripe. He's just so proud of that car. It's parked in the corner of the lot, farthest from the elevator lobby. Tommy positions himself halfway between the car and the lobby. Ghost walks to the Challenger, puts his hands on the hood and bounces it up and down until the alarm goes off. Then he sits on it.

I check my phone. Everything seems OK.

The alarm's louder than most. Ghost has got his hands over his ears.

After a moment the alarm goes off.

Ghost bounces up and down and the shrieking starts up again.

Then it stops.

Ghost bounces. It starts...

Then it stops.

And one more time...

Then it stops.

And one more time,...

But this time it doesn't stop.

It takes two minutes and seven seconds.

Street bursts out of the elevator lobby.

I check my phone. Everything seems OK.

He has a fob in his hand. He points it at the car and the alarm stops.

"Hey! What the fuck you think you're doing?" I hear him say as he strides across the parking lot.

Tommy moves into Street's path. "He don't mean no harm mister," he says, getting right up into Street's face.

I check my phone. Everything seems OK.

"Get out of my way, you bum." Street gives Tommy a shove and breaks into a trot towards his car. As soon as Street has passed Tommy, Ghost slides off the hood and races out of the parking area and down the street. For an ageing alcoholic who lives on the streets, Ghost is fast.

Street gives chase. We thought he might.

Tommy sticks to the script. "You'll never catch him, mister," he shouts as he runs over and jumps on the hood of the Challenger. The alarm screams again and Street turns. Right on cue, Tommy grinds his foot into the hood.

Street yells, "Get away from my goddamn car, you motherfucker." He runs back towards the car but Tommy jumps down and runs off in the opposite direction from Ghost. Street hits the fob again. His head swivels from Tommy running in one direction, holding on to his hat, to Ghost running in the other direction.

He strides back to his car and examines the hood.

He mouths something but he's too far away from Tommy for me to pick up what he says.

But I can make a good guess.

That was fun to watch.

I check my phone. Everything's perfect.

———

Two blocks from Eric Street's apartment building, I pick them up. They are both out of breath and both are laughing like clowns. "How'd we do Mr. Stammo?" Ghost asks.

I show them my phone and they peer at it. "Let's just say you earned yourselves a fifty buck bonus," I say.

"Fuckin' A!" says Ghost.

"That's one hell of a camera," Tommy says, handing me the cowboy hat.

I carefully extract the miniature camera with the very expensive lens from inside the hat.

"If you don't mind the little hole where the lens poked through," I say to Tommy, "you can keep the hat as a souvenir."

"Thanks, Mr. Stammo. You're alright." He plonks the hat on his head.

"You done good, guys," I say and hand three fifty-dollar bills to each of them.

"Thanks, Mr. Stammo," says Tommy,

"Yeah, thanks," Ghost adds. "And tell Rocky we're gonna find out the name of that drug dealer he took the pictures of this morning."

I make the call first and then put the truck in gear.

I've got to take these guys back to the downtown eastside and get back to the office.

Then the real work begins.

———

"WHAT ARE YOU DOING IN THE OFFICE ON A SATURDAY, Adry?" I ask.

"Lucy called me. She said you'd got a hi-res picture of Eric Street. I wanted to be in on the kill."

What a team!

I hand the tiny camera to Lucy and she connects it to her

computer. She opens the app and hits play. The image of the inside of my truck wobbles as Tommy puts on the hat with the camera inside.

"Skip ahead to three minutes," I tell her.

The image changes to the view from outside Eric Street's elevator lobby. Lucy turns down the volume so that the scream of the car alarm is bearable. We watch the elevator door open. Street strides into the lobby and through the glass door into the parking garage. We see him hit the fob and the noise of the car alarm stops. Street's image gets bigger as Tommy converges on him, soon his whole face takes up the screen as Tommy pushes in front of him. Lucy hits pause and Street's face is frozen on the screen. She clicks forward what looks like one second at a time. Then clicks back a couple of seconds. "Getting there," she says. She is now advancing one frame at a time. She stops and clicks back a couple of frames. Street's eyes are centred on the screen. "That's the money shot," she says. She zooms in and has a near-perfect image of Street's eyes. A couple more clicks of the mouse and there are two images on her screen. On the left is the banner from the Rasul Brigade website. She zooms in on the picture of the man with his head and face covered so that only his eyes show. On the right is the picture Tommy took less than an hour ago.

I'm no expert on pattern recognition but I'd bet my VPD pension on the eyes being from the same man.

I grab my phone and select my only contact with an Ottawa area code.

———

WE'VE NEVER HAD SO MANY PEOPLE IN THE OFFICE BEFORE. In addition to Jen and her boss Jim Sharkey, there's an RCMP

superintendent, in uniform, and two of his plainclothes officers, an inspector and a sergeant. Only Rogan's missing even
though I've texted him three times.

"Do you want us to wait for Cal?" Jen asks. From the
frowns of her colleagues, I'm guessing she just lost a couple
of brownie points.

"No, it's fine. Let's get started."

"Just before you do start," says the Super, "I wanted to
tell you how impressed we all are with your firm." Nods all
around from the assembled feds. "Not only did you put a
name to one of the terrorists—something we've been trying
to do unsuccessfully for about a year—but you've also made
the connection with this VPD detective too. On behalf of
both the RCMP and CSIS, I wanted to say how grateful we
are. If there's ever anything we can do for you, just call me."

I look around at the big grins on the faces of Lucy, Adry
and Zeke and I kinda think those grins are thanks enough.
But not quite. "Just doing our jobs," I say, "but if you ever
want to use our services..." I just leave it hanging and am
rewarded with a quiet nod from the Super. "OK, Luce," I say.
"Show them the pictures."

Lucy takes them through the video of Street and the
comparison of his eyes with the eyes on the Rasul Brigade
website. She does it so professionally that I can't keep the
big stupid grin off my face; I am just so damned proud of
my wonderful daughter. Which of course makes me think
of her brother. If only Matt had taken a different path, he
wouldn't be in Royal Oak cemetery. But I can't think of
that now. For now, I need to focus on Lucy. I'll think about
Matt later. Like I have every night for the last couple of
years.

The inspector's voice breaks my train of thought. "Can
you email me a copy of that video," he asks Lucy.

He hands her his card and she smiles and nods. A few keystrokes and she says, "Done."

"When we've had our lab look at it," says the Super, "we'll pick up Detective Street. Tonight probably."

"That's great," I say. "Can one of you let me know when he's in custody? I need to inform Micah Weston's lawyer. The detective who investigated his girlfriend's murder being in the same terrorist group as her brother will invalidate the evidence presented at Micah's trial. We'll have him out of Kent in a day."

I smile up at the Super. He looks at Jen's boss who holds his gaze for a moment and then looks at me for a long five seconds before taking a deep breath. What's going on here? "The thing is, Nick," he says, "you can't do that."

"Why the hell not?"

"National security. None of you can talk to anybody about this and certainly not to Micah's lawyer. You can't even tell your spouses." His gaze shifts to each of us in turn. "Do you all understand that?"

The three of them nod but I'm not buying it. "Wait a minute! There's a kid locked up in Kent Institution for a crime he didn't commit." I can feel my anger ramping up. "One of the prison gangs wants to kill him for fuck's sake. And you're telling me I can't use the *one* piece of evidence that will get him out of there fast."

"I'm afraid so," Sharkey says. "I don't like it any more than you do Nick, but one man's situation doesn't weigh much against the security interests of the country."

I bite back the words I want to shout at them and just sit in my chair and fume. If I use the one thing that will ensure Micah's release, these guys will be back here in no time with a warrant for *my* arrest. I fume some more. It doesn't help. When life hands you lemons...

"When *can* we use this evidence?" I ask.

"Believe me, Nick," Sharkey says, "as soon as we can release it, you'll be the first to know."

"And how long's that?"

He shrugs. He's government. It's never going to be quick. Maybe I can use this.

"If we can't use Street, can you put a rush on getting the DNA from the shirt? If Haasim Ajram's DNA is on it, we can—"

"It's not," Jen cuts in. "We put a rush on the DNA and got the results back an hour ago. There was DNA from Kitana Ajram, Micah Weston and from a third person. It wasn't Haasim or any of the other people we arrested yesterday. It wasn't Eric Street and there was no match in any of our databases."

Strike two. I can feel myself deflating.

There's silence for a while then Adry says, "That doesn't rule Haasim out. When I saw him at the Ajram's house, he was wearing a teeshirt but he had a long-sleeved, traditional-looking shirt underneath it. If he was dressed the same when he killed Kitana, the long-sleeved shirt could have kept his DNA off the teeshirt."

"You could be right, Adry," Jen says. "He was dressed like that when we arrested him yesterday."

"Yeah," I grunt. "But that just stops us from ruling him out. It doesn't prove that he *was* wearing it."

Zeke speaks for the first time. "That's right. But let's say Haasim *was* wearing the teeshirt over a long-sleeved shirt. The long-sleeved shirt might have kept *his* DNA off the teeshirt, but there's no way the teeshirt would have kept *Kitana's* blood off the long-sleeved shirt."

He's right. Good lad.

"It's a long shot," Jen says. "Kitana's murder was months

ago. Even if Haasim didn't throw away his long-sleeved shirt, it would have been washed a bunch of times since the murder. But blood is persistent, we might be able to pick up something." She looks over at the RCMP Inspector and he nods. He pulls out his phone and steps into our reception area. I can hear him snapping instructions to his crime scene people. It's official; I definitely don't like RCMP Inspector Patrick Wright.

"There's another possibility," Adry says. "Cal told us that a couple of guys were checking out his townhouse complex. They're probably other members of the Rasul Brigade. What if one of them was the one who killed Kitana? Cal got their licence plate, it was—"

She is interrupted by my phone ringing.

"It's Rogan," I say as I answer it.

He says three words that make my blood run cold.

17

CAL

Ten minutes earlier

It's a measure of my worry that I'm knocking on this particular door. I waited at Bridges until two but Tina never showed. I called her parents but they said they hadn't heard from her. I've been waiting at home for the last couple of hours trying not to panic. I keep telling myself that sometimes Tina forgets to charge her phone and that sometimes when she gets a lead on a story, she will disappear for a while as she tracks it down. But now I can't take my mind off a darker alternative. I've ignored Nick's texts about coming into the office.

The door opens. My smile is not returned by my neighbour but Biscuit wags her tail.

"Hi Martha, I'm sorry to bother you, but have you seen Tina today?"

She frowns. "Why?"

Part of me doesn't want to tell her. She is the font of all gossip in our townhouse complex and would love to spread the word of trouble in our mixed-race paradise. The worried part of me takes precedence. "She and I were supposed to meet for brunch today but she didn't show up and she's not home right now. I'm just worried that something might have happened to her. Have you seen her?"

"No," she says, looking down. "We haven't, have we Biscuit?" As she looks back up at me, there is a smile on her face and it's not a nice one. "However..." she leaves the word hanging for a beat, "you might want to speak to Karla. She was telling me about Tina making some sort of fuss outside on the street. Apparently, there was some shouting. Karla was quite upset; it was right in front of her house."

I thank Martha and make my way to Karla's door. Although Martha is a gossip, she's fairly harmless but her friend Karla has a mean streak. I try to avoid her and her husband whenever possible.

She opens the door before the sound of the doorbell has died. It's like she was lurking in her hallway, waiting for me to appear.

"Hi, Cal," she says with a big smile. "How are you?" I know this smile. If you were to look up passive-aggressive in Wikipedia there would be a picture of Karla.

"Hi, Karla," I say with as pleasant a smile as I can muster. "Martha said that you had seen Tina earlier today."

The smile is replaced by a phony look of concern. "You know me, Cal," she says, "I don't like to complain, but Tina was out there on the street at about eleven this morning, right in front of *my* house, making a very unpleasant spectacle of herself."

I push down my anger at the enjoyment she is getting out of telling me this and craft my words to keep her talking. "I am *so* sorry, Karla. Whatever was she doing?"

" I think she was walking to the supermarket, she was carrying that big canvas bag she always uses for shopping. You know, the one with the aboriginal design on it." She pauses.

I rein in my mounting frustration. "I know the one," I say as nicely as I can. "What happened?"

"There was a car parked right in front of my window. There were two men in the car. Men like Tina, you know." A worm of fear slithers through my gut. Her words must mean that the men shared Tina's skin colour. I think back to Thursday night and to the two Rasul Brigade men with whom I had the altercation. I feel the blood drain from my face.

"Oh my God," I say. "Were they in a white Toyota Camry?"

She can see the fear, writ large across my face. "I don't know," she says. "I can't tell the difference between cars. I think it was silver."

"Can you tell me exactly what happened? It's really important Karla." I'm sure she can hear the tone of pleading in my voice. She'll relish it when she tells the story to Martha.

"Yes, of course," she says. "As Tina walked past the car, the passenger called her over. She talked to him and I could see she was angry. In no time at all, they were shouting at each other. I heard her yell 'No way am I getting into your...'" She hesitates. "I won't use the actual word she used but let's just say she told him quite forcefully that she wasn't going to get into his car."

"What happened then?"

"The man in the car said something, I couldn't tell what it was but it must have had an effect on Tina. She stood stock-still for a moment, then opened the back door of the car and got in. The passenger turned around to face her so I couldn't get a good look at his face except that I *did* see he had a big, ugly scar on his cheek."

It *was* the men from Thursday night. The one with the scar must have threatened Tina with his Glock to force her into the car.

"Are you all right, Cal?" Her words filter through the fear that's coursing within me.

"Yes... No... What happened next?" I'm starting to babble. Gotta keep control.

"They just drove off."

"Can you tell me anything about the car, anything at all?"

"No, just that it was silver."

"You didn't get the licence plate?" A desperate hope.

She shakes her head.

"Thanks so much, Karla, I really appreciate it," I manage to say as I stumble away.

She says something but I don't hear it. I pull out my phone and dial Nick. He answers on the second ring.

I say three words. "They've taken Tina."

There's a pause as it sinks in. *"What happened?"* he asks.

I give him a précis of my conversation with Karla.

"Hang on," he says. I hear him repeat what I told him to whoever's in the office. The next voice I hear is Jen Halley. *"You're sure it was the same guys who were checking out your place on Thursday night?"* she asks.

"Yes, absolutely. But I think they were in a different car this time."

She thinks for a second. *"I forgot to follow up with the car rental company. You said you were going to do it. Did you get a name?"*

I feel the embarrassment at how I treated Hamid at Tuxedo Rent-a-Car. "Sorry. I blew it. He wouldn't tell me who rented that Camry. I just know that it was returned Friday morning."

I hear her talking with someone else for about a minute.

"Cal, an RCMP Inspector, Patrick Wright, is going to meet you at Tuxedo. How soon can you be there?"

"Why can't you guys just phone Tuxedo's head office and get the information or hack into their computer system or something?"

"We just checked that out. Tuxedo's a small local firm. They don't have a head office. The RCMP has a file on them, Patrick's boss thought it would be better to go there in person and not give them any advanced warning. Plus he's going to get a forensics team there to go over that Camry with a fine-tooth comb."

"I can be there in less than ten minutes. Tell Wright I'll meet him there."

She talks some more with her colleagues.

"He's organizing the forensic team right now and he said he'll meet you there in fifteen minutes or so."

"Great!"

"And Cal. Wait for him to get there, OK?"

"Sure. I'm betting the guy there is more likely to respond to an RCMP inspector than he is to me."

Feeling just a little less desperate, I hang up and head for the underground garage to get my car.

———

IN THE SEVEN MINUTES IT ACTUALLY TOOK ME TO GET HERE, I've worried myself sick at the thought of what the Rasul Brigade thugs might do to Tina. Not to mention that I've allowed myself to wallow in the guilt I feel that, for a second time since I've known her, my job has put Tina in danger. I just pray that she won't be physically harmed this time. I swear, after this is all over, I'm going back to my nice, quiet academic life at SFU.

The Healey looks a little out of place in the Tuxedo Rent-a-Car lot. I can see the white Camry. I wonder if the kidnappers rented a different car for today, a silver one. I'll know when Inspector Wright gets here and can use the authority of the RCMP to find out. Maybe I'll also find out why the RCMP has a file on Tuxedo.

The door of the office opens. It's Hamid. He pulls a bunch of keys from his pocket and locks the door. He heads across the lot. The lights flash on a small green Chevy as he unlocks the doors with his key fob. I can't let him leave before Wright gets here. We need access to his computer. I jump out of the Healey and walk on a path to intersect him. He sees me immediately and I see the look on his face change as he recognizes me. First anger, then fear. He casts a fast look around. Maybe looking for help in case I decide to attack him. I'll only attack him if I can't delay him from leaving.

I hold up my hands, palms forward, in a gesture that I hope says 'don't worry. I'm not going to hurt you.' When I get to within two meters of him, I stop. "I came here to apologize," I say.

"What for?" he says.

"When I was here yesterday afternoon, I was trying to find out who rented that white Camry over there. The reason I wanted to know who rented it is..." I pause. When I was here yesterday, how much did I tell him? Should I tell him about the Rasul Brigade? Maybe the RCMP file on Tuxedo is because they are suspected of supporting terrorists. If so, I can't tell them we are on to Rasul. Then again, it's not too likely. Canada isn't exactly a haven for terrorists; not so far as I know anyway.

When in doubt, go for the truth. "First I wanted to say I'm sorry. I implied that, because you have brown skin and your name is Hamid, that you might be a terrorist. That was *completely* out of line and I want to say that I'm truly ashamed and that I sincerely apologize to you."

He looks at me and blinks a couple of times. "Wow," he says. He shakes his head in a gesture of amazement. "You're not the first person to imply that. Imply? Hell, people have called me a terrorist to my face, more than once. And worse than that, too. But I gotta tell you, you are the first person who has ever come back to apologize." He smiles and nods. "Thank you, I accept your apology."

I feel like one weight has been lifted off my shoulders. Unfortunately, the other, greater, weight is still bearing down. "I know it's no excuse," I say, "but the reason I need to find those guys is that we think they *are* involved in a terrorist group and now it looks like they've kidnapped my girlfriend." I swallow hard, feeling my emotions bubbling up. Grief, frustration, anger at myself and fear for Tina all vie to be top of the heap. I bite my cheek, hoping to stop the tears that are threatening to escape.

He thinks for a second, blinks again and turns back towards the office. "Come on," he says.

I follow him across the lot. He unlocks the office door and holds the door open for me.

It takes him a minute to turn off the alarm and boot up his computer, then after a combination of taps at the keyboard and clicks of the mouse, he says, "Drew Gill." He scribbles on a piece of paper and hands it to me. It's an address in Surrey, Greater Vancouver's largest suburb.

"This is the guy who rented the white Camry?" I ask.

"Yes." He turns his screen around so that I can see it. I check the vehicle's licence plate. It's the same as the one from Thursday evening and the name's right.

"Drew Gill," I say. "Does that sound like the name of someone from the Muslim community?"

He laughs. "Definitely not. Sounds, well, kinda caucasian." He laughs again.

"Was the guy who rented the car white?" I ask.

"I have no idea," He looks at the screen again. "It was rented on Wednesday, my day off. And it was dropped off sometime between six o'clock on Thursday evening and eight o'clock Friday morning, which is when I got in. The keys were in the dropbox."

I take the paper with the address on it.

"Thank you so much, Hamid. I really appreciate it. And, again, I'm sorry." I extend my hand and we shake. "An RCMP Inspector is on his way here. Can you wait for him and give him the same information you gave me?"

"Sure. No prob."

As I run back to my car, my stomach churns. The guys in the Camry were definitely not white. I'm guessing that Drew Gill is a false name. The address is probably phony too.

But it's all I've got.

————

THIS SECTION OF 134TH STREET IN SURREY IS IN A NICE middle-class area with modern houses and well-tended lawns. With the sun setting behind me, I drive past the address scribbled on my piece of paper. It's a white house with a double garage and a dormer window on the upper floor. There is a new-looking black Honda Civic parked in the driveway and a man of around sixty is mowing the front lawn. I can tell by his bright orange turban and beard that he is a Sikh. Definitely not an Islamic terrorist. Definitely not a caucasian. This is definitely a dead end.

I stop the car and slam the wheel in frustration. For the hundredth time, I tap my Bluetooth earpiece and say, "Call Tina Johal." For the hundredth time, I get her voicemail. I've already left a slew of messages. No need to leave another one.

Well, I've wasted forty-five minutes driving out here; five more won't do any harm. It's not like I have any other leads.

I get out of the car, cross the street and take a few steps up the driveway. "Excuse me, sir," I say loudly so that he will hear me above the noise of his lawnmower. He turns, nods and takes his hands off the handle so that the electric motor shuts off.

"How can I help you, sir," he says walking over to me. He has a broad, kindly smile and I take an instant liking to him. He stops two or three metres from me.

"I don't know if you can," I reply. "I'm looking for someone named Drew Gill and I have this address for him. Do you know him or did he ever live here?"

"Ah," he sighs. "*Drew* Gill. Yes, he lives here. He is my son." He smiles at the confusion on my face. "When he was born, we named him Dhruv but he doesn't want to be associated with our religious heritage now that he's an adult. He legally changed it to Drew six months ago." He extends his hand to shake and then remembers we can't do that anymore. "I'm Jaswinder Gill."

"Hi Mr. Gill, it's nice to meet you." I shake hands with the air in front of me. "I'm Cal Rogan."

"Mr. Rogan." He nods his head, air shakes and smiles. "And what is it you want with my son?"

I don't want to tell him I think his son might be a kidnapper. "Is he home?" I ask.

"Not right now but he should be back later tonight."

I don't want to alienate Mr. Gill by asking some pointed questions about his son, so I say, "Just to make sure I have the right person, does Dhruv have a jagged scar on his cheek?"

The smile slides off his face. "Oh, no!" he says. His right hand comes up and strokes his beard. Once, twice, three times; clearly troubled. He looks me straight in the eye. "What trouble has he got himself into now?" He doesn't wait for a reply. "You'd better come in so we can talk." He walks towards his front door and I follow, slipping a mask out of my pocket and onto my face.

My head is spinning, trying to rationalize how the son of a Sikh would be part of an Islamic terrorist group? Unless... A theory starts to form... and it's not good.

Mr. Gill opens the door and leads me inside. The house is traditionally furnished and the smells from the kitchen make my mouth water. I haven't eaten since breakfast at the Ovaltine with Ghost and Tommy.

He ushers me into an immaculate living room and invites me to sit. "Can I offer you anything?" he asks. I politely decline, so he sits down opposite me. "Where do I begin?" He gathers his thoughts. "Some years ago, when he was a teenager, Dhruv had a good friend, they met in high school. Unfortunately, his 'good' friend was not so good; they got into some serious trouble with the law. Dhruv was not completely innocent in all this but it was his friend who was the instigator. It got so bad that his friend was sent back to India by his parents, to avoid a criminal prosecution." The story sounds eerily familiar and does nothing to disprove my theory. "We were glad to see the back of him. Not long after, we moved out here to BC."

My mind is working overtime thinking about Tina's chat with Ellie on Monday evening. "Did you happen to live in Belleville?" I ask.

"Yes. How did you know?"

"Was Dhruv's friend's name Balvir?"

"Yes." Amazement is written on his face. "It's Balvir who has the scar. As soon as you asked me if my son had a scar, I knew that Balvir must be back in Canada." He shakes his head and an infinite sadness descends onto his entire body. "Oh my God, what have they done Mr. Rogan?"

As much as I don't want to burden this good man, I have to tell him. "I'm almost sure that Balvir and Dhruv have kidnapped my girlfriend."

His eyes go wide. "Why would they do that?" he asks.

"Her and Balvir's parents arranged a marriage between them when they were—"

"Tina," he breaths. "Tina Johal. Is she your girlfriend?"

"Yes, how did you know?" I say.

"The Indian community in Belleville was quite small. I knew Tina's family, I remember when they broke off the engagement."

"Do you have any idea where Dhruv and Balvir might be? I need to find them before something happens to Tina."

His face takes on a sickly look. "You may be too late," he says.

"Why do you say that?" I realize I'm shouting.

"When Dhruv left the house this afternoon, he told me he was going out to drive a friend to the airport. He must mean Balvir. That boy is pure evil. He would do anything to get his own way. If he's going to the airport, then one of two things is true: either he will force Tina to go with him to India, or he will have already taken his revenge on her and is fleeing the country."

I feel myself freeze with fear. Seconds pass as a horror movie of possibilities plays on the screen of my mind. I see Mrs. Gill walk into the room. Her mouth is moving and her words reach me as though from a great distance. "What is going on?"

The words zap me out of my funk. I grab my phone and call Jen Halley. She answers on the first ring. "Jen, can you lock down the Vancouver airport?" I shout.

"What do you mean lock down the airport?"

I give her the abridged version of what Mr. Gill has told me.

"So, it's not the Rasul Brigade who's taken her?"

"What difference does that make? It's her former fiance, his name's Balvir... Hang on a minute." I turn to Mr. Gill. "What's Balvir's last name?" I ask him.

"Gujral," he says.

I repeat it to Jen. "He may be trying to force her to go with him to India." I can hear the panic in my voice and so can she.

"OK, Cal. Calm down," she says. It's the totally wrong thing to say to me but somehow I manage to control myself and not shout at her. *"Here's what I can do. I will put him on a watch list for all airports in BC and Alberta. And I will get the airport RCMP to look out for an Indian man travelling with a woman who may seem drugged or drunk or in a wheelchair."*

"What if he's travelling under a different name? Can't you just stop all flights to India?"

"No, I can't. And anyway, many of the people travelling to India from Vancouver fly through Toronto or London or some

other city. I can't stop half the flights leaving Vancouver." She pauses for a moment. *"We may not get him but if he's trying to force Tina to leave with him, that's not going to happen. Don't worry, Cal. Tina's not going to be flown out of Vancouver. And if Balvir Gujral is going anywhere using his own name, we will arrest him and take him in for questioning. Let me hang up now so that I can contact the right people to make this happen."*

"Ok," I say, as evenly as I can. "Thanks, Jen." As soon as she hangs up, my frustration and anger explode. "Fuck!" I immediately regret it. "I am so sorry," I say to the Gills. "I feel like I've violated your hospitality."

Mrs. Gill gives me a kindly smile and her husband says. "I would have said the same thing in your place."

I'm pretty sure he wouldn't have but I am grateful for his kindness. "Thank you so much for understanding," I say, feeling the anger drain away. I take a deep breath and realize I'm missing stuff. There are questions I should have asked before I grabbed the phone and called Jen. "You said Dhruv told you he was driving someone to the airport. Was he using his own car?"

"Yes, I don't like him driving mine," Mr. Gill says.

I remember my neighbour's description of seeing Tina get into a car. "Is his car silver?" I ask.

"Yes."

"What make is it?"

"It's a twenty-twenty Civic, like mine. I bought both cars together. He wanted a BMW but decided that a free Civic was better than paying for a BMW out of his own pocket."

"Can you tell me the licence plate number?"

"Yes," he says. "It's one number higher than mine. I registered them both at the same time." He gives me the number and I write it down in my notebook.

"I'm going to see if I can find them." I need to phrase the next question in a way that the Gills may be prepared to answer it. I have to put their son in the best light I can. "I have an idea that Balvir may have forced Dhruv to take him and Tina somewhere." I pause. They nod. Good so far. "Can you think of anywhere that might be? Dhruv's work? A storage unit? Someone's apartment?"

They shake their heads. "Dhruv didn't work," he says. "He lost his last job a year ago and moved back in with us. He has lots of big ideas but he's one of those people who's long on ideas, short on action."

Mrs. Gill jumps in. "Be fair Jaswinder. He has been talking about that real estate project for about three months now."

"It's all talk," he replies. "Where is he going to get the money to do it?" He snorts.

"He stopped talking to you about it because of that attitude of yours." She looks at him sternly. "He told *me* that he had a wealthy investor. Someone he trusts. Someone he's known for a while. They have already started working on it. He wasn't going to tell you until he could show you the finished project."

I get a flashback to Tina's story. "Doesn't Balvir come from a wealthy family? Could he be the investor?"

"He didn't say who the investor was but it could be, I suppose," she says.

It's a long shot but it's my only lead. "Do you know the address of the building?"

"It's an old warehouse just off south-east Marine Drive. Dhruv's going to renovate it and turn it into lofts." She gives me the address.

I stand up. "Thank you so much," I say. "I'll do anything I can to play down your son's role in the kidnapping." I give them a business card. "If there's anything you can think of that might help me find Tina, please call me."

They walk me to the front door. "Again, thank you both so much," I say. I open the door and step out.

Ten feet in front of me stand two men.

Their weapons are pointed at my chest.

18

TINA

Cal will find me. If I repeat it enough times it will come true. He must know I'm missing by now. It's been six or seven hours since Bal pointed his gun at me and forced me into Dhruv's car. Cal will work it all out. I have to keep telling myself it's true.

Bal's been gone for a while now. He told Dhruv he was going to 'make the arrangements.' What arrangements? Every time I try to guess, I frighten myself. He hasn't hurt me so far—apart from zip-tying me into the chair just a bit too tightly—but the hate in his eyes is a foretaste of far greater future pain.

There's only one way out. It hasn't worked so far but I have to keep trying.

"Could I have some more water please Drew?" He got angry before when I called him Dhruv.

He gets up and takes the plastic bottle off the metal desk and holds it to my lips. I'm not thirsty but I swallow a couple of gulps of the lukewarm water. "Thanks," I say. "I really appreciate it." He nods. I need to try a new approach. None of the others have worked.

I sense that he's not a hundred percent on board with my kidnapping. Every time I've tried to get through to him he's seemed like he's on my side but hasn't been prepared to do anything that would go against Bal's wishes, like loosening these damn zip ties. I have to find a way into his head.

I look around the abandoned office. The lone window has an iron grill over it and two of the window panes have spider-web cracks in them. They must have known this building was abandoned; they wouldn't have brought me here otherwise.

"Does Balvir own this building?" I ask.

"We both do." There's an element of pride in his voice. "We're going to redevelop it into lofts. Kind of a live-work space. Because of covid, a lot of people are working from home. I think it's going to be the new way of working. People who buy the lofts will be able to use part of the cost as a tax deduction if they're using it for work." It's the most he's spoken since we came here.

There must be a way that I can use this.

"That's a really cool idea," I say. Then I remember what he was like when we were in school. The other kids, especially Bal, would tease him for being a momma's boy. This is the way in. "Your Mom must be really proud of what you're doing."

It works. He smiles. "She is. I brought her here and she could see the potential."

"She would. She's very smart," I say. "I remember what a great cook she was, too. Do you remember those Nan Khatai cookies she used to bake? Oh my God, they were heaven. Does she still make them?"

"Yes," he laughs. "Every Sunday for tea."

"Really? That's amazing," I chuckle. "I always liked your Mom."

"She always liked you."

I let the thought sink in for a while.

This might just work.

"How would your Mom feel about what you and Balvir are doing to me right now?" I ask.

To his credit, he blushes.

"You've got to understand, Tina," he says. "I need Bal." I start to speak but he holds up his hand to stop me. "I've been a screw-up for most of my life. But when I got the idea for this development project, I knew I had a winner. I talked to some bankers and investors; they all turned me down. But when I called Bal in India, he thought about it for a while and then offered to finance the project. He put down the deposit on this place. He's promised to finance the whole development."

"You know he's going to hurt me, Drew. How would your Mom feel about *that*? You accepting money so Balvir can have his revenge on me."

"It's not like that. Bal isn't going to hurt you. He loves you. He told me. He just wants to take you back to India so that he can marry you. Just like he was always promised by your parents. You'll have a wonderful life, Tina. Bal's very rich. He'll treat you like a queen. He promised me that. I wouldn't have helped him otherwise."

"Don't be naïve, Drew. How's he going to take me back to India? Drug me and put me in his luggage? He won't be able to threaten me with his gun. He can't go through security with a gun in his hand. I'll scream bloody murder the moment we get into the airport." He starts to shake his head and opens his mouth but before he can speak, I barrel on. "Even if he drugs me, the airline staff are not going to let me on board if I seem drugged or drunk. And what's he going to use as a passport for me? He's conned you. He's not taking me back to India. He's got other plans for me. Plans that may even end in my death. And whatever he does to me will be on your head too."

"No, no," he says. "You've got it all wrong. It's not like that. He's chartered a private jet. He's arranging the details right now. You leave from the South end of the airport. There's not much security and the formalities are pretty lax for departing planes."

"Drew, you cannot let him force me to go back to India. If she knew, your mother would be so ashamed that you —"

The sound of a metal door slamming echoes through the warehouse. He's back.

"Please Drew, you have to help me. Please."

There is indecision written all over his face. Maybe...

The office door opens. "Let's go." Balvir strides into the room. "Everything is arranged. We have one hour." He pulls out a knife. It's one of those penknives with all the gadgets that I always associate with Boy Scouts. He flips open a blade and slices through the zip ties on my wrists. "Stand up," he orders.

"I need to go to the washroom."

He looks at his watch. "OK, but be quick."

I pick up my purse and walk across the office to the washroom. It's filthy and there is no running water. Balvir is staring at me. I make a point of slamming the door and pray that he doesn't come over and open it. I take two things out of my purse and do what I need to do. As I leave, I partially close the door and head straight towards Balvir. Dhruv has already left.

He grabs my arm and leads me to the door of the office.

I hear a rattling noise, like a fence being moved. It's coming from outside the building.

In one, last, desperate act of defiance, I open my hand and let one thing silently drop.

It won't do any good but it's all I can think to do.

19

CAL

"Put your hands on your head and kneel down!" I do as I'm told. Arguing with Emergency Response Team members is not a recommended practice. As soon as they have cuffed my hands behind my back and placed me face-down on the newly-mown grass in front of the Gills' house, they know I'm not a threat. It's safe for me to speak.

"I need to speak to Inspector Wright immediately," I say it loud enough to be heard from the vehicles on the street.

After a few long moments, I see a man in a suit trot across the lawn and stop in front of me. "Get him up," he orders. Hard hands haul me to my feet. He looks at me. "Rogan?"

"Yes. I—"

"What the fuck! Why didn't you wait for us at Tuxedo Rent-a-Car instead of coming in here like a cowboy." Inspector Patrick Wright is not a happy man.

"Yeah, I'm sorry. I got it all wrong. The people who took Tina aren't part of the Rasul Brigade."

He gestures towards the Gills, Jaswinder in his Sikh turban and his wife in her sari. "No kidding, Sherlock," he sneers. "Maybe you should have told us that *before* we got this address from the kid at Tuxedo and put together the ERT." He turns to the ERT team leader. "False alarm. Uncuff them all."

"Tina was kidnapped by her former fiancé and his friend. I think I know where they're holding her. It's in a warehouse in South Vancouver." I feel my cuffs being removed and pull my notebook from my pocket so that I can show him the address. "I know it's a huge ask, but can you redeploy the ERT there?"

"You're joking right?" He shakes his head in amazement, or maybe pseudo amazement. "You want me to redeploy an entire Emergency Response Team to a warehouse to take down someone who you *think* might be there, someone you *think* might have kidnapped your girlfriend. You cannot be serious. I'm in the RCMP Terrorist Unit. We don't do missing person cases." He looks me hard in the eye. "Asshole."

Part of me wants to plead with him.

A bigger part of me wants to punch that stupid sneer off his face.

The biggest part of me wants to get to Tina.

I stop only to apologize to the Gills before running to my car and burning a long strip of rubber down 134th Street.

———

IT'S SEVEN-FIFTEEN BY THE TIME I GET TO THE WAREHOUSE OFF south-east Marine. I circle the block but can see no sign of Dhruv Gill's silver Civic anywhere on the street. It's not behind the temporary construction fencing which surrounds the building.

Everything looks deserted. No light emanates from any

of the windows. I circle the building on foot until I find the gate in the fencing. It's chained and padlocked. Fortunately, it's not topped with barbed wire. I grab the top of the gate and climb. The gate rattles under my weight. Too loud. I freeze and check the building. There's no sign of movement; no door opens; no one at any window. I swing over the top and drop down on the other side as silently as I can.

I make my way towards the main door.

"Hey! Where do you think you're going?" The shout comes from behind me. I turn to see a man walking his dog. It's a Pomeranian. It yaps at me. Great, more noise. Just what I want. "I saw you climb that fence," the man barks at me. "Don't you know that's private property?" I glance back at the building. Still no sign of movement. If they're there, maybe they're on the other side. "Get out of there or I'll call the police." Hmm. Not such a bad idea. I'm still stinging from Inspector Wright calling me a cowboy. Maybe I can kill two birds with one stone.

I trot back to the fence so that I don't have to yell at him. "Would you please call nine-one-one and get the police here. I think someone is being held captive in there."

"Oh," he says. "OK. I'll do it now."

I turn and run back to the building. On this side of the warehouse, there is a long loading dock with three roll-up doors and a short flight of stairs up to a regular door. I try the door. It's metal and it's locked. No chance of opening it. I move onto the loading dock. Beside each of the roll-up doors there are a pair of buttons, one red, one green. I try both buttons for all three doors. Nothing. I have no way in.

I jump down from the loading dock and make my way around the side of the building. At the front is a door and a floor-to-ceiling window with the words 'Clarion Distribution' painted on the inside of the glass. I check the front door. No surprise, it's locked. I press my face to the glass and can just make out a lobby with a reception desk. To the left is a double door that must lead into the warehouse. Behind the reception desk is a stairway leading up.

I take a couple of steps back and look up. Above the front door are two windows. Light is streaming out. My heart kicks the inside of my chest. I couldn't see the light when I checked out the building from outside the fence because of the tree that covers the view of the windows from the road. My entire being tells me that Tina's up there.

I'm coming baby.

But how?

I think of the lock picks in my desk back at the office. I must remember to keep them in my car in future. I look up again. The bottoms of the window frames are about fifteen feet above my head.

This is a soon-to-be construction site. Maybe there's a ladder. A fast circumnavigation of the building crushes that hope. I look at the construction fencing. It's modular. Maybe I can remove a section of it and improvise a ladder. As I walk towards the fence, I have to cross a section of ground, covered with small boulders, surrounding what looks like some sort of ornamental pond with a fountain. I examine the fence. It's a bust. The sections are put together too tightly for me to budge. Even if I could, it would make a hell of a racket. It would alert the people in the lighted room above before I could get it up to the building and climb up to the window.

I look across the remains of the ornamental pond towards the door and the plate-glass window.

Oh. There *is* a way in. It'll be noisy but maybe I can use that to my advantage. I scan the ground in front of me and see what I need. It's the perfect size, about forty centimetres across. I bend down and pick it up. It's about twenty-five kilos. Perfect. I carry it to the front of the building and start swinging. One, small swing... Two, bigger swing... Three, getting there... Four, muscles strained to the max... Five, fight to keep my balance... and GO! I release the boulder and spin away from the window. As the plate glass explodes I take a fast step away but still feel a shower of tiny shards rain down and around me. I turn back. It worked. The hole in the window is more than man-sized.

I step carefully through the gap and make a dash for the reception desk. I flatten myself against the wall beside the stairway and listen. Silence. The people upstairs must have heard. Why are they not running down? Do they suspect a trap? I strain my ears. Do I hear scuffling?

Silence.

Then the realization.

I'm too late. They've gone.

Or maybe they were never here.

I silently take my first steps up the stairway. The fifth stair creaks and I freeze. Still silence.

The staircase terminates on a concrete balcony that looks down onto a warehouse floor. There is a partially open door to my right. Light is streaming out. I step to the door and push it fully open. It is, or at least it was, an open-plan office. There is an old metal desk in one corner and three spindly metal chairs in different parts of the room. Behind one of the chairs are the remains of a plastic zip tie. They *were* here! My blood boils at the thought of Tina being bound into that chair. If they have hurt her... I force the thought away. I need my mind working at maximum. I scan the room. There are some old posters on the walls and a file cabinet with one of the drawers open and empty. On the far side of the office is another door with a red mark on it. It's partially open and I can see a tiled wall. Bathroom.

Somewhere here there's got to be some clue as to where Balvir and Dhruv have taken her.

I walk over to the file cabinet. I check the closed drawers, also empty. There are some blueprints on the desk. I check them out, they're floor plans. The desk drawers are all empty.

Nothing.

Now what?

I think about the man with the yappy dog. If he called the police they'll be here soon. I was hoping they would arrive in time to arrest Balvir and Dhruv. Now they're going to find me in the process of breaking and entering. Time to go. I move towards the door and see something on the floor. Something white. I crouch and pick it up. It's a paper wrapper. The label tells me it contained a tampon. Definitely not something the kidnappers would have dropped. Did Tina drop it? Why here? Why not in the... I spring up and race across the office.

I recognize her strong handwriting, scrawled in lipstick on the bathroom mirror.

There are three words 'Private jet YVR' and a time '7:30.'

I check my watch and start running.

Twenty-five seconds later and I'm scaling the fence at the back of the warehouse. The man with the dog is still there and I can hear the sirens of the approaching cruiser.

As I jump down, the dog produces a tirade of yaps. "They're coming," the man says.

I don't bother to answer either of them as I sprint for my car.

I have just one shot at saving her.

If I haven't already blown it.

20

TINA

Private jets are the way to travel. I love this one. It's so quiet and so smooth. So much better than being on an airline. I forgot where we're going again. I'll have to ask Cal. I look across at him. But it's not Cal. It's Bal. Oh, that's funny. Cal, Bal. They rhyme. "Where are we going?" I ask but the words come out oddly. I giggle.

Bal looks stern. It makes me giggle some more. How long have we been flying? Feels like a while. We could be anywhere now. I like this.

Just floating in the sky.

Cool!

India! That's where we're going, I remember now. Of course. Bal's taking me to India. I'm not sure why. We must be halfway there by now. Maybe Cal will be there. That'll be nice... Cal, Bal. Still funny.

I hear a voice.

It's a nice voice, deep and calm.

Bal speaks to him. Not deep and not calm.

Mr. Deep and Calm answers and Bal's shouting now.

Bal's angry.

He stands up and he's talking to someone.

It's Mr. Deep and Calm. He's in a uniform and he's kinda cute. Wings on the uniform, lots of gold braid. Must be one of the pilots.

Oh, look! Lights on the ceiling.

They're making pretty patterns.

This is nice. I'll close my eyes until we get there.

Where is it we're going again?

I'm tired. But I can't sleep because everyone's shouting.

Why is everyone shouting?

I wish they'd stop.

Hey, they did stop. What d'you know, wishes *do* come true. Now I can sleep 'til we get there. Except that someone keeps shaking my shoulder. Please, let me sleep.

I hear a voice. Not Bal. Not Mr. Deep and Calm either. Nice voice though.

Whoever they are, they're still shaking my shoulder.

I force my eyes open.

Oh.

"Hi Cal," I say but the words don't come out right.

Cal... Bal...

I giggle.

It's still funny.

So why is Cal crying?

———

HOW MUCH DID I HAVE TO DRINK LAST NIGHT? I HAVE *NEVER* had a hangover like this. The microwave won't stop beeping. Why doesn't someone turn it off? And what's the microwave doing in the bedroom anyway?

"For God's sake turn it off Cal," I mumble.

"Tina," he says. I feel him squeezing my hand. "Open your eyes."

I do as he asks and the world rushes in.

This is not our bedroom.

"Where are we?"

"You're in VGH," he says.

"Why?"

"What's the last thing you remember," he asks.

I think about it and the memories rush in.

"Bal and Dhruv. They forced me into their car and took me to some sort of warehouse. Then Bal left for a while, for quite a few hours. Then he came back and took me somewhere else but I don't remember where." Why can't I remember? What happened next?

"Do you remember leaving a message in the bathroom at the warehouse?" Cal asks.

"Oh yes. About the plane. Did you find it?"

"Yes, I did." He has a big smile on his face. "If you hadn't dropped the wrapper on the floor, I would never have seen it."

"Why can't I remember what happened next."

"Balvir drugged you. I haven't seen the tox screen yet but it was probably Rohypnol or something like it."

"That's why I feel like I'm hungover?"

He nods.

I feel the smile spread over my face. "But you saved me."

"You can thank Jen Halley for that. After I saw your message on the mirror, I called her and persuaded her to have the RCMP stop all private jet flights out of the south terminal. We were lucky; there was only one jet that had filed a flight plan and it was already on the runway when the pilot was told to return to the terminal. When he did, they arrested Balvir and charged him with kidnapping you."

"Yes, I sort of remember being on a plane. I thought we were already flying." I comb through the tangles in my mind. One memory comes to the fore. "Were *you* there?" I ask.

"Yes. The warehouse was about twenty minutes from the airport. I made it in twelve. Jen had an RCMP officer there to escort me to the plane so that I could confirm it was you on board. They didn't want to arrest the wrong person."

I tell him he's my hero.

"I thought I'd lost you," he says.

He squeezes my hand and I see the start of a tear in the corner of his eye.

He takes in a huge breath. Holds it, then says, "Will you marry me?"

I know why he's asking me now and my heart already knows the answer. I've been expecting it for a while now.

I give him my answer.

I can't tell if that's what he was expecting.

21

CAL

Monday

As I walk into the office building, I see Zeke standing at the elevator. "I talked to Nick yesterday. You must be relieved you got Tina back," he says. Thank you Captain Obvious. I feel a nudge of shame. He's just being friendly. The elevator door opens and we step in.

"Thanks," I say. "It was touch and go. The plane she was in was third in line for takeoff as the control tower told the pilot to return to his hanger. If Jen Halley hadn't reacted so fast, he would have already been in the air."

"Whoa!" he says. "Is she home yet?"

"No, they kept her in for another night. I have to pick her up this afternoon."

An awkward silence descends and we both look up at the floor indicator.

"How was your Sunday?" I ask.

"Quiet. Had my second jab."

"Good… good."

The opening door saves us a second strained silence.

When we walk into the office, everyone else is there.

Adry and Lucy both give me big hugs and Nick says, "Glad you got her back, man. You done good."

If Tina had said yes, I'd be telling them about my proposal. I take a deep breath. Although I understand her reason—it makes total sense, I even agreed with her at the time—I still feel deflated. If, or rather when, I ask her again, will she—

"OK." Nick's voice breaks into my thoughts. "Morning prayers. Let's start with Micah Weston." At least he's stopped punishing me by leaving it to the last item on the agenda. He gives me a detailed rundown of the Saturday afternoon meeting with Jen Halley, her boss and the RCMP guys. He finishes with, "Bottom line: we don't have Haasim's DNA on the bloody shirt and we can't use the fact that Eric Street is a part of the same wannabe-terrorist group as Kitana's brother." He takes a big sigh. "National security," he says, making air quotes.

"Did they say we couldn't use the fact that her brother was in the Rasul Brigade and that they were all for executing women they considered adulterous?"

"No. They didn't say we couldn't use that," he says.

"Plus we've got this drug angle," Adry says. She counts on her fingers. "One: we have the lab report that it was crystal meth we found in the lab on Powell Street. Two: we have the evidence that Kitana had a key to the lab, plus, I've made a call to the owner of the building asking him to confirm it was Kitana renting it from him. If he doesn't get back to me today, I'll call him again. Three: we have a voice recording of the gangbanger, whose number was in her burner phone, acknowledging that she was supplying him with meth."

"Adry's right," I say. "And I know some more about the

guy. You remember I gave Melanie his picture? She called me yesterday evening. She printed out the picture and while she was visiting Micah, she showed the picture to his friend Blackbird. Blackbird knew who he was. His name's Casey. He's in the same gang as Guy Chang."

"That's good," Nick says. "It confirms what we already thought. But just because she was selling drugs to them, it doesn't follow that someone would murder her for it. No judge is going to release Micah just because his murdered girlfriend happened to be a drug dealer."

Nick's right. We need something more.

I think it over for a moment.

There might be a way.

I ask Nick about all the technical gizmos he has in boxes in the stationery cabinet.

I get the answer I want.

Nick wheels over to the cabinet and gets out two items.

One of them is a burner phone. I use it and when I hang up, I give them all a big smile.

———

I press the doorbell but cannot hear the ring. I wait fifteen seconds and, before I can hit the bell again, the faded-green door opens. I recognize the face. "I'm here to see Casey," I say.

"Who the hell are you?" he asks.

"Tell him it's Vince, Kitana Ajram's friend."

He looks at me and I pretend to feel intimidated by his tough-guy stare. "Wait here," he says, slamming the door in my face.

It doesn't take long.

The door reopens. This time it's the guy in the photo.

"Hi Casey," I say.

His eyes are slitted as he looks me up and down.

"Come in." It's the same deep voice.

He opens the door wide and steps back to let me pass. I walk in. The fixtures and fittings of the clothing store that used to operate out of this building are still here. Casey's sidekick is sitting on a counter cleaning his nails with a knife. What a cliché. He looks like an actor playing the part of a thug.

"How'd you know Kitana?" he asks.

"I helped her with the manufacturing," I say.

"Doesn't really answer my question, does it?" He has a slight accent that I don't quite recognize. Québéc maybe?

"I'm an assistant professor. I taught a couple of her classes."

He nods and thinks.

"How much can you supply?" he asks.

"I need to know something first." His eyebrows go up. "Kitana was killed because she was selling you the meth. How do I know the same won't happen to me?"

He smiles. It's not pretty; it doesn't reach his eyes.

"Because I know who killed her and it's not that dumb-assed kid in Kent." He chuckles. His chuckle's about as pretty as his smile. My mind races through the ramifications. If he knows Micah didn't kill Kitana, why is his colleague, Guy Chang, a.k.a. Goliath, a.k.a. Giant, trying to get to Micah?

"Who did kill her?" I ask.

"You don't need to worry about that. The man who killed Kitana is no longer a danger."

"How can you be sure?"

"Because when he killed Kitana, he was fucking with my business and..." his eyes drill into mine, "...no one fucks with *my* business. I made sure he was dead three days after her." This isn't what I was expecting. It's better.

"Who was it?" I ask.

"None of your business," he sneers. "And, talking of business, how much meth can you make for me?"

I need to play along with him. He's the key to finding out who really killed Kitana. "How much do you need?"

"Can you do fifty kilos?"

Holy crap. That's a lot of meth. I do the math. That's a street value of between one and two million dollars. I need to give him the right answer now. I don't know a lot about crystal meth but I know how the drug business works.

"Yes," I say. "But not all at once"

"Go on."

"Five kilos by the end of the week. Fifteen kilos by the end of next week and thirty the following week. Same price you were paying Kitana."

After a beat, he says, "Deal. Call me the day before the first delivery." He stands and walks to the door. He's not long on social niceties. He lets me out onto Gore and I turn towards Hastings where Nick's truck is parked.

Now I know why Casey and Goliath want Micah dead. With him out of the way, no one is going to try and prove him innocent, no one will ever know who Kitana's killer really was and no one will try to find out who killed the killer.

Casey will never tell me who killed Kitana but he did let one thing slip. He told me he killed Kitana's killer three days after Kitana's death. There aren't that many murders in Vancouver. It won't take us long to find out who it was. Proving it will be a whole other thing. But if we can prove it, Micah will be free.

I turn onto Hastings, walk the few paces to Nick's truck and climb aboard.

"Attaboy, Rogan," he says. "Perfect audio and perfect video." I remove the Rotary Club lapel pin—with its tiny camera, microphone and three-inch-long wire attached to it —from my jacket, hand it to him and he lovingly puts it into its case. "If we can prove who really killed Kitana, that poor kid will be out of that hell hole in no time flat."

"It's a big if."

"You're right, but let's take the first step."

He puts the truck in gear and accelerates down Hastings.

———

JIM GARRY TUGS GENTLY ON HIS PONYTAIL AS HE THINKS OVER what we've told him. He opens his mouth to speak but is interrupted by his wife. She comes into their living room with a tray containing three coffees and a plate of cookies which look suspiciously like Nick's favourite chocolate digestives. She's a few years younger than Jim and she has an impish smile and an accent, which I think is Australian.

She looks at her husband with a fond smile. "Don't get used to the idea of me making coffee for your clients," she says. "I'll only do it for Nick and Cal."

Jim gives her a fond smile.

She gives us our coffees and puts the plate of cookies on my partner's lap.

I take a sip. The coffee is superb.

When she has left, Jim says, "The recording of this Casey character saying that he killed someone is evidence that *he's* a killer. But his assertion that the man he murdered was Kitana's killer is just hearsay, I'm afraid. There's no way I can use that in court to get Micah released."

Nick wipes a cookie crumb from the side of his mouth. "Yeah, we were kinda guessing you'd say that. However, Rogan did an internet search while we were driving over here. There was an article in the Vancouver Sun. Three days after Kitana's murder, the body of a suspected gang member was found. They didn't give a name. I'll follow it up with Steve Waters at VPD. Maybe we can find some evidence, but I'm not too confident."

"It looks like a long shot, for sure," Jim says. "What about Kitana's brother?"

"Also not looking too good," I say. "His DNA wasn't on the bloody shirt. He's got motive and opportunity up the wazoo, but we don't have any solid evidence."

"Of course, our best shot is that pain-in-the-ass detective, Eric Street?"

Nick and I exchange glances. He can't say what he knows; Jen Halley's boss told him and the rest of the team, in no uncertain terms, that they could not mention anything about Street's arrest for his membership in the Rasul Brigade. I wasn't there at the time, so in effect, Nick has already broken the law by telling me.

"Guys?" Jim has spotted something's going on.

"Let's not talk about Micah Weston's case for a moment, Jim," I say. "Let me ask you a purely hypothetical question."

Jim nods. He knows where this is going.

"Let's say you had a client who had been found guilty of, I don't know, let's say... shoplifting. And suppose the person who had the most damning evidence against your client had fabricated that evidence. And let's also say that you couldn't mention to the court anything about this person for reasons of national security. What would you do?"

Jim knows exactly what I'm saying.

"First," he says, looking from me to Nick and back again,

"I would advise anyone who knows anything about this hypothetical national security matter, to say nothing to anyone about it."

He puts his head back and stares at the ceiling for a long while. There is a muscle in his cheek pulsing as he clenches and unclenches his teeth. The only sound in the room is Nick biting into a third cookie.

Finally, Jim speaks. "This hypothetical national security matter, would the ban on talking about the matter be permanent?"

"Probably not," Nick says, "but with the feds, who knows how long it might last?"

Jim scratches his bearded chin. "I know a judge who likes to exercise his mental acuity around the nuances of national security. I might just talk to him about this hypothetical story you just posited and see what he might do, hypothetically, of course. Meanwhile, you should follow up on this dead gang member and see if you can link him to Kitana's murder."

I'm cautiously hopeful about Jim Garry's ability to get around the national security issue. But if he can't, all we have left is this dead gangbanger. I'm a lot less hopeful about that working out.

22

NICK

S teve Waters looks haggard and it's not just from the pressure of being an inspector in a police department that could do with a lot better funding. I've got a good idea why he's looking like this and I'm wondering how he's going to react when I tell him that Stammo Rogan Investigations is partly responsible.

He smiles as I wheel into his office. "Hey, Nick. Good to see you. Are you here to tell me you're going to take the case manager position? Please say you are. I need some good news right now."

"That's not what I came here to talk about but it is good news. We may have solved a murder case for you."

"Which case?"

I pull out the thumb drive and hand it over. "Before you watch it, I need to give you some background. Rogan and I have been retained by Micah Weston's family to try and prove he didn't kill his girlfriend Kitana."

His eyes narrow. "That was Eric Street's case," he says and the haggard look returns. "Would this have anything to do with why the RCMP arrested him on the weekend?"

I think of Jen's boss and his warning to us that we couldn't speak to anyone. "Might be," I say.

"What did he do?"

"They told me I can't speak about it. National security bullshit."

He sighs. "What *can* you tell me?"

"We discovered that Kitana Ajram was manufacturing that crystal meth you told me had been on the streets."

"You are kidding me," he says.

I shake my head. "No, I'm not. She was a genius-level chemist. She was super ambitious and wanted to go to Harvard but needed a ton of money to be able to afford it. The video on that thumb drive is Rogan talking to the guy she was selling the meth to. Take a look at it."

Steve plugs it into his computer. Once his anti-virus software gives him the OK, he plays the video and I hear Rogan's conversation with the gangbanger, Casey, all over again. When it ends, I say, "We checked on it. There was an article in the Vancouver Sun about a gang member killed three days after Kitana's death. It's gotta be the guy he was talking about. I was thinking about an exchange of information."

"He's the guy in the picture you sent me. The one I sent on to Domenic Dixon in the drug unit. Dom told me they don't have a name for him."

"That right," I say trying not to sound too smug. "I can give you his first name and the address where you can find him and you've got his confession right there in the video."

"You said an exchange of information. What did you want in return?" he asks.

"Everything you've got on the guy he killed, the guy who he said killed Kitana."

He thinks it over for a couple of seconds. "Sure, why not. You first."

"The guy's name's Casey. He's part of the George Walsh gang." That makes Steve's eyes open wider. I give him the address on Gore Street. "That's where we took the video," I say. I give him a grin. "Your turn."

He turns back to his computer and taps away at a few keys. The printer on the credenza behind him starts to spit out paper. "The dead guy's name is Georgi Volkov. Small-time member of the biggest Russian gang in the city. I'm printing out his file for you. He was a low-level dealer. I don't see him as Kitana's murderer. Not to mention the fact that we've got rock-solid DNA evidence that your client did it."

"It makes sense that he's in a rival gang. If the Russians learned who was making the meth for Walsh's gang, they'd want to cut off the supply."

"Good luck with that, Nick. Aren't you forgetting the DNA evidence?" He's the one sounding smug now.

But I can out-smug him. "Unfortunately, I can't give you the details 'cos of the national security BS, but Street's evidence is going to be thrown out."

The haggard look returns at the mention of Street's name. He turns around, pulls the file off the printer and hands it to me. "You didn't get this from me," he sighs.

"Thanks, Steve, I appreciate it." I drag my fingers in front of my lips like I'm pulling on a zipper.

"Could we talk about you coming back to the Department now, Nick?"

"It sounds great, Steve, but not just now. I need to get this Micah Weston case behind us. When it's settled one way or another, we can talk."

He's about to object when his phone rings. He looks at

the caller ID. "My boss," he says. "More fallout around Eric Street."

Saved by the bell.

"You take it," I say. "I'll get out of your hair."

I wheel out of his office.

I can't wait to get my nose into this file on Georgi Volkov.

23

CAL

I pull the Healey into the parking garage below our condo and reverse into my parking space. I hop out and run round to open the door for Tina. She always pretends to object on feminist grounds but I know she likes that I open doors for her. I take her hand and help her out. She slips her arms around me and kisses me gently on the lips. I try not to think about where she would be now if that plane had taken off with her and Balvir on board.

I pull the soft top into place.

"It was fun to drive with the top down," she says. "It cleared the smell of the hospital off me." I put an arm around her and we make our way to the townhouse without running into Martha and Biscuit, or worse, Karla.

As I open the front door, I say, "We should make up for missing lunch at Bridges on Saturday and go there for dinner tonight."

"Sounds wonderful," she says, stepping in and dropping her bag on the hall floor. She looks into the living room. "Ellie not home from school yet?"

"She's staying with Sam tonight. I thought it would be nice for just the two of us to have dinner."

She hugs and kisses me. "We should make a reservation."

"Already done. It's for seven o'clock."

"Mmmm." She looks at the watch on her slim wrist. "Not for another three hours." She puts her arms around my neck and kisses me again. "I wonder what we can do to pass the time." She kisses me again but much more passionately this time and I feel myself reacting to the way she's rubbing her body against mine. "I'm glad you're happy to see me," she whispers in my ear.

"I love you."

"And I love you, Cal Rogan."

As I carry her upstairs, she takes my ear gently into her mouth and sends me into overdrive.

———

I RUN MY FINGERS GENTLY OVER THE SCAR FROM THE KNIFE wound she sustained almost a year ago. It was the result of my investigation into a missing teenager. If Tina's kidnapping by Balvir had been because of our current case I don't know what I would have done.

In an effort to banish the thought, I say "We should think about getting up and getting ready for dinner."

She takes my hand in hers. "In the hospital," she says, "when you proposed I said no because I didn't know if you were just proposing because of what had happened with Balvir or whether you just felt you should. I was also worried that maybe the drugs they had given me might warp my judgment."

"That's OK," I say.

"So..." She gives me a smile. "Can a girl change her mind?"

I can feel my heart beating.

"Of course," I say.

She takes a deep breath. "Cal Rogan, will you marry me?"

"Yes, I will."

I pull her close and can feel her heart beating too.

I don't remember ever being this whole.

24

CAL

Tuesday

I'm saving the big news until the end of 'morning prayers.' Nick gave me the file on Georgi Volkov, the Russian gangster whom Casey said killed Kitana. It's the only decent lead we've got at the moment and I'm not too sure how decent it is. Volkov was a bit low down on the chain to be assigned an assassination job unless he did it on his own initiative to get himself a promotion.

I listen to them reporting on their various cases. Most are the usual, run-of-the-mill assignments, which are the bread and butter work of every investigative agency, but two of them are interesting enough that I wouldn't mind working them myself. With the term just about finished at SFU, I could certainly spend the summer working some cases. And the extra money could go towards the wedding.

Nick winds up the meeting with his usual. "Any other business?"

I break the usual pattern. "Yes," I say.

Nick's eyes light up. "Please tell me it's a new case with a client who's loaded."

I can't help chuckling. Stammo Rogan Investigations is a huge success financially, thanks to Nick's management skill. A skill I would never have imagined that he possessed. He has a nose for lucrative business and manages to convince clients that we're the firm to get the job done.

"No, something else entirely." I pause and look at them, waiting for the moment just before Nick's impatience puts his mouth in gear. I see it appearing on his face. "Tina and I are getting married."

There is a stunned silence broken first by Adry. "OMG," she says. She stands up to give me a hug but stops short, undecided. "Oh what the hell, you and Nick have had both shots and the rest of us have had our first," she says. I stand up and she hugs me and Lucy jumps in and hugs us both. "I'm so happy for you Cal," she says. Zeke gets to his feet and shakes my hand. "That's terrific news, buddy. I'm sure you guys are going to be super happy." He pats my back and gives me a big smile. I've waxed hot and cold about Zeke but right now, he's got a checkmark in the good-guy column.

As they release me, I look at Nick. I can tell he's happy for me but frustrated that he can't leap out of his wheelchair to shake my hand. I step over and take his proffered hand and he pulls me down so that he can hug me with his left arm. "Smartest decision you ever made, Rogan," he says. There's a catch in his voice. Ever since he came out, he's been with Stewart, who was his nurse at VGH after he got shot in the gut by a crooked arms dealer. It was a year and a half ago. Stewie's a great guy and they are a great couple, but Nick is old-fashioned in many ways and I get the sense he hasn't been able to embrace the idea of gay marriage just yet. I whisper to him, "You should think ab—"

"What are you guys so happy about? Celebrating that you fucked me over?" Jen Halley is standing in the doorway in a dark blue suit with an even darker look on her face. Another flashback to a year and a half ago.

Nick is the first to speak. "What do you mean, fuck you over? We don't fuck over our friends, Jen. You know that."

"I got a call an hour and a half ago. It was from a BC Supreme Court judge. He told me I had to be in his chambers at ten o'clock this morning to explain my reasons for withholding information that could exonerate an innocent man. I wonder where he got that information. I'm guessing it was from someone in this room and I'd like to know who because I want to know who to have charged for violating the Security of Information Act."

"No one here spoke to any judge," Nick says.

"No doubt," she fires back. "But someone must have talked to Micah Weston's lawyer so that he could talk to the judge. Which one of you has been talking to him?"

"Nick and I went to see him, Jen," I say. "The reason was to discuss our theory that a drug gang killed Kitana."

"And you expect me to believe that you didn't talk to him about Eric Street?"

"Believe what you want but here are the facts." I hold up one finger. "We went to see Micah's lawyer." Up goes the second finger. "We talked about our findings on the drug gang theory." Third finger. "*He* asked *us* if we had anything he could use to refute Eric Street's evidence." Fourth finger. "We refused to answer and Street's name was not mentioned again." All completely true. And I'm sure we don't want to waste Jen's valuable time getting into a long discussion around what hypothetical questions may or may not have been posed.

"Because you refused to talk about Street, the lawyer

must have known something was up." Her voice oozes with frustration and more than a soupçon of sarcasm. "That's why he went to speak to the judge."

"Damned if we do and damned if we don't?" Nick says with a snort. "You can't accuse us of doing something wrong just because we did exactly what you told us to do, i.e refuse to talk about Street. Jim Garry's as sharp as a tack. It's not our fault if he worked out that two and two equals four."

After a long five seconds of glaring, Jen's anger visibly deflates. "I suppose," she sighs and shakes her head. "They're making me the spokesperson to go see the judge, so if something goes wrong, I'll be the scapegoat."

"Fuck 'em," Nick says. "If it weren't for you, we never would have brought the Rasul Brigade to their attention and they wouldn't have the nice juicy arrests they've just made."

"Yeah, you're right. Sorry, you guys." She checks her watch. It looks like a Rolex but she's on a federal government salary, so it's probably a knockoff. "I gotta go see the judge. Let's get together later for a drink." She sweeps the room with a half-smile and leaves.

When the front door closes behind her, Nick grins. "Nice way to dodge a bullet Rogan," he says.

"Yeah, but was it true?" Adry asks.

"One hundred percent," Nick replies. "The name Eric Street, or anything about him or to do with him, never left our lips."

Zeke laughs. "I believe you one hundred percent. However, I'm betting one thing that did leave your lips was the word hypothetical." He was a cop. He knows how the game's played. I give him another check in the good-guy column.

"No comment," Nick shoots back.

"Never mind all that," Lucy says. "I want to know when

the wedding is."

"We haven't set the date yet. I haven't even told Ellie or Sam yet." A little worry slithers through my gut. Ellie loves Tina but how will she feel about the marriage. They say every child of divorced parents wants the parents to get back together again. And Sam, how will she take it?

Nick breaks into my thoughts. "We should go out for a drink after work this evening and celebrate. Everyone free?" That gets yeses all around. "Good," he says. "Now... on the Micah Weston case, we might get lucky. The judge might be able to get CSIS and the RCMP to admit that they are holding Eric Street for being part of the same terrorist group as Kitana's brother. If he does, Street's evidence is compromised and Micah's a free man. We can hope for the best but we've gotta be prepared for the worst. Rogan, you've got to dig into this Georgi Volkov guy. If he *is* the one who killed her, we're gonna need some solid evidence."

"You're right," I say, "but it's not going to be easy. Volkov was killed a few days after Kitana so the trail's pretty cold at this point."

"Now that we've wound up the Hillside case," Zeke says, "if it's OK with you guys, I'd like to help on Cal's case."

Nick and I exchange glances and he nods. "Sounds good. Might as well get in a few more billable hours."

"Talking of which," Lucy says, "I billed Melanie for last month. Our terms are net but she hasn't emailed the money. Could you remind her please, Cal?"

"Will do," I say. I feel a stirring at the thought of talking to Melanie, maybe even meeting her to pick up a cheque... *What the hell am I thinking? I just got engaged.* The thought of Tina washes away the thoughts of Melanie. I remember a promise I made to her six days ago; a promise I have yet to keep. Plus there's an errand I need to run.

"OK Zeke," I say. "First thing this afternoon, let's get to work on Georgi Volkov. There's a couple of things I need to do first. Let's meet right after lunch and make a plan."

"Perfect," he says. "It'll give me time to do a bit of research into this Volkov guy."

I head out of the office to do some important shopping and keep a promise.

———

I HAVE VERY MIXED FEELINGS ABOUT BEING HERE. FIVE DAYS ago on our way to dinner, Tina and I went to an NA meeting and she made me promise to attend meetings more regularly. I'm here to keep the promise but, deep down, I don't think I *need* to be here. My drug-taking days are behind me. Sure, I think about heroin a lot, probably every day, but there is no way that I'm going down that path again. I'm also having serious doubts about the effectiveness of these twelve-step programs.

On the other hand, it was in this very room that I met Tina just a year and a half ago. I smile at the memory.

"Would anyone else like to share?" the grey-haired lady asks.

I put up my hand. Tina suggested that I should not just go to meetings, but think about sharing my experiences for my own sake and to help others in the program.

I walk up to the podium and smile at the assembled faces. "Hi, my name's Cal. I'm an addict."

"Hi, Cal," comes the response.

As I tell them the story of my life as a junkie ex-cop, I notice that one person in the crowd is particularly engrossed in my words. I've always been good at speaking in public—and as a lecturer at SFU, I've honed my skills—but this guy seems to hang on to my every utterance. He's around thirty, well-dressed in casual clothes but, judging by the shoes he's wearing, he spends a lot of money to achieve that casual look. He looks like a professional. Maybe a banker, except that a banker would be in a suit. Perhaps he's something in high tech. A sudden intuition tells me his drug of choice is coke. I try not to get distracted by his stare and get through my story, finishing with, "and I met my soon-to-be-wife in this very room..." I check the date on my watch and smile, "...seventeen months ago today. Thanks to her, I've been clean ever since. Thank you."

I get a big round of applause as I walk to my seat. I put my hand in my pocket. The purchase I made is still there. I grin like a fool as I sit in the rickety, church-basement chair.

After the chairperson has wound up the meeting, a couple of people thank me for my share and, as I help stack the chairs in the corner, I notice the young, well-dressed guy looking at me from across the room. He nods at me without smiling, turns and walks out the door. Odd.

Something tells me our paths are starred to cross again in the near future.

————

"Where is everyone?" I ask as I walk into the office.

Zeke looks up from the file he's been studying. It's the file Nick got from Steve. "Nick's wining and dining a potential new client. Adry and Lucy took a late lunch; they should be back in half an hour or so."

Covering my disappointment that Adry and Lucy are not here, I ask, "Find anything in the Georgi Volkov file?"

"Yeah, a couple of things. He was a long-time member of the Russian gang. The first entry in the file was for beating up a kid at school when he was fourteen. The kid was beaten pretty badly, spent two days in the hospital. Volkov wasn't charged because the kid he beat up turned out to be selling drugs to his fellow students. The Crown Prosecutor reckoned that would make it easy for any decent defence lawyer to get him off.

"Over the years he was charged with a number of crimes, all violence and drug-related and all small-time stuff. He spent a couple of stretches as a guest of BC Corrections, one for eighteen months and another for three years."

"Sounds like a charmer," I say.

"Yeah, totally." Zeke smiles. "But I did find out something interesting. His body was found in the alley behind a bar in the downtown east side. Turns out the bar is owned by his father."

"That's harsh. Killing someone and then leaving the body for his father to find. That Casey character is worse than I thought. Was the father a member of the gang too?"

"Nick checked with Steve Waters. The father doesn't have a record, so we don't know if he is part of the Russian gang. Maybe they're using the bar for money laundering and the father's going along, either willingly or unwillingly."

I think it over for a second. "What I don't get is this," I say. "The Russians discover that Kitana Ajram is manufacturing high-quality crystal meth for George Walsh's gang, so they decide to eliminate her. Georgi Volkov kills her, either on his own initiative or on orders from the gang. So, how does Casey find out that Volkov was the killer?"

"If we knew that, then we'd have the proof we need that Micah's innocent," Zeke says.

"So how do *we* get that proof?"

"Could you find a pretext to meet with Casey again," he

asks. "Maybe to talk about delivering the meth he thinks you're manufacturing for him."

"He wouldn't even tell me Volkov's name let alone how he knew Volkov killed Kitana."

He leans back in his chair and stares at the ceiling for a moment. "Maybe we should try and falsify the hypothesis," he says, almost to himself.

"What do you mean?"

"I studied physics at UBC. The scientific method says that when you have a hypothesis about something, you should try and falsify it, in other words, try and prove it wrong. If you can prove it wrong, it saves a hell of a lot of time trying to prove it's right. Maybe we should try and falsify the hypothesis that Volkov killed Kitana."

"But if we do that," I say, "we'll have one less thing for Jim Garry to present to a judge as a reason to set Micah free."

"Yes but as it says in John 8:32 'Then you will know the truth, and the truth will set you free.'"

He's right. "I'm pretty sure Casey was telling the truth about Volkov but if he wasn't, it would save us a lot of time."

Zeke stands up. "Let's go see the only lead we've got, Volkov's dad."

"Why would *he* speak to us?" I ask.

He smiles. "Let's talk as we walk." We head out the door and, as he locks it behind us, he says, "My parents were born and brought up in what was then called Leningrad. They were able to escape from the former Soviet Union in the late 1970s. One of the reasons they defected was that they were deeply religious Russian Orthodox, in fact, they still are. When I was born they named me after the prophet Ezekiel and they changed the family name from Petrov to Stone— it's a literal translation—because they thought it would be better for me to have an English-sounding name." We step into the elevator. "Despite the name change, they were still very attached to their culture and I spoke Russian before I spoke English. They made me study Russian every day after school and go to church every week. If anyone can get through to Georgi Volkov's father, it's me."

"How do you plan to get him to open up to you?" I ask.

When he tells me, I feel a smile spread across my face.

———

ZEKE PARKS RIGHT IN FRONT OF THE NEVSKY BAR AND GRILL. It looks clean and well-kept despite the fact that the building itself is old and ugly. "Ironic," Zeke says with a chuckle. "Nevsky Prospekt is an avenue in St. Petersburg; it's renowned for its opulent architecture."

We step inside. As my eyes adjust to the darkness, I get an immediate sense of its Russianness. There are small icons on the walls, the décor is predominantly brown and red-tasselled velvet, and behind the bar is something you won't see in any other bar: a samovar. Although it is after two, several of the tables have people at them still eating lunch. There is no host desk or maitre d' but a young waiter comes over and addresses us in Russian.

Zeke answers him and I hear the name Volkov among the words.

"*Da*," the waiter says and gestures towards an older gentleman sitting behind the bar. He is dressed in a rather out-of-date suit and has flowing, grey hair.

"*Spasibo*," Zeke says.

We walk to the bar and Zeke hands the man a business card. After exchanging a few words in Russian he says, "My colleague doesn't speak Russian, would it be OK if we spoke in English?" Volkov nods and Zeke continues, "We've been hired by the Russian-language newspaper, Vancouver & Us. They've asked us to look into the deaths of a number of Russian men whose murders the police haven't solved. One of the names they gave us was your son Georgi."

"Police don't care," Volkov says. "It's because Georgi got in trouble when he was younger. Went to prison. Police don't give a damn." His voice is heavily accented.

"I'm really sorry about you losing your son," I say. "I'm a father too and I don't know what I'd do if my daughter were killed."

He nods. "Thank you. Yes, is very hard."

"The police told us he was part of a gang," I say. "Is that true?" I watch him like a hawk.

"It was true, yes. But Georgi changed. He left gang. He came to work here, with me." A tear starts to form in the corner of his eye. "He even returned to church."

Either he's telling the truth or he's the best actor I've ever seen.

"Do you have any thoughts as to who might have murdered your son?" Zeke asks.

"Gang, probably. They don't like when people leave."

"We heard a rumour it might have been a rival gang. Do you think that's possible?"

He shrugs. "Maybe."

"Can you tell us about the days leading up to his death?" I ask. "Was there anything unusual? Did he seem worried or upset? Georgi was killed on a Tuesday. What happened on the weekend before he was killed?"

"He was with Church. I don't know word in English. *Ubezhishche*."

"He was on a retreat," Zeke translates for me.

"When was it?" I ask.

"He left on the Friday at noon and was back Sunday night."

"Where was the retreat?"

"Church has place in Manning Park." Manning Park is over two hundred kilometres from Vancouver. If what Volkov says is true, there is no way his son killed Kitana Ajram on the Saturday.

"Which church was it?" Zeke asks about a half a millisecond before me.

"*Sankt Nikolas.*"

"I know it well," Zeke says.

"You've been very helpful Mr. Volkov," I say. "Is there anything else unusual that happened in the time before Georgi was murdered?"

He shakes his head. "*Nyet.*"

We say our goodbyes and leave.

"Your idea of falsification worked," I say. "Unfortunately."

"Don't give up hope," Zeke says. "Let me drop you back at the office and I'll drive over to Saint Nikolas and try and falsify Georgi Volkov's alibi. Who knows. Maybe he drove back to Vancouver, killed Kitana and then returned to Manning. He could do that in five hours or less."

Zeke is clearly more of an optimist than I am. I was really hoping that we'd find evidence, or at least an indication, that Georgi Volkov was a viable suspect in Kitana's murder. But I'm pretty sure there is none. I believe what his father just told us.

"You go over to the church and I'll walk back to the office. I need the fresh air and the exercise won't hurt either."

I put my hand in my pocket and what's in there makes me feel a lot better.

———

LUCY GIVES ME A BIG SMILE AS I WALK THROUGH THE OFFICE door. "Hi Cal," she says. Her general cheeriness is infectious.

I smile back at her. "What are you so happy about?"

"Oh, you'll see," she giggles. She gets up from the reception desk and follows me into the main office. Adry and Nick are sitting at their desks with smiles that match Lucy's.

I look from Nick to Adry and back again to Nick. "So I'm guessing you closed the deal over lunch."

"'Course I did," Nick chuckles. "Don't I always? Biggest assignment we've ever had. I got a fifty grand retainer."

"That's amazing." Now the big grin is on my face too.

"Yes, it is," says Adry, "but that's not why we're grinning like fools."

I wait for her to tell me and they all start laughing.

"What?!" I say.

And they all laugh some more.

Finally, Nick pulls himself together. "Jim Garry called. The judge had a long interview with Jen in his chambers then he had a Zoom meeting with her bosses and some RCMP bigwigs. The upshot is that the judge is going to overturn the verdict on the basis that Street's evidence at Micah's trial is invalidated by his association with Haasim Ajram and the Rasul Brigade. The judge called Kent and ordered them to put Micah in protective custody until his release. Jim says the kid will be out of there this week."

I sink into my chair. "Thank God for that." I feel like a weight has been lifted from my shoulders. We'll likely never know who killed Kitana but it's almost certainly either her brother or some gang member. Poor kid didn't know what she was doing when she started doing business with George Walsh's gang. "I was about to give up. There's no actual evidence that her brother killed her and Georgi Volkov was a bust. I will be so glad to see Micah outside of Kent." This is what it's all about: righting wrongs. The grin that has crept onto my face is so broad, it almost hurts.

"So here's the plan," Nick says. "We're all going out to dinner tonight to celebrate, significant others included. I persuaded Jen to join us and Jim Garry is coming with his wife. Lucy booked a table for twelve on the patio at Lift for six-thirty. It'll cost a bundle but it's a fraction of our final billing to Melanie Weston."

Zeke walks in and wonders why we're all grinning like fools, so they have to repeat it.

Déjà vu all over again.

I check my watch. With the case just about closed, I've got a free afternoon.

But not before I show Adry and Lucy what I bought today.

———

I DON'T KNOW IF IT'S JUST TREPIDATION OR ACTUAL FEAR. As I think it over, I can see that it's both. Sam and I have known each other for over seventeen years and we were married for seven of them. We were blissfully happy from the day we met until about six months after the time I first took heroin. My love for her and Ellie and my longing for us to be a family again was what sustained me through detox, rehab and recovery. Two years ago we almost made it back together and about a year ago, when she moved back from Toronto, she indicated that she was interested in rekindling our relationship.

The trepidation I have is about how Sam might be hurt by my news that Tina and I are getting married.

The fear is that, as much as Ellie loves Tina, she'll reject our marriage because she will see it as the final nail in the coffin of any dream she has that Sam and I would one day reunite.

The thought of Sam and Ellie united against me really hurts. Could I actually bear it?

I press the doorbell. I'll know very soon.

I hear rumblings from inside and Ellie's voice yells, "I'll get it."

The door swings open and she gives me a double-take. "Dad! What are you doing here?" She steps forward and gives me a hug.

I wrap my arms around her. "I want to talk to you and your mom about something."

I feel her tense a little. She whispers, "Mom's MS is really bad at the moment. It's not anything that's going to be stressful for her is it?"

Now I'm torn. Stress is one of the factors that can speed the advancement of MS. If I tell Sam now and she reacts negatively, will it have an effect on her disease? But if I don't tell her now, she is going to learn about it soon enough anyway.

Ellie senses my hesitation.

She steps back and looks into my eyes. "Is it bad news, Dad?"

"No. Quite the opposite." Although I don't know if Sam will view it as good.

"Great!" The concern washes out of her face. She links her arm in mine and hauls me down the hallway. "Let's tell Mom."

As soon as I see Sam, I struggle to keep the shock out of my face. It's just a couple of weeks since I saw her last and she seems to have aged ten years. She's in her wheelchair, sitting by the window.

"Hi, Sam."

"Hi Cal, how are you?" Even her voice sounds weak.

"I'm fine. But how are *you*?"

She shrugs. "It is what it is," she sighs.

Ellie drags me over and pulls me down on the sofa next to her.

"Dad has some good news, Mom," she announces.

I put my arm around her and give her a big hug. "Can I speak to Mom first, sweetie? Just the two of us?"

She looks at me, frowns, then looks at Sam who gives her a tiny nod. "Sure," she says dragging the word out. She gets up. "I'll be up in my room, finishing off my homework. Text me when you want me to come back down again."

When I hear her feet running up the stairs, I say, "How bad is it, Sam?"

She waits until she hears Ellie's door close. "It's cyclical. I have good days and bad days. Some days I don't even have to use my cane. Others are well..." She taps the arm of her wheelchair, "...like this." She emits a long sigh. "But I have to admit that the overall trajectory is downhill."

"What does your doctor say?"

"He says the path of the disease is unpredictable but reading between the lines, I doubt I'll see my fiftieth birthday."

Sam will be forty-one next month.

"I am *so* sorry," I say. I wonder how much of the stress I caused her, during my drug-addicted years, accelerated the progress of the disease. "Does Ellie know?"

"She's a smart kid. She can see that it's getting worse but I haven't told her how long. I don't think she's ready for that. She's mature for her age but she's not even twelve yet."

After I got clean, five years ago, I read everything I could about MS. My mind runs a movie of the next nine years. It won't be that long until Sam's spending all of her days in a wheelchair. Who will look after her? Her parents are getting on in years and won't have the physical strength to care for her. I think of all the years during which I loved her and she loved me. Does that mutual love create a debt between us? Is my share of that debt to help care for her when the time comes? If I'm married to Tina, how will I juggle my priorities?

Sam's voice breaks into my thoughts. "So, what's your good news?"

The trepidation I felt has become a dull ache but there's no way I can avoid the subject now.

I look her in the eye. "I proposed to Tina," I say.

Try as I might, I can't gauge her reaction. She smiles brightly, too brightly maybe. "What did she say?"

"She said yes."

"Congratulations, Cal." She beams at me.

"Are you OK with it?" I ask.

"Of course. Why wouldn't I be?"

"I dunno. I..."

"Text Ellie and get her down here," she says. The beam is still on her face but I can't tell how sturdy it is.

Almost the instant after I press 'send' on the text, I hear Ellie coming downstairs like a herd of elephants. She bursts into the room and bounces down onto the couch beside me. "So what's your big news?" she demands.

I take a deep breath. This is it. "I asked Tina to marry me and she said yes."

"OMG!" she yells and throws her arms around me. "That is sooooo cool, Dad."

Relief washes through me.

"Can I be a bridesmaid?"

"I don't know how fancy a wedding we're going to have but you'd have to talk to Tina about that."

"Oh, I will." She laughs and looks towards Sam. "Isn't it great, Mom?"

Sam still has the same beam on her face. "Yes, sweetie, it is."

"I have to see Tina! Can I go with Dad this evening?"

"Sure." Sam sounds uncertain. "If it's OK with Dad."

"Of course," I say. "The whole firm is going out for dinner at Lift. We're celebrating because it looks like Micah Weston will be getting out of jail this week."

"I *knew* you'd find him innocent, Dad." She jumps to her feet. "Let me get my backpack and we'll go." She races out of the room.

"Thanks, Sam," I say. "I wasn't expecting her to want to come home with me. Will you be OK."

"Of course. It will give me some time to catch up on my reading."

There is an awkward silence.

Sam breaks it with, "Did you go down on your knees and slip a ring on her finger?"

"No. In fact, I just bought the ring today."

Her eyebrows go up. "Can I see it?"

I get up and take the box from my pocket. I pop it open and show her the ring I bought on my shopping trip this morning.

"Oh Cal, it's beautiful." She reaches up to touch it but stops and puts her hand back in her lap. "Tina's very lucky." She smiles but I can't un-hear the sadness in her voice.

I struggle to find something to say. Shakespeare comes, but not to my rescue.

Ay; or else 'twere hard luck, being in so

preposterous estate as we are.

Is Sam's and my relationship a preposterous estate?

Ellie springs back into the room and banishes the uncomfortable thought.

"Let's go," she says. Then runs over and hugs her mother.

I blink away a tear as I see Sam, sitting in her wheelchair by the window.

———

"THERE'S ALWAYS ROOM FOR ONE MORE, ESPECIALLY WHEN IT'S Ellie," Nick says.

"I don't know, Nick," Zeke jokes with a big grin. "There was a time when thirteen people sat down to dinner and it didn't work out too well for a couple of them."

Ellie looks puzzled at the laughter. She's a product of religion-free education.

The waiter comes over for our drink orders. Lift no longer has Trash Panda on the menu but I'm more than happy with an Off the Rail pale ale.

When our drinks arrive, Nick taps his glass with his fork. I look at the big smile on his face and think back to what he was like when we worked for VPD. Back then, a smile was a rarity and when it did appear it was usually laced with cynicism. Even though he will now never walk again, he is the happiest he has ever been.

"I'd just like to thank everyone for working so hard on the Micah Weston case. Because of your work, an innocent kid is going to be released from prison this week."

"Hear, hear!" Jim Garry raises his glass and salutes all of us.

Ellie, who is sitting on the other side of Tina, gives me a big thumbs up.

"I also have another big announcement," Nick says. "Adry received the upgrade to her BC Security Licence. She no longer has the 'under supervision' category. She is a fully-fledged private investigator."

Adry blushes as everyone cheers and Jason gives her a big hug.

I look at Ellie. She is clapping louder than anyone. If Ellie is to have a detective role model, Adry would be a good choice.

Nick continues. "Although Adry was never a police officer, she has a bigger gift for detective work than many officers I've worked with." He looks directly at me and squints, which gets a couple of laughs. "Plus, she's a match for every one of them when it comes to dealing with unruly suspects. Until I met her, I'd never even heard of the Israeli martial art, Krav Maga. I've seen her use it twice and she's amazing."

Nick looks at me and raises his eyebrows. I nod.

I clear my throat. "As some of you know, I proposed to Tina and, for some crazy reason, she accepted, so I just want to make it official." I haul the ring box out of my pocket, take out the ring and slip it on her finger.

"Oh Cal," she says, "it's beautiful." She hugs me and I feel Ellie's arms around both of us.

I hardly hear the cheers and shouts of 'Congratulations.'

"One more announcement," Nick says. "As the managing partner of Stammo Rogan Investigations, I officially order Cal and Tina to take the rest of the week off and celebrate."

Tina looks at me and smiles. "We'd better do what the boss says."

Nick's announcements over, people start to chat. Jim Garry and his wife, Ginny, are sitting opposite us. "Can I see the ring," she asks. Tina extends her hand and smiles broadly at their obvious approval.

"I hear you recently had a bit of an ordeal, Tina," Jim says.

"Yes," she says. "But my hero rescued me." She puts her arm around my shoulders and hugs me.

"Cal said that at first, he thought the kidnappers were members of that terrorist group," Jim says.

Tina giggles. Putting on an imitation of her mother's Indian accent, she says, "That's because all brown people look alike to Cal."

I laugh, as much from relief that it wasn't the Rasul Brigade who kidnapped her. Then a sobering thought takes over: if they had kidnapped her, she probably wouldn't be alive.

I shake off the thought and change the subject. "So where shall we go for our mini-vacation?"

"I've never been to Lake Okanagan. Let's go there," Tina says.

"It's beautiful," Ginny says. "You'll love it."

"Done!" I say. "Tomorrow morning we can drop Ellie off at school and drive there. We can have a late lunch beside the lake."

"Hey," Ellie says. "Aren't I coming too?"

"It will have to be dinner beside the lake," Tina says. "Tomorrow morning, I have to go to the Crown Prosecutors office to tell him about Bal and Dhruv kidnapping me. I want to see those guys in jail for what they tried to do to me. Especially Bal."

I think of Micah getting out of Kent Institution.

Then I think of Balvir and Dhruv taking his place.

I get a horrible feeling that at least one of these cases is far from over.

25

CAL

Monday, six days later

It's not like me to be the first person in the office but, after the most relaxing and wonderful five days in the lovely little town of Penticton—with its six breweries and uncountable wineries—I'm ready to rumble. I have more than two months to decide whether to return to SFU in the fall and some investigation work is appealing. Maybe I'll work part-time and finish my Ph.D. part-time.

I fire up my computer and manage to navigate my way to the app that Nick recently purchased where—among a bunch of other stuff I have yet to learn—I can get my phone messages. I really preferred those pink slips of paper telling me who had called but I guess I have to move with the times. There's no message from Melanie Weston. I'd kind of expected her to call and say thanks for getting her brother out of jail. According to a text I got from Jim Garry, on Thursday the judge overturned the verdict in Micah's trial and he was released from Kent that same day.

I was glad Melanie didn't call me on my cell while we

were away. Tina is very intuitive and I think she might have guessed how close I came to being unfaithful.

There's a message from Inspector Domenic Dixon of the VPD drug unit. I call him back.

"Hey, Dom. Cal Rogan. You called."

"Hi, Cal. Yes. I wanted to thank you for passing on that address on Gore Street."

"My pleasure. Did you pick up that guy Casey?"

"No, we didn't. The place was abandoned. But we did get prints. When we ran them we came up with a bunch of guys we've had on the radar for a while and we had a match on the guy in the picture you sent us."

"Casey, right. One of George Walsh's scumbags."

"Turns out Casey's not his name. He's Yuri Antonov."

"Really? I didn't know Walsh hired Russians."

"Antonov doesn't work for Walsh. He works for a Russian gang run by a guy named Vadim Borisovitch Drozdov. They're big into crystal meth."

"Are you sure?"

"Yes. One of the prints we found matched a guy we just arrested. He was facing a murder charge and he struck a deal for a reduced sentence. He told us that Drozdov's gang were the ones who were selling all that high-quality crystal meth that was on the streets."

"Not Walsh's gang?"

"No. Ever since Walsh has been locked up in Millhaven, his gang has been falling apart. Anyway, I just wanted to thank you for giving us the heads up on the Gore Street location."

We say our goodbyes and hang up. I think of Zeke and the scientific method. Maybe I should have falsified that it was Walsh pushing the meth. If it wasn't Walsh, why was Goliath all over Micah? It doesn't—

"Hey Rogan. How was the vacay?" Nick wheels into the office with a big smile on his face.

"Great!" I respond as he makes for the coffee machine.

"Now you're back at work, I've got a job for you." He's all business this morning. "Melanie Weston still hasn't paid her bill yet. I called her a couple of times and left a message. Maybe she didn't recognize my caller ID and thought is was a scam call. Do you want to call her and get her to cough up? I know she's rich and all, but rich people don't always pay on time."

"On it," I say. I feel a little bit of dread that maybe she will want to meet in person to pay. I really don't want the temptation. I pull out my phone and dial her number. A computer answers the call. *"The number you have reached is no longer in service."*

"What number did you call her on Nick?"

He rustles through the papers on his desk and reads off a number. It's the same as the one I just called.

"And you got through to her voicemail?"

"Yeah," he says.

Why would she cancel her cell number?

Maybe the press were hounding her about her brother's release from Kent.

———

IT'S THE SAME DOORMAN WHO WAS HERE ON MY PREVIOUS visit. "Good morning, sir," he says as he opens the front door for me. "Are you here to see Ms. Weston again?" He has an impressive memory.

I glance at his name tag. "Thank you, Chad. Yes, I am."

"Is she expecting you, Mr. Rogan?" Even more impressive. I guess the rich can afford to hire the best.

"No, but it's urgent that I see her."

A slight frown crosses his face. He's too polite for it to be disapproving. "I don't think she's home at the moment." The frown is joined by a hint of puzzlement. He picks up his phone and dials. Fifteen seconds slip by, never to return. He hangs up. "As I thought, she's not in."

"Did you see her leave this morning?"

"No, sir," he says.

"Then why did you think she's not in?"

"I saw her leave on Friday with a friend. She said she'd be away for the weekend. I guess she's not back yet."

There's no way she went away for the weekend with a friend on the day after Micah's release. "This friend," I ask. "Was he tall and skinny?"

"Yes, he was."

Micah.

"Did they say where they were going?"

He looks undecided. The people who hired him for this job would not want him to give out information about the people who live here.

I pull out my wallet and extract a business card. I hand it to him. As he examines it, I surreptitiously withdraw five twenties and roll them into my right hand. "It's very important that I contact the man she was with. If there's any way you can help me…"

There is a conflict on his face. "I'd like to help you sir but we are not allowed to give out any information about our residents…" he pauses for a moment, "…or their *boyfriends*." The tone of his voice and the look on his face tell it all. He has a thing for Melanie. Who wouldn't?

"I understand," I say and reach out my hand to shake. As he takes my hand, he feels the roll of twenties. I keep hold of his hand. "I don't need to know where Ms. Weston went, but

I do need to speak with the man she was with. Can you help me, Chad?"

He looks at me for a long three seconds and buckles. "I heard him say to her, 'Let's go to my place then.' For some reason that made her laugh and he joined in. I could hear them still laughing as they got into the elevator down to the parking levels."

I let go of his hand leaving him grasping the hundred bucks. "I appreciate it, Chad," I say. "And if it makes you feel any better, the guy she was with wasn't her boyfriend. He was her brother."

He gives me a genuine smile of appreciation.

"Thank you for saying so, sir, but I'm pretty sure you're wrong about their relationship."

"Why do you say that?" I ask.

"I have a sister and she and I would never..." a red glow creeps into his cheeks. "Let's just say we wouldn't behave the way they did."

Maybe the guy wasn't Micah. There's no shortage of tall skinny men. I pull out my phone and do a search of the CBC website. Sure enough, there's a picture of Micah Weston in an article about his trial. I show it to Chad. "Is this the guy?"

He looks closely and frowns. "I'm not a hundred percent sure, but I'd say yes."

I thank him for his help and leave. Poor Chad. He's definitely out of Melanie's league but a guy can hope, right? His feelings for her must have led him to misinterpret the relationship between Micah and his sister.

If I'm going to collect our fees, I know where I need to go next.

———

I PULL INTO THE DRIVEWAY, HALF HOPING TO SEE MICAH'S Lamborghini. I don't, but I do see Melanie's Lexus. Hopefully, I can get her to do an email money transfer of the funds she owes us, then get out of here before anything weird happens between us. I don't really understand why she was so flirtatious with me. As much as I'd like to think it's my raw animal magnetism, I don't think so. I'm as far out of her league as Chad the doorman.

The door opens.

"Oh," I say. Not Melanie. Not Micah. "Hi." I search my memory. "You're Melanie's friend, Peter..." Searching...

"Lighthall," he supplies the answer.

"Of course," I say.

He gives me a warm smile. "I recognize the Austin Healey but..."

"Cal Rogan," I say.

"Of course, how can I help you?"

This makes sense. Although he's a lot older than Melanie. He's definitely in her league.

"I'd like to speak to Melanie," I say.

"Huh," he says. "You and me both, Cal."

"She's not here?"

He looks long and hard at me. "Let me guess," he says. "She owes you money."

My face supplies the answer.

"You'd better come in," he says. I follow him into the living room with the wood carvings, wondering what the hell is going on here. He gestures for me to sit down. "So tell me," he says, "how do you know Melanie Weston?"

"I'm a private investigator. Our firm found evidence to exonerate her brother of a crime he didn't commit."

"The murder of his girlfriend in my garage," he says.

"*Your* garage?" I ask. "You're not Melanie and Micah's father."

He laughs but it's not fuelled by humour. "No. I am, or rather I was, her landlord."

"She told me her parents owned this house."

"It transpires she told a lot of people a lot of things," he says.

"How long did she rent from you?"

"For over a year."

"You continued to rent to her even after the murder?"

"Sit back," he says. "It's a long story. I recently retired and decided I wanted to fulfill a childhood dream and visit the Amazon. I put the house up for rent for seven thousand bucks a month." Melanie showed up and offered me seventy-five hundred if I'd include the use of my Lexus SUV. I agreed." He smiles ruefully. "I've got to admit it's hard to turn down someone who looks like Melanie. I kinda liked the idea of her living in the house.

"She paid the rent, as regular as clockwork, on the first of every month by email transfer. After two months our trip was organized and my wife and I headed off to Peru for six months; we figured it would be safer than Brazil. Part of the trip was to spend time living in the rainforest with no cell-phone service, no internet and no TV. I emailed Melanie, saying that we would be out of contact for a while and that if anything happened, like a plumbing problem or a broken appliance, she could fix it and deduct the cost from the rent.

"Our trip was amazing. We even got to spend some time living with some of the indigenous people. When we finally emerged from the forest, returning to so-called civilization was a bit of a culture shock—for example, having ten thousand emails in my inbox—and it wasn't until about a month later that I discovered that after the first three months, Melanie had stopped paying the rent. I contacted her and she gave me a sob story about her brother being in trouble—she omitted to mention that he was on trial for murdering his girlfriend in my garage—and she promised to have the rent payment up-to-date in a month. I talked to my wife about it and we decided it was only money and we should finish our trip and deal with it when we got home. Which is exactly what we did and, after quarantining on returning to Vancouver, I went to see Melanie. That was when you and I met—what was it?—ten days ago.

"She was apologetic about the problem and gave me a cheque for the full amount of the rent owed, post-dated two days later on the Saturday. I didn't deposit it until Monday and, as you might guess, I got a call from my bank Wednesday morning."

"The cheque bounced?"

"Like a kid on a pogo stick. I called her several times but just got voicemail, so I came over here to find the place deserted. By coincidence, as I was leaving, my next-door neighbour walked by with her dog. That was when I learned about the murder. I don't know about you Cal, but she conned me out of thirty-seven thousand five hundred dollars."

Knowing how Nick is going to react to this bit of news is starting to make my head explode. "My partner negotiated a substantial bonus, contingent on us getting her brother released, so she owes us about the same amount."

"When you're tracking her down, if you can get her to pay what she owes me, or at least some of it, I'll be happy to pay you a finder's fee."

As I leave his house, I begin to worry about what other lies Melanie Weston might have told us.

———

"YOU HAVE GOTTA BE FUCKIN' KIDDING ME!" NICK IS MADDER than a wasp in a jar. "She scammed us into believing she could pay us for getting her brother out of jail. Who does that? If she'd have been straight with us, we might even have done it *pro bono* or at least for a moderate fee."

"Well, at least we got Micah out of Kent." Adry's trying to sugarcoat the situation.

"Yeah, but we still got screwed." Nick shakes his head in disgust.

"Wait a minute," Adry says. "Didn't she say her parents were the ones who were loaded? Maybe we should try them."

"That was probably a lie too," Nick says, not about to be mollified. "But why don't you check 'em out anyway, Adry? Just in case."

A silence descends as we all process what's happened.

Zeke is the first to break it. "If she lied about the money, I wonder what else she might have lied about?"

"I was just thinking the same thing. Any ideas about what?" I say.

"You and I went to get a picture of that Casey character. The only reason we knew of his existence is from Kitana's burner phone, a phone that Melanie gave you."

"Oh Jeez," Nick says. "The only reason we knew that Kitana was manufacturing crystal meth in the first place was because Melanie gave you what she said were Kitana's notes and formulas."

"Which got us to the address on Powell Street where I found the meth," Adry says.

"What if we've been set up?" Zeke says. "What if it wasn't

Kitana making the meth? What if it was Micah and Melanie?"

His words send a spear through my gut.

"Maybe," he continues, "we should try and track down that Casey character, see if he's really in George Walsh's crew. Maybe he's an actor hired by Melanie to pretend to be a gangbanger and to implicate Kitana."

"He's not an actor," I say. "I talked to Domenic Dixon of the drug unit this morning. The guy's a gangbanger alright. His name's not Casey, either. It's Yuri Antonov; he's Russian. It's not Walsh's crew who have been selling meth on the street. It's a Russian gang run by some character named Drozdov."

"What!" I see the shocked look rush onto Zeke's face. "Drozdov?" he says.

"Yeah. Do you know him?" I ask.

"No, I've never heard of him, but didn't you say that the guy protecting Micah in Kent was called Blackbird?"

I nod. "Yeah, why?"

"Drozdov means blackbird in Russian."

A second silence appears to let us all process what this means.

Puzzle pieces start to click in place in my mind.

Nick is the first to speak this time.

"Oh crap," he sighs loudly. "We're idiots. You're right Zeke, we got the whole thing back to front. We thought Walsh's gang was buying meth from Kitana and wanted to kill Micah in revenge for him killing her. But it's the other way round. It's the Russians who are selling the meth. They must have been protecting Micah because it was *him* who was supplying them with the product."

"Makes sense," Zeke adds. "The Russians wanted Micah out of jail so he could get back to making the meth for them.

Melanie and Casey—or should I say, Yuri—hatched up this whole plan to falsely implicate Kitana in the drug trade. Even supplying us with a substitute killer in the form of the late Georgi Volkov."

"Melanie played me like a fiddle," I say. "She brought up the religious angle on the drive back from Kent. Kitana must have told Micah about her brother's fundamentalist leanings. Melanie planted the seed in my mind and she must have been over the moon when we discovered that Haasim Ajram actually *was* an extremist who believed in killing adulterers. Then she and Casey/Yuri provided all the evidence for us to finger Kitana as the drugmaker. She provided us with two alternative killers. It was pure genius." It makes way too much sense. "Micah was doing engineering at UBC," I continue. "That's how he met Kitana, the genius-but-naïve chemistry student. He used her. He seduces her and then picks her brain so that he could work out how to manufacture the meth. She was probably too in love with him to suspect what he was doing. When she finally works it out, he kills her to shut her up."

"It makes sense," Adry says. "Both Kitana's mother and her friend Sarah said that just before she died, she was worried about something. She must have discovered how Micah was using her."

Nick weighs in. "Eric Street could have been telling the truth. He said he didn't trick Micah into putting on the bloody shirt to get his DNA all over it. Micah just got lucky when we got the evidence thrown out because Street was mixed up with Kitana's brother in the Rasul Brigade."

"Holy fuck!" I say. "We just got a murderer out of jail."

"Now what are we gonna do?" Nick asks.

We all stare blankly at each other.

26

ADRY

L angley is where Melanie said her parents lived. It's a fairly big suburb but there are only three families named Weston. The first two I visited were a bust and as I draw up to the home of the third, I can see that Nick's hope —the Westons being rich enough to cover what we are owed —is also a bust. I park the car on the street and make my way up the short driveway to the modest bungalow. Although it's small, it seems very well maintained and the front yard is lovingly tended. It reminds me of my parents' home. I press the doorbell and hear the chimes inside.

The woman who answers the door looks around fifty. She is quite tall and was probably striking in her youth but her face bears lines of perpetual worry and has a severity to it.

"Can I help you?" she says.

"Good afternoon," I say with my warmest smile. "Are you Mrs. Weston?"

"Yes."

"Could you help me? Are Micah and Melanie Weston your children?"

She doesn't reply but the look that crosses her face is a mixture of surprise and anger. It gives me my answer. "I need to speak with them," I say. "It's very urgent."

She looks me up and down, her lips pursed.

"Micah is in prison and I haven't seen or heard from Ruth in years."

"Ruth?" I say.

"Ruth! That's her real name." The severity is in her voice now.

Hmm. Ruth and Micah. Books in the old Testament. Maybe that's my way in.

"By the grace of God," I say, "Micah has been released." She draws in a sharp breath at my words. "I was wondering if he might have come home."

Through the mix of emotions cascading across her face, she manages to say, "You had better come in Miss...?"

"Locke. Adriana Locke."

She opens the door wide enough for me to enter, then closes it. In the dimness of the hallway, I can see several pictures. They are all of beatific faces surrounded by halos. She leads me into a small but spotless living room and gestures me to sit in an armchair. As I sit, I see on the wall opposite a large crucifix. It gives me just a little flush of guilt at the lies I am going to have to tell, in order to get what I want.

"So, Miss Locke, what is the connection you have with my... with Micah and Ruth? And just why precisely are you here?"

Every successful lie flies close to the truth. "I belong to an organization which tries to help people who have been wronged in some way. Mel— I mean, Ruth brought to our attention that her brother was in prison for a crime he didn't commit."

"Oh, is that what she told you?"

"Why do you say that, Mrs. Weston?"

"Ruth is a liar and a manipulator and worse."

"But in this case, she was right. We were able to show that the detective who investigated the murder was not credible. Micah was released last week."

She thinks this over and the severity of her face softens a little. "I'm glad he is innocent of that at least. Even if he has broken all of the other nine Commandments..." she looks up at the crucifix and adds as an afterthought, "...thanks to his sister."

This is a thread worth pulling. "Was Ruth a bad influence on Micah?" I ask.

"Were Lot's daughters a bad influence on Lot?" She says it as though to herself.

I've read bits of the Bible but I don't know what she means by that remark. I ask her but she ignores my question. "Did you come all the way out here to tell me about Micah's release?" she asks.

"Partly," I lie. "But also because Ruth owes my organization rather a lot of money."

"Well I'm very sorry about that but I can't help you," she says. "My husband and I are not wealthy. The pandemic has crippled his business and we have two mortgages on this house." She stands. "So unless there's anything else..."

"Do you know how I might contact either Micah or Ruth? Is there any place you know of that they might have gone to?"

"We expelled Ruth from our lives when she was nineteen and have had no contact since. Micah left, under her spell, not long after. I neither know nor care where in the world they have taken themselves."

She leads me to the door.

I check my watch. I'll be going against the afternoon rush hour so I should be able to get back to the office to find an answer and pose a worrying proposition.

———

AS SOON AS I WALK INTO THE OFFICE THEY ARE ALL OVER ME. Nick and Cal both speak at the same time. "Do the parents have money?" from Nick. "Was Micah there?" from Cal.

"No and no," I tell them.

"So it was a big fat zero," Nick sighs.

"Except for a couple of things the mother said." That got their attention. "She's like super-religious. She told me Melanie is not her real name, it's Ruth. We were talking about them and I asked if Melanie/Ruth was a bad influence on Micah. She said something like, 'Were Lot's daughters a bad influence on Lot?'"

Nick and Cal just look confused but Zeke says, "Holy crap, that's sick." We all turn towards him. He gives a little grin. "My parents were super-religious too, except they were Russian Orthodox. They made me read the Bible from cover to cover. Ironically, that's what made me stop believing." His grin broadens as he looks at our expectant faces. "So..." He's milking it. "In Genesis, when Lot and his family flee the destruction of Sodom and Gomorrah his wife looks back and gets turned into a pillar of salt and after a while, Lot and his daughters flee into the mountains. They live alone in a cave. The daughters basically start to get horny so they get old Lot drunk as a skunk and screw him."

"Ewww," I say. "Does that mean Melanie seduced her brother? That's icky."

"Makes sense to me," Cal says. "The doorman at her

apartment building saw them together and thought they were lovers, not siblings."

"Incest is illegal isn't it?" I ask. "They should be locked up."

Nick's eyes bore into mine. "Adry, did you know that fifty-two years ago in Canada, what Stewart and I do in the privacy of our own home was illegal. Should *we* be locked up?"

"No, of course not, but that's different."

"No, it's not. I think incest itself is OK provided that both parties are informed, consenting adults. We always think of incest as a parent and child thing which *is* completely sick, those parents should be thrown in jail until they rot. But between adults, why not?"

"OK guys," Cal says. "As much as I enjoy discussions on moral philosophy, let's leave it until we're all sitting in a bar one evening. Adry, you said there were a couple of things; what was the other one?"

"At the end of our conversation, their mother said she didn't care where in the world her kids were. It made me think that if they've made a ton of money manufacturing drugs for Blackbird's gang, they could be anywhere in the world. Maybe we should just write this whole thing off."

"No!" "No way!" Cal and Nick speak simultaneously.

"I don't give a shit about the money anymore," Nick says. "We're never gonna see a penny of it now. In a minute I have to pick up that phone and talk to the VPD, the Crown Prosecutor's office and the judge. I'm gonna tell 'em we got it all wrong. Then we're gonna find these sleazeballs *and* some solid evidence on them *and* I don't care how we do it. And do you know why? It's because I don't want Stammo Rogan Investigations to be the private eyes who got a murderer off scot-free."

"I'm a hundred percent with Nick," Cal says.

"But how are we going to find them?" I ask.

"I'm not sure yet," Cal says with intensity. "The journey of a thousand miles begins with a single step. And I sure as hell know what our first step is."

27

CAL

Tuesday

When I walk through the door I see them immediately. They are sitting at our usual table surrounded by food. Each has a plate laden with eggs, bacon, sausage and toast. Between them is a plate of corned beef hash, which they both dig into, and there are two bowls containing the remnants of what was once cereal.

I sit at the table. Four eyes swivel up from their plates.

"Hey, Rocky. How's it going eh?" says Ghost.

Tommy's mouth is too full to speak; he just waves a hand at me.

"Thanks for calling ahead and telling the waiter to feed us, Rock. He normally won't serve us unless we show him we can pay." He chuckles. "And right now, we can't."

"No prob guys."

I think of my call to the waiter. Although out of context, it brought to mind a line from Anthony and Cleopatra.

Then, world, thou hast a pair of chaps, no more;
And throw between them all the food thou hast,

He certainly did that.

Right on cue, he comes over but I decline his offer of coffee and ask for the bill.

"Listen, guys," I say. "You remember the picture I took of the guy from that building on Gore Street?"

"Sure Rock. We still got it don't we Tom?" Tommy nods vigorously. "We tried to find his name but we didn't have no luck. We seen him a couple o' times too. Talking to some guys. Tommy walked up close to 'em but they was talking some foreign language, so he didn't know what they were saying."

"They were speaking Russian. I found out his name. It's Yuri Antonov."

"I told you it was Russian," Tommy says proudly.

Ghost nods and forks a big scoop of hash into his mouth.

"Thing is, guys," I say. "I need to know everything I can about him, especially where he hangs out." I place an envelope on the table. "There's two hundred bucks each in there for you, together with a bunch of photos of Antonov. I want you to hand out the photos to as many of your friends as you can trust. If anyone comes up with anything I can use, *they'll* get two hundred and *you'll* get another two hundred each." He grabs the envelope and it disappears into the voluminous coat he always wears.

Tommy gives me a big toothless grin. "We'll get on it right after breakfast, Rock."

Ghost gives me the thumbs up. "Fuckin' A," he says around his mouthful of hash. Then he gets a thoughtful look on his face. "You know what, Rock. Me and Tommy appreciate the cash but you don't have to be always paying us. We're happy with a good meal now and again."

These guys are the salt of the earth. "Just think of it as a *quid pro quo*," I say.

"A what?" Ghost asks.

"Something for something," Tommy says. "You scratch my back, I'll scratch yours."

"I didn't know you were a Latin scholar, Tommy," I say with a chuckle.

He grins. "Not exactly a scholar, Rock. But not *everything* the nuns taught us was bad..." His grin fades and is replaced by a deep sadness. "Just most of it."

Tommy is too young to have been sent to one of the infamous residential schools that Indigenous Canadians were herded into by the thousands, right up until the nineteen-seventies. The last school closed its doors in 1996. "Which school Tommy?"

"Just a regular Catholic school," he says. "My dad was another story. He was sent to the St. Mary's Indian Residential school. He was lucky enough to come out alive; lots of the kids didn't. But I tell you Rocky, he came out broken. Used to beat my mom and us kids. For some reason I'll never figure out, he sent us all to Catholic school. Even though it was the eighties, they still treated us like shit because we was native." He gives a sardonic grin. "Made me the man I am today."

I reach out and give Tommy's arm a squeeze, he responds with his usual cheery smile.

"I gotta go guys. Call me as soon as you get anything, OK? Anything at all."

I get up, tap my phone on the waiter's payment terminal and head out the door. As I sweep through it, I almost barrel into a guy coming in. He looks a bit too well-dressed for the Ovaltine. He also looks vaguely familiar but then again, the downtown east side is a tight-knit little community and, from my time living on the streets, everyone here looks a little familiar to me.

I cross Hastings and walk along to Gore. Zeke's car is parked a hundred metres down the street, right opposite the building where I met Yuri Antonov when he was posing as 'Casey.'

I get into the passenger seat. "Anything?" I ask.

"No. I've been parked here since about seven and there's no movement from that building. Your buddy from the drug unit said it was empty when they raided it. I think it still is."

"OK. Let's go and see if we can find anything that the drug squad missed."

We get out of the car. "You know what, Cal?" Zeke says as we cross Gore. "If I was Melanie and Micah, I'd be out of the country by now. Certainly out of Vancouver."

"They might very well be," I say. "But I don't think they've flown the coop yet. With Micah's arrest and trial and then prison he was out of circulation for months. Blackbird and his gang must have run out of their crystal meth inventory. They are going to want payback for protecting Micah while he was in Kent and that payback will come in the form of a new supply of meth. If he and Melanie want to flee the country, they are going to need a ton of cash. My bet is they're going to be in Vancouver for a while longer, manufacturing meth for Blackbird's gang. And with him in jail, Antonov might well be their contact."

"He'd better be," Zeke says, "'cos he's our only lead."

I ring the bell beside the green door. No sound emanates from within. From my last visit, I know the doorbell works but that you can't hear it from outside. It must ring on one of the upper floors. I wait sixty seconds, check up and down the street, then withdraw my trusty lock picks from my pocket. I confiscated them from a thief when I was in uniform and somehow they never made their way into the evidence locker. Zeke moves his body to shield me from prying eyes as I bend down and work on the lock. Seventeen seconds. Not a record but still pretty good for an amateur. I rip off the crime-scene tape, left by the drug unit, push the door open and we step inside. We wait, straining our ears for any noise from the upper floors. Despite the complete lack of sound, I can't shake the feeling that we are not alone in the building.

The silence is shattered by the pinging of my phone and Zeke's voice.

"I think it's clear," he says. "Let's check it out."

I check my phone. It's a voicemail from Ghost; it can wait.

The ground floor is as it was when I was here just over a week ago. Zeke and I check the fixtures and fittings of the shop that used to be here. The drawers are empty and the cupboards are bare. We check the stock room, kitchen and toilet in the back. The only evidence we find is that mice have been using the building as their home or more precisely, as their toilet.

We climb the stairs to the top floor. The stairs and the landings are littered with all sorts of detritus: bits of paper, cardboard, items of clothing and things too fierce to mention. The abandoned apartment is empty. It smells musty and yields nothing other than a broken knife in a kitchen drawer.

The apartment on the middle floor shows some sign of habitation. In the kitchen, there are a couple of fold-up metal chairs like the ones I see at NA meetings. I feel a twinge of guilt that I'm not doing three meetings a week and resolve to go to one later today.

On the counters, there are various fast-food containers

and a mixture of plastic and styrofoam cups. This must be where Yuri and his gopher waited for me to discover them. Not for the first time and probably not for the last, I marvel at how well Melanie set me up. In the bedroom are some mattresses and the living room has a rickety card table and some more metal chairs. Zeke walks over to a chest of drawers and checks through them methodically but comes up blank.

"Well this was a big fat bust," I say. "Sorry to waste your time, Zeke."

"No prob," he grins. "You know police work, you got to kiss a lot of frogs before you find a prince."

"Ain't that the truth," I say. "Let's go."

I step through the apartment door into the hallway and come face to face with the barrel of a SIG Sauer P226.

"Freeze!" the gunman says.

I freeze.

Over the pounding of my heart, I assess the situation.

In less than half a second I observe all I need. One: There's no movement behind me. Zeke hasn't followed me into the hallway yet. Good. If they didn't hear our conversation they may not know he's there. Two: the face behind the SIG is tattooed with designs featuring Russian script. Three: two steps behind him is Yuri's sidekick who likes to clean his nails with his knife; not great positioning for them. Four: I walked out of the apartment just as the gunman was about to enter it, so my nose is no more than twenty-four inches from the barrel. Five: Russian gang members are not known for spending time indulging in compassionate thoughts prior to pulling triggers.

With every joule my adrenaline can muster, my left fist comes up and smashes into the back of his right hand. The gun discharges and over the ringing in my ear, I hear the thwack of the bullet burying itself in the drywall. Before he can recover, I open my fist, grab his wrist and snap his right hand into the air. I hear the clatter of the SIG falling to the floor as I step forward and slide my right arm under and behind his bicep then clamp my right hand over my left. I push down on the wrist and up on the bicep until I hear the satisfying click of a dislocating elbow and the equally satisfying howl it evokes.

Yuri's gopher is rushing me with his blade drawn.

I disentangle myself and step back. My foot catches on something and I topple over backwards. All the breath whooshes out of me.

Sidekick grins. He's in the catbird seat. He's too smart to attack me on the ground. Instead, he changes his hold on the knife so that he can throw it. In this instant, I know he's an expert at more than just cleaning his nails with that blade. He draws back his throwing arm.

"Freeze NOW!"

Zeke's voice stops him in mid throw. I cut a glance at Zeke. It wasn't his *voice* that stopped the throw of the knife. It was the SIG he scooped up off the floor.

I see the internal debate on Gopher's face. To throw or not to throw, that is the question. My inside turns to jelly at the thought of that knife slicing through me. I flashback to the knife Roy used to wield. I've always hated knives.

"DROP IT!" Zeke yells.

I see Gopher's throwing arm tense. Oh God, he's going for it.

The SIG roars. Zeke saw it too.

Gopher crumples and his knife clatters across the floor.

All the tension washes out of my body.

Well...

That was an exciting six seconds.

Tattoo-face whimpers and Gopher groans.

"Thank God he's not dead," Zeke sighs. "I'll call an ambulance."

As I get to my feet, I see what I tripped on. It's a filthy, old black hoodie, probably discarded by someone who squatted here. It fits right in. But as I stumbled over it, I must have moved it because I see something sticking out from underneath it. Something that definitely does *not* fit right in.

It's probably not important but I bend down, pick it up and slide it into my pocket.

"I'll call Domenic Dixon of the drug unit," I say. "He'll want to get his hands on these guys."

I pull out my phone and notice the voice message from Ghost. I must remember to call him back later.

As Zeke and I make our calls, I reflect on the fact that less than sixty seconds ago, we thought our visit here was a bust.

We both hang up and look at each other.

"Thanks," I say.

"You'd do the same for me," he says.

We both nod. Enough said.

An odd look passes over his face. "So…" he says. "We came here to find Yuri Antonov but ended up with these two losers who probably work for him." He looks over at them. "They seem like they're in a lot of pain. Maybe we should… oh, I don't know… maybe ask them where we might find their boss."

I'm not sure I like where he's going with this. "Interrogate them?" I say.

"Yeah," he says, wandering over to Tattoo-face. "Guantanamo-style," he says. He kneels down grabs the guy's wrist. "Where can we find Yuri Antonov?" he says and twists.

The Russian whimpers.

Zeke twists harder and the Russian yells out in agony. "Fuck you," he shouts.

This is not right.

"You just have to tell me where he is," Zeke says. Another twist evokes a scream this time.

"Enough, Zeke." I'm feeling sick to my stomach. "We're not going to use torture to get what we want."

He looks hard at me. I get the nasty feeling he's getting off on this and I can see in his eyes that he's not going to be persuaded by the moral argument. He just saved my life but I'm not going to let him continue this 'interrogation.' "Anyway," I say, "they're Russian. Russian gang members never rat their colleagues out. You know that."

He lets go of the Russian's wrist and nods. The moral argument may not have worked but the practical one did. He stands up. "Sure," he says. He starts to make his way down the stairs. "I'll open the door for the paramedics and the police. You can keep your eyes on the scum."

Just when I was starting to like him.

———

IT'S ALREADY TWELVE-FIFTY. THE PATROL COPS ONLY RELEASED Zeke and me when Domenic Dixon of the drug unit finally showed up and vouched for us. The Balmoral pub is one of Ghost's and Tommy's favourite hangouts but they have been in here for a couple of hours with cash in their jeans. I am not too hopeful of a cogent conversation. However, Ghost's voicemail was compelling.

"Hey, Rock," Tommy slurs. "Look Ghost, i's Rocky."

"Heeeeyyyyyy, Rocky," Ghost grins. "Did'ja get my voicemail?" At least he remembers he called me. But will he remember what he called me about?

"Yes, thanks Ghost. Who was this guy you saw?" I say. He just stares back blankly. "The guy in the voicemail..." I prompt him.

"Oh, yeah. In the Ovaltine." An even broader grin breaks out on his face. "That was a great breakfast, by the way. Thanks again Rock. Roy'd be real proud of the way you turned out."

"Yeah," Tommy echos. "Good old Roy. I haven't seen him in a while. Did he go somewhere, Rock?" Roy's been dead for years but Tommy's too far gone to remember.

I'll need to coax the information out of Ghost. "In your voicemail, you said that there was a guy in the Ovaltine asking about me?"

"Oh yeah. It was odd." His head nods sagely and I pray he doesn't go off on a tangent. "Just as you was walking out, he was walking in. To tell the truth, he looked a bit out of place in there. Well-dressed he was."

I remember passing by someone as I left. His face was vaguely familiar.

"What did he do?" I ask.

"It was funny. As soon as he got through the door, he looked back out the window, like he was watching you. Then he walked back out. We could see him through the window. He was standing on the sidewalk looking across Hastings to where you was walking, wasn't he Tommy?"

"Yeah..." Tommy nods slowly. "Who we talkin' about?"

"Fer Chris' sakes, Tommy. You know, the guy who came into the Ovaltine after Rocky left."

"Oh... yeah," Tommy says, clearly unconvinced.

"Ghost," I say. "This is important. Did he follow me?"

"No, he din't."

"Are you sure?"

"Hundred percent," he says. He picks his beer glass off

the table and drains it, wiping his lips on the sleeve of his coat.

"How can you be so sure?" I ask.

"'Cos he stood out there for a while watching you and talking on his phone but then he came back in."

I'm getting a bad feeling brewing in my gut. "What did he do then?"

"He goes over to the waiter, slips him a twenty and asks him something, then the waiter nods his head in our direction and he comes over."

"Ooooh, *that* guy," Tommy says. "I remember *him*. He scared the shit outta me."

"Fuckin' A. He was one scary dude."

"What did he say to you?"

"He asked us what you was talking to us about but we din't tell him, did we Tom?"

"Nah, we just said you was a friend from the old days."

"We jus' told him we'd known you for years and you'd often meet us here and buy us breakfast."

"Then he gave us like a long, hard stare." Tommy's a bit more lucid now.

"Creeped us out," Ghost adds. "Then he gets up and goes and has a chat with the waiter, like he was checking out what we said."

"Did he ask you guys anything else?"

"Nah. After he finished with the waiter he just turned around and fucked off out of there. Didn't even look back at us."

I absorb all that they've said. Whoever he was, he was following me. But for how long? Could I have been under surveillance? Hell, does he know where I live? A sliver of fear cuts through me. I wonder if—

"He sounded funny," Tommy breaks into my thoughts.

"Yeah, you're right, he did," Ghost adds. "I'd forgotten that. He had like a foreign accent."

The sliver becomes a pike. "Was it a Russian accent?" I ask.

Ghost shrugs, "I dunno."

But Tommy gets animated. "Yeah, that's it. I should have known he was a Ruskie. I know 'cos one of my teachers in high school was one. He had the exact same accent. Jus' like that other guy you talked to us about."

It makes complete sense. Micah and Melanie will know that we're going to track them down, so they've got Blackbird's guys keeping tabs on us. Mine and Zeke's encounter with the gang members this morning will have confirmed it. The well-dressed Russian must have seen me walking towards Gore Street and set his thugs on us.

We now all have targets firmly attached to our backs. Not just us but our families too.

———

"Don't get me wrong, I love staying at hotels and dining out, but are you sure you're not overreacting just a little bit." Tina gives me her quirky grin and takes a sip of the Cabernet.

"I told you, Nick and I and the others spent the whole afternoon discussing it at length. We agreed this was the way to go. The average gang might think twice about killing one of us, but Drozdov's gang would do it in a heartbeat and, sometimes, Russian gangs will make a point of taking out their victim's family members too."

The grin slides off her face and, as my words sink in, horror strolls on. "So how long do we need to hide out? The rest of our lives?"

"No. Once we track down Micah and Melanie West—"

"Whoa, whoa, whoa. Why do *you* need to do that? Why not let the police find them? If you back off and tell this Drozdov character that you're done with the whole thing, we can get back to normal. No one's paying you and Nick to find Micah and his sister. Why don't you just focus on your other clients? Or you could quit, enjoy the summer and go back to completing your Ph.D. and teaching full time."

Nick and I discussed the backing-off option too. How can I explain to her why we rejected it? Neither of us can bear to be forever known as the jerks who got a guilty man out of jail. We'd be a laughingstock in law enforcement circles. No one in the VPD or RCMP would give us the time of day ever again. If anyone's going to put this right it *has* to be us. It's what we do, damn it.

I take a deep breath. "You're a journalist. If you were working on a story about some political malfeasance which could put you in danger, would you back off?"

"Yes!" She says it emphatically then scrunches up her face. "No!" Equally emphatic. She's angry, but not at me. I can see the internal struggle. "I don't know." The frustration in her voice draws the attention of the other diners in Earls.

"It won't be forever. When we track them down, we'll hand over all the details to the VPD. They'll arrest them and interrogate them. Micah and Melanie are opportunists, not career criminals. They'll buckle and give up the rest of the gang members. Then they'll be off the streets and we won't be in danger any longer."

"You had *better* be right," she says.

"I am, you'll see." I say it with a confidence I don't completely feel. I reach across the table and take her hand. "I won't let anyone hurt you."

She smiles. "You'd better not," she says. "Otherwise my Dad will likely kill you."

I remember the episode in Hong Kong. "Or your mother."

"*And* my mother."

I squeeze her hand. "I love you."

Her eyes soften... but her sharp wit doesn't. "Of course you do," she says.

28

CAL

Wednesday

We're meeting in a conference room in the offices of Arnold Young. I've known Arnold for over thirty years. He manages the affairs and the estate of my late best friend's late father. An estate from which I receive a healthy monthly allowance on the condition that I don't lapse back into my heroin addiction. Arnold still stands ramrod straight even though he must be well into his seventies now. He is well connected with Vancouver's wealthiest and has been a great source of lucrative client referrals for Stammo Rogan Investigations.

"If there's anything you need," he says in his clipped, very British accent, "just ask my receptionist. Mr. Rogan has told me the circumstances; please feel free to use this conference room for as long as you wish." He closes the door quietly behind him.

"He called you Mr. Rogan," Adry says. "I thought you said you'd known him a long while." Adry's sharp brain doesn't miss much.

"He's called me Mr. Rogan since I was twelve."

"Yeah," Nick grumps, "he shows Rogan way too much respect." He pulls his laptop from the bag on the side of his wheelchair. "Morning prayers," he announces. "First item on the agenda: the Micah Weston case. Yesterday afternoon, we all talked about it and agreed we'd track him and his sister down, even though it puts us all at risk. You've all had time to sleep on it, if you want to withdraw from it say so now. This gang is dangerous and no one is going to think any less of you if you decide that the risks for you and your family are too great."

"I'm in." Zeke and Adry say in unison.

"Me too," Lucy says.

"Good, we appreciate it don't we, Rogan," he says and I nod. "Our big new project doesn't start until Monday and I talked to our other clients and told them that we needed to delay their cases for a couple of days. So it's a full-court press to find Micah, his sister and as many of his gang-banger friends as we can identify and turn them all over to the VPD. Lucy is going to stay here, get this place organized into a temporary office and provide support for the rest of us. We're going to go out onto the streets, rattle some cages and see if we can find this Yuri Antonov. He's Drozdov's man on the street and if we can find him it's gonna lead us to Micah and Melanie and their drug lab." He puts his unopened laptop on the conference room table and wheels towards the door. "We've got five days until Monday morning, so let's get out there. Be careful... but find those scumbags."

I open the conference room door and he wheels out like an infantry general in his tank.

It's just about five years since we started this business

and Nick has transformed from a jaded cop into a natural leader. Even I feel inspired.

My phone beeps.

It's a three-word text from Ghost.

———

FOR TWO GUYS WHO WERE WELL ON THEIR WAY TO BEING incoherently drunk at one o'clock yesterday afternoon, Ghost and Tommy are surprisingly chipper this morning. Ghost's grin goes from ear to ear and Tommy's smile resembles the top of the wall of a medieval fort: as many gaps as teeth.

"We found him, din't we Tommy?" Ghost proclaims.

Tommy nods and I'm all ears.

"Yuri Antonov?" I ask.

"Yeah. The dude in the photo, right?"

I can feel equal parts of elation and trepidation. "Where does he hang out?" I ask.

"We din't find out where he lives. But we saw him, eh."

"When was this?" I ask, the trepidation coming to the fore.

"Yesterday evening," Tommy says proudly. "On Hastings."

The elation part is gone now. "No offence, guys," I say, "but you'd had a few brewskis by one o'clock, Are you *sure* you saw Antonov yesterday evening?"

Clearly taking no offence, they grin. "Jeez, Rocky," Tommy says. "We don't drink twenty-four-seven. Well, not often anyways." He chuckles. "Not long after you left us in the Balmoral, we had a final drink and then took off to Oppenheimer Park. We've got a tent there." Oppenheimer Park is a tent city for many of the residents of the downtown eastside. Although there are a bunch of people who think the park is an eyesore and would like to see it cleared of the homeless and their meagre belongings, a kinder city council tolerates it. "We had a sleep for a couple of hours and then we started patrolling the neighbourhood."

Ghost takes up the story. "We was at it for a couple or three hours, 'cos we knew you was keen to find the dude. Then we saw him, right outside the old police station. He was talking to three guys. We recognized all three of 'em."

"And you're sure it was Antonov?"

"I fuckin' am," Ghost says, reaching into the pocket of his voluminous coat. He pulls out one of the pics I gave him. "That was him, wasn't it Tommy?"

"That was him, for sure."

The elation is starting to creep back in.

"Did you see where he went?"

"Course we did." There's pride in his voice. "He talked to the three guys for a while then he got into his car and drove off."

"What was the licence plate number?"

"Oh... Sorry, I didn't see. Did you Tom?"

"Nah. Stupid of me! I shoulda checked it out."

I try not to show them my disappointment. "No problem guys," I say. Big problem. "Next time you see him, try and get the licence plate for me, OK?"

They nod, crestfallen. "I can tell you the make and model though," Tommy says.

Maybe not a complete bust.

"It was a Lexus LC500, a white one. The five-litre, not the hybrid."

He sees the surprised look on my face. "I may be homeless, Rocky, but I know my luxury cars, don't I Ghost?"

"You sure do. I tell you Rock, every couple of weeks

Tommy walks over the Burrard Bridge and checks on all them car dealerships. He knows stuff about cars, I can tell you that."

"Thanks Tommy," I say, "that's good to know. A car like that stands out." Tommy grins and nods. "You said you knew the people he was talking to?"

"Yeah," Ghost says. "Two of 'em were street dealers. I don't know their names but they've been around for a while. But the third one I do know. Name of Henry. Used to live near us in Oppenheimer. He got a job as a steer and started making a bit of money, so he moved out of the park into the Lion Hotel."

A steer is the low man on the pole in a drug team. His job is to scour the streets, looking for people who need a fix and steering them towards the dealer he works for. He gets a small commission for his efforts; not a lot, but certainly enough to move into a flophouse like the Lion.

"Do you think he might talk to me? Tell me where I can find Antonov?"

"He might do. Since he's been steering, he's been a bit cocky about who he knows and how he's makin' money. He won't tell you for nothing, so a little bit of cash might grease the wheels."

"Do you guys know where to find him?" I ask.

Tommy gives his big grin. "Does a bear poop in the woods?" he says.

"Great! I'm going to go to a cash machine. You guys get hold of Henry and text me where to come and meet you. If I find where Antonov hangs out, there'll be a nice little commission for you guys."

Tommy grins and nods.

"Fuckin' A!" says Ghost.

———

IF YOU LOOKED UP THE WORD WEASEL IN AN ENCYCLOPEDIA OF slang, you'd see a picture of Henry front and centre. When Ghost makes the introduction, he asks, "You a cop?" His shifty eyes make a scan of the seedy coffee shop we're sitting in.

"No. Used to be but not now." I say it in a way that indicates maybe I was thrown off the force.

He nods. "Ghost says you want information. How much you paying?"

"Depends on what you've got. You know Yuri Antonov, right?"

"Yeah, sure. Me and Yuri are tight." I almost laugh at the thought that someone as high up the feeding chain as Antonov would be 'tight' with a low-level jerk like Henry.

"I have a business proposition for him. How would I go about finding him?"

He thinks about this for a while. "Tell me what it is and I'll ask my man Yuri if he's interested."

"Doesn't work like that, Henry," I say. "*This* is how it works: I give you two hundred bucks and you tell me his address. If I cut a deal with him, you get a bonus of five hundred and, if you want me to, I tell him how helpful you were in setting the whole thing up. Maybe *he* pays you a bonus too." I pull out my freshly loaded wallet and extract two hundred.

He licks his thin lips and I watch the conflicting emotions battle across his face. Avarice and fear are the primary combatants. The latter wins round one. "Nah. Mr. Antonov is very private." It's no longer 'my man Yuri.' "He don't want nobody knowing where he lives. No matter what deal you do with him, he'd kill me if I told you anything."

I withdraw another hundred. "I don't need to tell him where I got the address." The fear seems to ease and his mind is working overtime. I withdraw a fourth hundred. He licks his lips. I take out my last hundred and return the wallet to my pocket. The back of my hand brushes against the plastic that I found on the floor at the Gore Street building; I'd almost forgotten about it. I fan out the five one-hundred-dollar bills.

"OK, OK. Here's the deal," he says. Avarice wins round two. "I don't actually know the address." I fold the bills and start to slide them into my pocket. "Wait a minute, wait a minute. We can still do a deal," he says, an air of panic in his voice as he sees the money start to disappear.

I pull the bills back out. "How can you help me if you don't know the address?" I ask.

"I can get it from my buddies for sure, I just don't know which one it is—" the words tumble out of his mouth before he realizes he's let something slip.

"What do you mean, you don't know which one it is?" I ask.

His eyes flick left and right, giving a pretty good impression of a hunted rodent.

"Well..." I prompt him. I wait a beat, then put the money back in my pocket and turn away.

"Which hotel," he blurts out. "All I know is that he lives in a hotel downtown, I just don't know which one." Electricity fires up my spine. I hardly hear his next sentence. "Just give me the five hundred and I'll find out for you."

I try to keep the excitement out of my voice. God, I love this job. Forcing a straight face, I stand up. "Come on guys," I say to Ghost and Tommy. "This guy knows nothing." I take one of the hundreds, drop it on the table and look into Henry's shifty eyes. "That's for taking the time to see me.

Ghost and Tommy told you there'd be some money for you and that's it. You can thank them later."

I turn and walk out of the coffee shop, my compadres in tow. We walk down Pender towards Main. "That was a bit hasty there, Rocky," says Ghost. "I think he coulda come up with the address."

"Yeah, Rock," Tommy agrees. "Maybe you shoulda kept trying."

The grin let loose on my face is so broad it almost hurts. "No need guys. I already know."

"How?"

"Hang on," I say and hold up my finger while I make a quick phone call. Bingo! I smile at them. "I know where he is because I'm a good detective," I chuckle.

I take the money still in my hand and give them two hundred dollars each. "This is a downpayment," I say. "I've got more paying work for you, starting in about an hour. And, if you've got a few reliable friends who might like to help, bring 'em along."

As always, Tommy grins his thanks and Ghost says his signature expletive.

———

"Jeez, Rogan. That was friggin' fast," Nick says. "How did you track him down?"

"Ghost and Tommy found some low-level steer who let slip that Yuri Antonov lives in a hotel downtown."

"But how did you know which hotel?" Adry asks.

"When Zeke and I were in the abandoned building on Gore, I tripped over an old hoodie someone had left on the floor. If Zeke hadn't been there I might not be around to tell the story. As I was getting up, I spotted a piece of plastic on the floor. I remember thinking it looked a bit out of place. So I picked it up and put it in my pocket. It was a keycard for the Hyatt Hotel. Antonov must have dropped it."

"Bit of a long shot, Rogan? What if you're wrong?" Nick says.

I can't stop a grin from spreading across my face. "Not such a long shot. What are the chances of finding a hotel keycard in a building that was basically being used as a squat? We know that Antonov was there because that's where I met him, back when we thought his name was Casey."

"Fair enough, but you could still be wrong," Nick says as my grin broadens, much to his obvious irritation. "One of the squatters may have found it and just thrown it on the floor. It could have been there on the floor before Antonov even went there."

"True, true, all good points," I say. "That's why I called the Hyatt and asked to speak to Mr. Antonov. They put me through to a room. I just got voicemail, but it confirmed he's staying there."

"Why didn't you say so in the first place?" Nick explodes. He glares at me for a second, then his anger dissipates into a grin. "Dork!" he says.

"OK boys, you've had your fun but what do we do next?" Adry says.

"Our priority is to track down Micah and Melanie and prove they are working with Drozdov's gang," I say. "With Drozdov in Kent, Antonov's almost certainly the top gun on the streets. If anyone can lead us to the Westons, it's him. I'm going to stake out the Hyatt until I see him, then follow where he leads me. Tommy also told me that Antonov's car's a white Lexus LC500, which will be easy enough to spot."

"The Hyatt will be a pig to stake out, though. We could take turns helping you," Nick offers.

"Great, I might need some backup but I've got Ghost and Tommy and hopefully one or two of their buddies to help me. I think the best thing to do is for you guys to get back to work on all our other cases so that we don't go broke in the interim. I'll call in if I need any help."

"Just do it quick, Rogan. The sooner we can get Drozdov's gang off the streets, the sooner we can all go back to working in our own office and living in our own homes."

No pressure there.

———

NICK'S RIGHT ABOUT THE HYATT BEING A PIG FOR A STAKEOUT. It sits in Royal Centre which, in addition to the hotel, has office towers, a shopping mall and a bunch of restaurants. Someone can leave the hotel and get onto the street through one of eight possible exits.

Right at one of those exits is a small McDonald's. I'm sitting at a table, surrounded by Ghost's army. In addition to him and Tommy, there are four of their friends. They are enjoying a lunch of burgers, nuggets and fries, washed down with shakes, Coke and over-sweetened coffee. They are eating like there's no tomorrow and a couple of them look like they really haven't eaten in days.

When they get down to the baked apple pies for dessert, Ghost addresses them. "OK, guys. Listen up," he says. "Rocky here's gonna give you your assignments. All you gotta do is sit in the place he tells you and watch out for the guy in the picture he's gonna give you. If you see the guy, you just call Rocky."

I hand out pictures of Yuri Antonov and give each of

them a burner phone with my number in it. "If you see this guy walking in or out of the hotel, call me immediately," I say. "Ghost is gonna come round from time to time and check with you to make sure everything's OK. He'll bring you dinner at around six. At midnight, we'll all meet here for another meal and you'll get paid a hundred and fifty bucks apiece." A murmur of appreciation runs around the table. For these guys, a hundred and fifty bucks is more than they can earn in a week. "Tommy's going to sit out there on the sidewalk and watch the exit here and the steps that come down out of the hotel lobby." I give each of them a location to occupy. Each will sit with an empty coffee cup in front of him and beg for spare change. Except to the occasional, kindly soul, they will be all but invisible. Homeless people are the ultimate surveillance operatives... providing they don't sneak a drink or fall asleep. It's Ghost's job to see that doesn't happen.

They all troop out to take up their positions.

I make my way to the hastily-rented, grey Honda, parked at a ridiculously-priced parking meter on Burrard Street, outside Staples. It is parked so that I can watch the exit from the hotel parking for a white Lexus LC500. It was Adry's idea to rent the Honda. If that Russian guy who questioned Ghost and Tommy in the Ovaltine has been following me for a while, he may know that I drive an Austin Healey, which is just too out-of-the-ordinary for a stakeout.

Now for hours of boredom.

———

As soon as I sit behind the wheel, my phone buzzes. It's Tommy. So much for the hours of boredom. "Yeah, Tommy," I say.

"Rocky, I seen him. He just walked right past me."

"Yuri Antonov?" I say. "Which direction?"

"Nah. Not Antonov. The other guy. The one in the suit who questioned me and Ghost in the Ovaltine. He's coming towards you." I look straight ahead. I see a well-dressed guy of about thirty heading towards me. *"You should be able to see him now, Rock."*

"I see him. Good work, Tommy." I hang up.

He is heading in my direction, scanning the parked cars. I recognize him. He's the guy who was at my NA meeting last week. The one who was taking in everything I said. I think back to yesterday morning. As I left the Ovaltine, I nearly bumped into someone. It's him. This is the guy who has been surveilling me and he's been doing it for over a week. He's good and that's bad. Does he know that Tina and I are staying at the Pacific Palisades? I need her to get out of there. His eyes pass over the car parked in front of me and lock onto mine. He smiles a friendly smile and walks towards me. Who is this guy? Tommy had said that he had a Russian accent but he doesn't look like a gang member. He looks like a businessman or maybe a well-dressed cop. He leans down beside my driver's door and with a grin signals me to wind down the window. I comply.

"Mr. Rogan," he says. "Please, unlock the car doors." Not something I would normally do, but I see what's in his hand. I unlock the doors. It's always wise to pay attention to Mr. Smith and Mr. Wesson, especially when accompanied by Mr. Silencer.

He gets into the back seat. "Drive to the downtown eastside," he orders. His accent is slight but it sounds Russian to me. "And please do not try anything clever or heroic. Remember we know how to find your girlfriend, not to mention your ex-wife and daughter."

With his words raking my gut, I start the car. As I wait for the traffic to abate enough to let me pull out of the parking space, I see Tommy running into the hotel garage.

———

HE STOPS SPEAKING RUSSIAN INTO HIS PHONE. "TURN RIGHT, into the alley," he says. I do as I'm told. He has guided me to one of the many alleys which are home to the drug addicts of the downtown east side. It's not too many years ago that I slept in this very one. There are a couple of people sleeping here now, huddled under filthy blankets. "Stop," he says as we draw parallel to a garbage bin. Ten metres beyond the bin is a black Chevy Suburban.

As I put the car in park, I feel the pressure of the silencer on the back of my neck. He speaks into his phone. "*Seychas zhe.*" We wait ten seconds and a door opens in the grey wall beside the garbage bin. It looks like the back entrance to a shop or a restaurant. A guy the size of a house steps out.

The Smith and Wesson nudges the back of my head. "Get out of the car and leave the keys."

As I obey, the big guy takes my elbow, in a hand the size of a lion's jaw, and leads me into the building. The door slams. Nobody knows where I am.

We are in what looks like a storage room. The walls are concrete and lined with shelves, all empty. In one of the four mismatched chairs is a small man. He is tied up and his face is a bloody mess. He is having difficulty breathing. It's Henry, the weasel who let slip that Yuri Antonov lives in a hotel.

This does not bode well for him.

Me neither.

The House still has my elbow in his paw and Mr. Well-

Dressed has followed us in and still has his gun levelled at me. I calculate. The grip on my elbow has eased; the gun is not within my reach but I could probably kick it out of his hand; I will have to disable the House within a half-second of kicking the—

"*Syad!*"

I am forced down into one of the chairs, the only one with arms. Moving fast for someone so big, the House ties me into the chair. He doesn't use rope but long pieces of cloth, like a bedsheet cut into six-inch-wide strips. Rope leaves obvious abrasions on the skin, cloth doesn't. He leaves my left arm to last, rolls up my sleeve and then secures my wrist to the arm of the chair with more strips of cloth. He immobilizes my left arm with several strips leaving only my hand and the crook of my elbow exposed. I remember where I first set eyes on Mr. Well-Dressed and my guts turn to jelly as I work out where this is inexorably leading.

He gives a stream of orders in Russian.

While he's not looking at me, I wriggle my right hand— no way I can move the left one. There's not much give in the cloth that's binding it to the arm of the chair but I start working it. The only way I'm getting out of this is if I do it myself.

The House says "*Da.*" He walks over to a table in the corner of the room. Hanging on the wall beside the table is an oil-cloth raincoat. At one time it was expensive but it is now old and well-worn. He puts it on and picks up an extra-large pair of leather gloves from the table. As he does this, I work my right hand against the restraints. I think I'm making progress.

Somehow, the giant squeezes his hands into the gloves. Leaning against the wall is a length of metal pipe. As casually as if he were opening an umbrella, he takes two steps towards Henry and smashes the pipe into the side of his head. The skull collapses with a sickening crack and blood spatters everywhere. My stomach heaves; it's all I can do not to throw up. I focus on the pain in my right wrist as I try to pull it free.

The House takes the pipe and places it carefully on the table in the corner. He takes off the raincoat and the gloves and puts them in a black garbage bag, together with a few other items on the table. Other than the pipe, the only thing left on the table is a small cardboard box.

I have an idea of what's in there and I redouble my efforts.

With a nod at Mr. Well-Dressed, the House takes his garbage bag and lumbers into the alley. The door slams and I hear my rented Honda drive off, less than five minutes after it arrived.

"So, Mr. Rogan, you have made the mistake of interfering in the affairs of Mr. Drozdov. A fatal mistake I am afraid." He gets up and walks over to the table. With his back to me, I work at freeing my hand; it's my only chance, no one knows where I am. He continues in his slightly-accented, pedantic voice, "Do you remember when you first saw me? At your Narcotics Anonymous meeting. You very kindly told us about your predilection for heroin." He takes a syringe out of the cardboard box and heads back towards me. "Here's what's going to happen. You are going to die of a massive overdose of your drug of choice." He grabs a chair and puts it facing mine. "You'll be found dead in the alley outside. When the police investigate, they will find the dead body of your friend Henry. Henry was stupid enough to try and find out where Mr. Drozdov's associate, Mr. Antonov lives. He asked one question too many. So we asked *him* some questions. Your name came up." He sniggers. "Tell me, Mr. Rogan, did you really think you could do surveillance on Mr. Antonov without being seen?" He sits down and shows me the syringe. It isn't an injection needle. He flicks and presses the crook of my elbow until he finds an artery. He inserts the needle, withdraws blood and walks over to Henry's body. "When the police investigate in here they are going to find your blood..." he drips blood onto Henry's jacket, "...here and..." he drips blood on the ropes binding him, "...here and here on the floor." He empties the syringe and drops it in the box on the table before taking out a second, larger one. He crouches down on the floor beside the body and fills the second syringe from the substantial amount of Henry's blood that has pooled on the floor beside him. He puts the syringe of blood on the table.

He takes five items out of the cardboard box. A needle, a spoon, water, a lighter and a large flap of heroin. There's enough in there to murder a horse. As he cooks up the dose, he says, "So here's what's going to happen." The bastard is enjoying this. "I'm going to inject this heroin into you. You'll enjoy it a lot, for maybe a minute or two, until you slip into a coma. When that happens, I'm going to do four things. I'm going to cut away all those strips of cloth binding you. I'm going to squirt Henry's blood on you. It won't withstand a thorough blood-spatter analysis but I don't expect the police will bother with that. Then I'm going to put a small cut in your hand using the knife we found in Henry's pocket. Lastly, I'll take that metal pipe and grip your lifeless hands around it transferring your bloody fingerprints onto the murder weapon."

While he has been speaking, I've almost stretched the cloth strips enough to free my right wrist.

The heroin's cooked up and he sucks it up into the

needle. Expertly he points it skyward and depresses the syringe just enough to expel any air. A tiny droplet of heroin appears, glittering at the point of the needle. I remember the desire that droplet evokes. The knowledge that the heroin is ready to be injected, ready to take away the pain and feed the Beast inside. And even though I know the dose he plans to inject will kill me, a tiny sliver of me wants the peace that only heroin can bestow. Then I think of Ellie and Tina and then all of me wants to live.

I have about five seconds to free my hand. I work at it as he walks over and sits in the chair facing me, our knees touching. He reaches forward to feel for the injection site and I pull my right arm back with every ounce of strength I can muster. It won't budge. My only option is to try and topple the chair, maybe break one of the arms. I start to rock from side to side. At least he can't inject a moving target.

He just shakes his head like a teacher mildly irritated by a misbehaving child. He puts the needle on the floor, stands and steps around behind my chair. In one swift movement, he pulls the chair backwards and deposits me on the ground. Then he rolls the chair so that I'm on my righthand side. He kneels on my left arm and I feel him tapping and probing.

"Please, no! Don't do this, please." I struggle with every ounce of strength I have left.

Then I feel the jab of the needle and know I'm going to die in this room.

Nobody knows where I am. I'm going to die alone.

"You've solved your last case, Mr. Rogan."

His words dissolve in the bliss sweeping through me.

29

TOMMY

He walked right past me but thank Christ he din't notice me. It's not Antonov but it's that fancy-dressed, Russian guy who was in the Ovaltine. The one who sounded like old Mr. Kossof from high school. Better give Rocky a heads up. I pull out my phone and tell him. Better stand up so I can see where the Ruskie goes. Jeez, he spotted Rock, he's walking towards his car. He stops by Rocky's window. Fuck! He's got a gun. He's getting into the car. This is bad.

Better call Ghost and tell him. But what can he do? I gotta find out where he's going but even in this traffic, I can't outrun a Honda Civic. Rocky starts to pull away from the curb. Only one thing to do. I run into the vehicle entrance for the hotel and run to the first cab. He's sittin' there waiting for some rich dude to drive to the airport. I can see he don't like the look of me, so I jump in the back real quick so as he don't have time to lock the doors. Just as he turns around and starts to give me a hard time, I pull out the two hundred bucks Rocky gave me this morning. I wave it at him. "If you can follow that car, this two hundred's yours."

He looks at the money and looks at me. "What car," he says.

"Drive out onto Burrard and I'll point it out," I say. He puts the car in drive. "Quickly!" I tell him.

He hits the gas and drives onto Burrard. Almost hits a rich-looking guy as he crosses the sidewalk.

I lean forward and point. "That silver Honda Civic at the lights."

He pulls up two cars behind Rocky. "Half now," he says.

Fair enough. I peel off five twenties and drop 'em on the passenger seat.

I open my phone and dial Ghost.

"Wassup, Tom?"

"That Russian guy in the Ovaltine yesterday morning, he just carjacked Rocky. I'm followin' in a taxi. What should we do?"

"Let me think." Good. Old Ghost's a thinker. He'll know what to do. He only takes a moment. *"Keep after him, I'm gonna call Mr. Stammo."* He hangs up.

"You say a Russian carjacked your friend?" The taxi driver asks.

"Yeah. Real bad dude he is too."

"I'm Ukrainian. Goddamn Russians carjacked half my country. I won't let the bastard get away." The Civic does an illegal left onto Georgia and the taxi follows. Funny how you can find a friend when you need one.

I sit back and buckle up my seatbelt.

We go four blocks before Ghost calls back. *"I couldn't get through. The office phone had a recorded message. I think Rocky said something about they was moving to a different office for a while."*

"What about his cell?"

"Don't have it."

"So what we gonna do?"

"Let me have another think." He goes silent for while and doesn't talk again until we're on the Georgia Viaduct. *"OK, I got an idea,"* he says and hangs up.

The Civic pulls off the ramp at Main and we follow. As we come to the lights we're right behind it. The Russian's in the back seat, so he won't see us in the mirror. We follow him down Main and still no call from Ghost. At Pender, the Civic takes a right and then turns left down an alley. The taxi driver pulls over beside the curb. "If I follow him down there he'll see us," he says.

"OK, buddy. Fair enough. You've been great." I drop the rest of the money on his passenger seat and hop out. I run to the entrance to the alley. The Civic's stopped about halfway down. Now what do I do? Ghost would know. Why ain't he calling me?

A guy the size of a friggin' mountain walks out of a doorway. He takes Rocky's arm and steers him into the building, the other guy follows.

"Did you see the size of that guy?"

The voice makes me jump. It's the Ukrainian taxi driver. He's standing beside me and looking down the alley. I get to take a look at him for the first time. He's about six feet tall and big. Not big like one of them guys who spends all their time in the gym, but big like a factory worker. He sticks his hand out. "Nikolai," he says.

I shake. "Tommy. Pleased to meetcha."

"What you think we should do?" he asks. His Ukrainian accent sounds kinda Russian.

"I'm waiting for my buddy to call back. He always knows what to do."

He thinks this over. "Let's go," he says and starts down the alley.

We get down to where the Civic's parked. We can see the door they went through.

"We have a conundrum," Nikolai says.

"A what?"

"A puzzle. If we don't go in, they may do something bad to your friend. If we do go in, we are faced with one man with a gun and the other man big enough to eat us both for breakfast."

It's a puzzle alright. One I can't solve, fer sure.

Nikolai goes over and listens at the door for a moment, then comes back.

"Just talking," he says. He gives a kind of a shrug, then looks off into the distance for a while. "I'm not a big fan of police but maybe we should call them. What do you think?"

"I dunno, the police are always breaking my—"

My phone rings. Saved by the bell, eh?

"Ghost?" I say.

"Hi Tommy, this is Steve Waters. I used to be Cal's... uh, Rocky's partner when he was with VPD. Do you remember me?"

"Yeah. I remember you, Constable Waters." Rocky's partner was good people; not like some of 'em.

"Clarence called me, said Rocky was in trouble." I almost chuckle. I'd kinda forgotten Ghost's real name, he hates it.

"Yeah, some Russian gangster's kidnapped him, got him in a building." He asks me the details and I tell him as clear as I can.

"Stay where you are, I'm sending a squad car." He hangs up.

Just as I'm telling Nikolai, the big guy comes out of the building. He's got a black garbage bag in his giant hand. He just ignores us. As far as he's concerned, we're just alley people, not worth his time. I look at my new buddy. He's eyeing the big guy like he's trying to make a decision. He shakes his head. "Too fuckin' big," he mutters.

Somehow the giant squeezes himself into Rocky's rented Honda. As he drives off I notice a Chevy Suburban parked just past the garbage bin. Nice wheels. Them Russians have some nice cars. I remember Yuri Antonov's white LC500. That reminds me of something. Ghost and me didn't get the licence plate. I ain't gonna make that mistake a second time. I look at the Chevy's licence plate and say it three times over in my head.

Nikolai breaks my concentration. "I'm worried about your friend in there with that Russian," he says. "Russian gangsters are killers."

"Yeah, I know." I wish Ghost was here to work it all out and tell me what to do. "Are you thinking we should go in there and try rescuing him?" The thought of that Russian dude's a bit scary. Maybe he's got some other guys in there with him, as well. And I ain't no hero. "Or should we wait for the cops to get here?"

He doesn't answer for a second, just puts his head on one side, then he says. "I don't hear sirens."

"Whatcha think we should do?" I ask.

Before he can answer, the door bangs open. The Ruskie comes out and he's dragging something behind him. It's a body. He drops it halfway through the doorway so it jams the door open and he starts to walk towards the Chevy.

"Hey, you!" Nikolai shouts and runs at him. The Russian turns and just as Nikolai's about to grab him, his fist shoots out. Nikolai stops dead in his tracks and grabs at his throat where the Russian hit him. Before you know it, the Russian kicks the poor bastard right in the crotch.

As my new buddy doubles over, the Russian's eyes are looking right at me. There's no doubt he remembers me from the Ovaltine. I turn and run.

I'm going as fast as I can but I can hear his footsteps

gaining on me. A life of booze and fast food ain't helping me none. When he catches me I'm a dead man. I can hear his breathing now. This is it.

Then his footsteps stop.

I sneak a quick look over my shoulder. He's turned around and he's running back. Back towards the black Chevy. Then I hear them. The sirens. I ain't a religious man but I sure as hell thank God right now.

I start to run back. Not as fast as I was running away but as fast as I can go. By the time I get to where Nikolai is, the Chevy is pulling out of the alley onto Hastings Street.

Nikolai is getting to his feet. "You OK?" I ask. Silly fuckin' question now I think of it.

"Check your friend." His voice kinda growls through his damaged throat.

He's right.

I trot over to where Rocky's lying on the ground. He's on his back halfway through the doorway. He don't look good. For one thing, there's a needle still jabbed in his arm. His face is white and looks kinda sweaty. "Rocky!" I shout and poke his shoulder. Nothing. Coming out of his mouth there's some white stuff, looks like the foam on a good head of beer. Jesus, I don't think he's breathing.

I've lived on the streets long enough to have seen this a few times.

A car screeches to a halt. The cops. They get out of the cruiser, hands on the butts of their guns. For once, I know exactly what to yell. "Overdose here! My buddy needs Narcan. Fast!"

The woman cop responds the quickest. She reaches into the car and comes out with a couple of boxes. She runs over and kneels down beside Rocky, opens a box and takes out the plastic thing that always reminds me of a kid's toy rocket ship. She jabs it up Rocky's nose and presses the plunger down with her thumb. Nothing. Maybe he twitched. I ain't too sure. We wait for a few seconds, then she pulls out the second one. "I can only give him two, maximum," she says to me as she puts it up the other nostril. She jabs her thumb down and with a big gasp of breath, he half sits up. His eyes are wide, wide, open but the pupils are like tiny black dots.

He sinks back down with a groan and lies there breathing in gasps. But at least he's breathing.

"We'll need an ambulance, fast!" she yells at her partner and I can hear him on his walkie-talkie thing. She gently takes the needle out of Rocky's arm. "You did alright," she says to me with a big smile.

As I get to my feet, I look around but don't see Nikolai. Straight away, two more cop cars arrive. An older guy with stripes on his sleeve gets out of one and walks over. I've seen him before; he's always around. Everyone calls him Sarge. He walks over and looks down. "Rogan." He says it like he's not surprised. That's not fair. Rocky's worked hard to stay clean. There's no way he'd take heroin.

"Don't say his name like that," I say. "Some Russian gangster shot him up."

He turns and gives me that look. The look the cops have been giving me for years. Back in the day, they'd usually add words like 'drunken Indian' or 'redskin bum.' Some of 'em still think it. I look him right in the eye. "Rocky was tracking down a Russian gang. I saw the guy kidnap Rocky and bring him here. It was my buddy who called Rocky's old partner, what's his name, Steve Waters and told him that Rocky had been taken. I'm the reason you're fuckin' here now. So don't look at me like I'm some piece of shit."

He nods his head towards the door. "Took him in there?" he asks.

"Yeah."

He takes out his gun and calls one of his buddies over. They disappear inside just as the ambulance pulls up. That was quick.

I get out of the way so the paramedics can do their work. These guys are friggin' heroes. They've saved thousands of lives in the downtown east side over the years.

Rocky still seems out of it but at least he's alive. "Do you know his name?" one asks.

"Rocky Rogan. Rocky's his nickname. His real name's Cal."

They check him out for a bit then bring over the stretcher on wheels and lift him onto it. But before they can take him and put him in the ambulance, the cop, Sarge, comes out of the building. He looks a bit pale. He says something to one of the paramedics, then he pulls out a couple of plastic bags and puts 'em over Rocky's hands. Now he's cuffing Rocky's wrist to the rail of the stretcher.

"What the hell is that all about?" I ask him.

He just nods at his partner who cuffs *me*.

"I wanna lawyer," I say.

They just laugh.

————

FEELS LIKE I'VE BEEN IN THIS GODDAMN ROOM FOR HOURS. Every so often someone puts his head in the door, looks at me and walks out. A couple of times I've tried to tell 'em about the Russian but they just ignore me. I wish old Ghost was here.

The door opens again but this time it's Cal's old partner.

"Thanks for waiting, Tommy," he says.

Like I had a choice!

He puts a Wendy's bag on the table. "I thought you might be hungry."

He's right. I am hungry. Hadn't even thought about it until now. "Thanks, Constable Waters."

He smiles. "My pleasure, it's the least we could do for you."

I open the bag. Burger, fries and a Coke. Perfect. Well, almost perfect. A beer or two would sure help to wash it down but I don't reckon that's gonna happen.

"Tell me what you know, Tommy," he says, opening a folder he brought in with him.

I take a big bite out of the burger and chew on it slowly to give myself some thinking time. I remember Ghost telling me there was some bad blood between Rocky and this guy. I can't be sure whose side he's on. I suck up some Coke. I can't decide.

"How's Rocky?" I ask.

"Alive. Just. He's in St. Paul's." That sends a shiver through me. That's where Roy died. Rocky was with him at the end. Someone should be with Rocky.

"Is anyone with him?"

"His partner, Nick Stammo."

"Good, good," I say. "Is he alright?"

"We're hoping. Listen, Tommy, if you want to help Rocky, you need to tell me everything you know."

Can I trust this guy? As I try and figure it out, I remember what my foster Mom used to say before she passed. *"When in doubt, Tommy, tell the truth."*

I tell him everything I know about the stakeout, the carjacking and me following the Russian to the downtown east side.

He takes it all in and writes it down on a piece of paper

in the folder. Then he says, "Tell me about when the Russian guy left."

I tell him about how he dropped Rocky's body in the doorway, punched Nikolai in the throat and chased after me. Then I remember! "He stopped chasing me when he heard the cop cars. He ran back to his SUV and drove off—"

Before I can go on he asks. "Do you know the make?"

"I can do you better than that. It was a black Chevy Suburban, twenty-twenty-one model I think." He goes to speak again but I hold up my finger. "And I know the licence plate number too."

"What?"

Ah-ha. That got his attention. I tell him the number and he writes it down. He stands up. "Let me get this out to all units," he says.

Time for the old *quid pro quo*, as Rocky would say.

"Why did that Sergeant handcuff Rocky and me?" I ask.

He looks at me. He can probably hear the anger in my voice. I know *I* can. He thinks for a bit and then says, "Do you know a guy named Henry Little?"

"Yeah," I say.

"He was in that room Rocky came out of. His head had been cracked open with a length of pipe. The pipe was covered with blood and Cal was covered in blood spatter. We don't have the DNA analysis back but we've confirmed it was Cal's prints on the pipe. Henry had a knife on the floor beside him and Cal had a knife wound on his hand."

"The Russian musta done it," I say. "He musta framed Rocky. I've known Rocky a long time and he ain't no killer. Hell, he was your partner for years, you must know Rocky couldn't have done this."

He looks at me for a long while. It's like he's thinking he knows something I don't know.

"And why would Rocky wanna kill Henry," I add. "Henry was going to try and find out—" I cut myself off. I don't know if Rocky wants the cops to know about Yuri Antonov.

"Find out what, Tommy?"

"I dunno. All I know is Rocky had no reason to kill Henry. Henry was gonna help him."

"Maybe," he says. He scratches his chin for a moment. "Stay here while I get uniforms searching for the SUV." He leaves with his folder under his arm.

By the time I finish my burger and fries, he's back. When he sits down opposite me his face is serious.

"OK, Tommy," he says. "The licence plate you gave us is for a black Chevy Suburban. It's registered to a corporation." He gives me a long, kinda suspicious look. "Were there any other witnesses to this Russian guy?"

"Yeah, I told you, Nikolai. Ask him."

"So who is this Nikolai?"

"He's the taxi driver. I jumped in his cab at the Hyatt and we followed Rocky and the Russian to that building in the alley. Nikolai tried to stop the Russian but the Russian hit him in the throat."

"Thing is Tommy," he says, tapping the folder, "no one at the scene mentioned anyone other than you being there in the alley."

"Well, he was there!"

"If you say so, Tommy."

Bastard thinks I'm lying. "Yes, I do fuckin' say so," I shout at him.

He just gets up and leaves.

The door clicks behind him.

30

NICK

Jeez. Rogan looks like shit but I manage to smile as I wheel into his room. Tina's already here. She gets up from her chair beside his bed and hugs me. I hug her back and I'm glad he's got her in his life. I wheel up to his bed and see the handcuffs. "Hey, Cal, how are you feeling?"

He gives a half-smile. "A bit disoriented and starting to get some pain."

"What happened? I got a voicemail from Ghost and when I called him back he had some story about you being carjacked and that Tommy had followed you in a taxi. He told me he'd called Steve. So I called Steve and he told me you were here. I called Tina and came right over."

He looks confused. "Tommy followed me?" he asks.

"Yeah. Jumped in a taxi at the Hyatt and followed your rental car."

"I'm alive because of Tommy and Ghost?"

"I suppose. What happened?"

He tells me the whole story and I listen without interrupting. When he finishes, I ask, "What's with the cuffs and the uniform outside your door?"

"I guess they're buying the frame-up that I killed that guy, Henry."

"Oh, this is BS on steroids."

I pull out my phone.

Steve and I have a heated conversation.

I dial again.

Jim Garry picks up on the first ring.

31

ADRY

Thursday

He grins. "OK, Miss. Mr. Stammo said you're in charge so I'm at your service." He pulls himself to his feet and gives me a little bow.

"Thanks, Ghost. Nick and Cal have told me a lot about you."

"Uh-oh." The grin widens.

"And it's all good." I like Ghost. Cal once called him an honest rogue and I suspect that fits him like a glove.

"First, a huge thanks for calling Steve Waters at VPD yesterday. Your call saved Cal's life. The gangster who kidnapped him pumped him full of heroin to make him OD. Last night, Nick managed to find out from Inspector Waters that Tommy's in custody in Cambie police station."

"Why would they arrest Tommy?" he asks indignantly.

"He wouldn't say. But Nick has asked our lawyer, Jim Garry, to go represent him. He should be with him right now."

Ghost chuckles. "Tommy'll like that. All the scrapes he's had with the law but he's never had a lawyer."

"Anyway," I say, "I'm going to take over the surveillance operation and follow Yuri Antonov if we can spot him or his car."

"Alright, sounds good to me."

"First thing is breakfast. Let's pick up some food and make sure you and your guys get fed. Nick said that I can give them each the hundred and fifty they were promised for last night, so they know they're going to get paid."

"The food would be great but forget the cash. These are all good guys but if you put cash in their hands right now, they'll be off to spend it before you know it. Give it to 'em at the end of the day. They got my word they're gonna be paid and my word means something on the street."

We load up with McD's—Ghost seems to know what each of his guys will want—and we deliver it to each of them. Ghost introduces me and I thank each of them for getting here so early, then Ghost gives a little pep talk to each one of them. This guy's a natural leader.

That done, he gets into his place and I head for my car.

Now the wait begins.

———

IT'S OFFICIAL. STAKEOUTS ARE THE MOST BORING THING EVER. I can see why they always have two cops on a stakeout—just to keep each other company. The only way I've kept my sanity is by listening to music and podcasts. It feels like I've been here for most of a day but it's still only eleven o'clock.

My yawn is cut short by my phone.

"It's Dave," the voice says. He's one of Ghost's guys. His position is on the sidewalk near the exit from the Hyatt's

garage. He's sitting with a coffee cup in front of him and a cardboard sign that says, 'I'll tell you a joke for a buck.' *"I can see that Yuri guy getting into his white car."*

"Great work, Dave." I hang up and start my engine. After a second or two, I see the white car pulling out of the hotel. I check the picture I printed from the Lexus website. It's the same car for sure. So much for boredom. My heart's pounding now. He pulls onto Burrard and I pull up behind him. Using the hands-free, I call Ghost and tell him I'm following the car. Then I call Nick. No reply so I leave a message.

The lights change and the Lexus accelerates up Burrard. I follow at a distance, trying to remember all the tips Nick gave me about how to follow another car without being spotted. At the old BC Hydro building, he moves into the left lane and I do the same, making my lane change so that there's a car between us: Nick's tip number three. The flashing left-turn signal at Nelson is green and as the Lexus takes the turn it changes to orange. The car in front of me stops. What an idiot! He could have easily made that turn. I resist the temptation to hit the horn; Nick's tip number two was 'don't draw attention to yourself.'

I take deep breaths trying to contain the road rage. I've lost him! My first job following a suspect and already I've blown it! A millennium seems to pass before the light flashes green again. As soon as I get onto Nelson, I accelerate past the idiot and strain my eyes to try and see the Lexus. There's no sign of it. The lights on Nelson are synchronized so if you drive at the right speed they will be green all the way. Antonov could have turned off anywhere, heading either north or south. I could slow down at every intersection and check to see if he's turned off but then I would lose the advantage of the synchronized signals. I'm going to go for broke and assume he headed down Nelson for the Cambie Bridge.

The traffic gods are rewarding me for having led a good life; each signal changes to green as I approach but there's no sign of the Lexus. He either turned off, probably at Howe, or he's over the bridge and could be going south on Cambie or be somewhere on Broadway.

As I accept defeat, my phone rings. I check my car display. It's Nick.

"Sorry Nick, I lost him."

"Don't worry, it happens," he says. *"We'll get him another time."*

"I just feel like I've let down the team," I say. "I should have—"

My heart skips. I see the Lexus. He's waiting at the last light before the bridge, right in front of a panel truck; that's why I couldn't see him. He drove just that fraction too slow and got caught by the last signal. I tell Nick. *"Atta girl,"* he says and I grin.

I slow down so that I won't pass Antonov. As the light changes, he shoots away and I take up a position a few car lengths behind him. I follow him over the bridge and along Cambie.

"How's Cal?" I ask.

"Conscious now but he's going through withdrawal. Tina's with him."

"Good. Where are you?"

"I just got home. I was about to catch a couple of hours of sleep. I was up all night at the hospital."

As we cross King Edward, the Lexus signals and moves into the left lane. I do the same but this time I don't wait for a car to move in between us. I'm not going to be caught like that again.

"We're turning onto Midlothian," I say.

Nick grunts.

We go about two hundred metres.

"He's signalling a left turn again."

"That's into the parking lot for Nat Bailey stadium. It's too early for a Canadians game." He's quiet for a second then says, *"Don't follow him. You'll be too obvious. Carry on along Midlothian and do a U-turn as soon as you're out of his line of sight. Then drive back and pull into the parking lot."*

The Lexus is waiting for the traffic coming in the opposite direction to clear before making his turn.

I tell Nick.

"What car do you drive?"

"A Nissan Micra, silver."

"Good car to use in a tail," he says. *"Nice and anonymous. Better than that old English car of Rogan's."*

The road curves left and the traffic gods are still with me. There's nothing coming so I hang a U-ie and drive back. I turn right where the Lexus turned. On my right is the stadium and to my left is the Hillcrest Community Centre. I can see the Lexus parked in the parking lot between the buildings.

Antonov is getting out. As I get closer, I can see that he is tall and cute in a bad-boy way. He's carrying a purple gym bag and heading towards the Community Centre. Fortunately, he doesn't even glance in my direction... yet.

I relay all this to Nick. "What should I do now?" I ask. "Should I follow him or just wait in the parking lot for him to come out?"

He thinks for a moment before answering. *"You should wait in the parking lot. It would be safer."*

His tone of voice disagrees with his words. "Screw that," I say as I park. "We're following Antonov so he'll lead us to

Melanie and Micah. One or both of them might be in the Community Centre. I'm going in."

"It would be better if you didn't," he says half-heartedly.

"Like *you'd* wait in the parking lot," I chuckle. He sighs.

I get out of my car and jog towards the doors.

"Stay on the line. I'm gonna get you some backup," Nick says. My phone beeps.

The only time I was in the Hillcrest Community Centre was years ago. I was there to watch my brother play little league hockey. I walk through the doors into the large atrium. Thanks to Covid, it's not teeming with people. There are a few lining up at the front desk to my right and some people further away but I don't see Antonov. I walk through the atrium. There's a corridor to the left, with signs pointing to a gym and a seniors' centre, but it's empty. Ahead is the hockey rink and a café with tables. My target is not among the people at that end. It's like he walked through the doors and vanished.

I turn round and look back. To the left of the main doors, there is an entrance to the pool which I didn't notice when I walked in. It's the only place he could have gone in the time between walking into the Community Centre and me following him in. Could it be that Antonov just came here for a swim in the Olympic-sized pool? I walk back in that direction and as I get closer, I see him. He's coming out of the pool area and heading straight towards me. He's alone and his head's down in his phone texting or something, so he doesn't see me. Thank god for our addiction to tech. With what I hope is a smooth movement I turn and join the lineup at the front desk. Out of the corner of my eye, I see him walk out through the front doors. He was in here for no more than three minutes.

I head after him. I step through the doors and see him

striding towards his car. He's still focused on his phone and he's no longer carrying the purple bag.

My phone beeps. *"Adry, I'm back. I'm heading for my truck and Zeke's on his way too. I've conferenced him into this call."*

"He's leaving already and I'm following," I say. "He was in the pool area for less than three minutes and he doesn't have the purple gym bag he took in."

Nick says. *"Maybe the bag has money in it. What if Micah or Melanie is there? It could be a payment to them for drugs."*

"If I go back in and check, I might spot one of them but I will definitely lose Antonov."

"Decision time," he says.

Zeke says, *"If the bag was money to buy drugs, Antonov would be walking out with a different bag with the drugs in it. Gangs don't pay in advance, it's a cash-and-carry business."*

"Antonov has reached his car," I say. "What do you want me to do?"

Nick hesitates for just a second then decides. *"Zeke's right. I don't know what the story is with the purple bag, but you need to keep following Yuri Antonov."*

It feels like the right decision... I think.

I walk to my car and as I get in, Antonov starts to pull away from his parking spot.

I wait for a few seconds and follow.

"I know my car's not that noticeable, but I'm worried he'll spot me."

"I know how to solve that problem," Zeke says.

When he tells me his solution I feel a whole lot better.

A nother rivulet of pain pushes out a groan. As the heroin starts to dissipate, the withdrawal symptoms tighten their clamps on me. Tina strokes my forehead. She's been here all night but she still looks as fresh as a daisy. God, I love this woman.

My nurse said they are ready to discharge me with a prescription for Tylenol 3 but I am still cuffed to the bedrail.

"Maybe we should go away again for a while, Cal," Tina says.

"I can't." I rattle the cuffs.

"They can't be seriously thinking you killed that guy."

I look deep into her eyes. "They're as serious as a heart attack," I tell her.

"Not anymore!"

We both turn to the sound of Jim Garry's voice. He's standing in the doorway with a big smile on his face.

Standing behind him is a uniformed officer talking on a cellphone. After a moment he says something, hangs up and hands the phone back to Jim. He walks across to my bed and unlocks the handcuffs. Without a word, he slips them into the pouch on his belt and walks out.

Tina gives Jim a hug, which he obviously enjoys, and asks him, "How did you pull that off?"

"Following Nick's instructions, I went to see your buddy Tommy first thing this morning. He told me about the taxi driver he got to follow you. Tommy remembered it was a dark blue taxi. I called Maclure's Cabs and they verified they had a driver named Nikolai. I met with him and got him to sign an affidavit that verified Tommy's story of the Russian dragging you out of that building and fleeing the scene. I immediately went to see Inspector Waters and persuaded him that it would be better for the VPD to release both you and Tommy right away. He agreed."

"Just like that?" I ask.

His brow wrinkles. "Yes," he says. "It was easier than I thought it would be."

I sit up in bed, managing to avoid groaning at the pain, and extend my hand. "Thanks Jim, we owe you."

He shakes my hand and grins again. "You don't owe me anything... well, not until you get my bill at the end of the month." Who says lawyers never joke about money.

He leaves and Tina helps me get dressed.

"Now you're no longer handcuffed, how about we go away for a while," she says

"I still can't."

"Why not? This gang knows how to find you. What's to stop them coming after you again? Or me?"

"The only way to stop them is to put them all in jail. That's what Nick and I are going to do."

Even as I say it, I can hear my own words from her point of view.

"I almost lost you," she says, hugging me. I see a tear

form in the corner of her eye. "I don't know if I can live with the thought that you are constantly risking your life."

Somehow the thought that my life is at risk doesn't bother me too often. But gangs like this one will not hesitate to take the lives of the people their enemies love most.

Going away for a while makes sense on the face of it, but Tina and Sam and Ellie and I can't spend the rest of our lives hiding from them. Nor can Nick and Stewart and Lucy and Adry and Jason and Zeke.

Sometimes, you have to make a stand.

33

ZEKE

Adry's directions are perfect. I hang a left onto Cambie and pull in behind her. The white Lexus is three cars ahead. "I'm behind you now," I say.

Her voice comes through my earbuds. *"I see you. He's all yours."*

She takes the next left. If Yuri Antonov was starting to suspect he was being followed by a cute woman in a silver Micra, those suspicions will be laid to rest. He continues on Cambie going south. I report in to Nick, who is now in his truck heading in my general direction.

As we approach forty-first avenue, he pulls into the right lane. I switch lanes too and now I'm directly behind him; it's not my favourite position for a tail. When the lights change, he doesn't turn right but continues straight and then pulls into the parking lot for Oakridge Centre. I follow him up two parking levels and when he parks in the first available slot I keep going until I find a free spot. It's on the other side of the aisle about ten metres from him.

I tell Nick exactly where we are parked.

Antonov doesn't get out of his car. Is he suspicious of me

because I followed him into the parking lot? He's a cautious puppy for sure, but this isn't my first rodeo. I get out of my car and head towards the blue door leading into the shopping mall. I walk right past his car without a glance in his direction. I get to the blue door and as I open it, I hear the solid click of his driver's door closing. Without looking back, I cross the tiny lobby and go through the second door and into the mall. I'm on a mezzanine floor that has the medical offices. I take the escalator down to the main floor of the mall.

Fighting the urge to check behind and see if he is following me I walk briskly into the mall. There are shops on either side but I head for the information desk that sits in the middle of the aisle. Fortunately, I've shopped here a couple of times and have a good sense of the layout. I smile at the young man behind the desk. "Excuse me, can you tell me where I can find the White Spot restaurant," I say like I'm a tourist. Nick and Adry are still on the line but they don't speak.

As I knew he would, he points over my right shoulder. "Just down there on your left," he says. It gives me the perfect cover to turn around and look back down the way I just came. Sure enough, Antonov is heading in my direction. I try not to sigh in relief.

I turn back to the young man. I need to play for time. "Thanks so much," I say. "And can you tell me what time the mall closes?"

"Yes, sir. We close at nine."

"Great. Are you open until nine on the weekends too?"

As I say the words, Antonov strides past me without giving me a glance. Success!

I don't register the young man's answer, I just thank him and follow my quarry. He is walking fairly fast and I let him get a little bit ahead. He comes to an intersection and turns left. I don't want to lose him, so I speed up. As I turn the corner, I see that he is heading towards a decorative water feature in the middle of the wide aisle. It is a line of small fountains and the water they eject laps up against a low brick wall.

I hear Nick's voice in my ear. *"What's happening Zeke?"*

I don't want to draw attention to myself so I just whisper, "Hold," and hope Nick can hear me.

Antonov stops and looks in the fountain for a second. He slips his hand into his pocket for a moment and takes it out again. Then he turns around and sits on the brick wall, facing the stores to my left.

It's an odd thing to do and he looks uncomfortable doing it. My problem is that I'm getting close to him. I walk to my right and step into a jewellery store. It's a perfect position. I can see him but he is mostly facing away from me. As I watch, I see him look up and down the aisle.

"Can I help you, sir," a young female voice says.

Without taking my eyes off Antonov, I say the first thing that comes into my head. "Yes, I'm looking for a watch for my girlfriend."

"What?" Nick says in my earbuds.

"How much were you thinking of spending?" she asks.

Antonov puts his hand into the water. He splashes his fingers for a moment.

"Sir?"

"What's happening, Zeke?"

I look at the shop assistant. She's very pretty—but then again it's Oakridge so she's bound to be—and for a second I can't take my eyes off her.

"How much were you thinking of spending ?" she asks again.

"Oh, I don't know. What would you recommend?"

I drag my eyes back at Antonov. He's still sitting there waggling his fingers in the water. The shop assistant takes my arm and leads me towards a counter. "Look at these. We have some lovely watches here."

I notice that none of the watches have price tags. That spells expensive.

I turn to look at Antonov but her grip on my arm is firm. She moves closer and I can smell her perfume. "Would she like something like this?" She waggles her wrist at me. She is wearing a watch and a slim, diamond tennis bracelet which looks like it's worth my annual salary. The watch is lovely but...

"Excuse me a moment," I say and pull my arm from her gym-fuelled grip so that I can see Antonov.

He stands up, shakes his wet hand, puts it in his pocket and marches off, back the way he came.

I give a quick glance and a smile at the mystified girl. "Sorry," I say and walk out.

"Where are you, Nick?"

"I've just parked three cars down from Antonov's Lexus. What's going on?"

"I'm not sure I know, but he's heading back to the car park. I'm not going to follow him. I think if I do, he might make me as a tail."

I get to the intersection with the aisle I entered on. I take a peek around the corner and sure enough, he's marching in the direction of the escalator back up to the mezzanine floor.

"He'll be walking into the parkade in about a minute," I say. "He's all yours now, Nick."

34

NICK

Odd. What's going on? "Roger that," I say to Zeke. I watch the blue door. "Zeke, when he clears the parkade, I want you to get in your car and tag along but stay way back. My truck is a bit too distinctive. If I follow him for too long he'll make me for sure. I may need you to take over the tail again. You too Adry."

They both say. *"10-4."* Cute.

Antonov pushes through the blue door and walks straight to his car. He pulls out of his parking space and heads downwards. I wait a few seconds to let him get a little ahead and follow. He gets to the bottom floor of the parkade and heads west. It's OK for me to follow him here. Half the cars leaving the parkade will leave this way. I give Zeke the all-clear and follow the Lexus onto forty-first going west. Pulling into the right lane, I let a couple of cars pass me. They are a buffer between him and me.

We stay in formation for a good while, until he crosses West Boulevard. He comes to a stop and signals a left turn into an alley. There's no way I can follow him without him noticing me. The traffic coming towards him is pretty heavy.

He's not going to be making that left turn too soon. I pass him on his right and hit the gas. I just make the lights at Yew. My tyres squeal as I make a left onto Yew and then another left onto forty-second just in time to see him pull out of the alley and cross the road into the parking lot of the Kerrisdale Community Centre. What is it with this guy and community centres?

I update Adry and Zeke. I gotta say, I never really liked earbuds but they are great when you're running a tail.

The parking lot has two entrances. He's pulled into the one farthest from me so I hang a right and park as far from him as I can. In an instant, I have our good camera, telephoto lens attached, in my hands. I start snapping shots like one of the paparazzi. He gets out of his car and looks around. Maybe looking for a tail... or perhaps cops. His glance sweeps past me but doesn't stop to look directly at me, so I'm pretty sure he hasn't made me. He walks into the community centre.

Zeke's voice says, *"I'm parked on Yew Street. I can see you in the parking lot."*

"I'm at a meter on forty-first," Adry says.

What a team!

"Zeke, I'd like to get eyes on him in there. Adry followed him at Hillcrest, so I don't want to risk her being recognized. Can..."

"I'm on it."

I drag my eyes away from the entrance to the community centre for a second and look towards Yew. I see Zeke half-limping, half-jogging across the grass towards the centre. He passes in front of me as he goes through the car park but doesn't look at me. Good man.

I take a picture of him entering the community centre.

"Not in the lobby area," he says into my earbuds. I hear a

creaking noise and then the slam of a door. *"Not in the gym."* He's silent for a moment, then, *"We may have a problem."*

"What?" I ask.

Silence.

I wait a beat. "Zeke?"

I hear him give a little cough like he's clearing his throat. He's telling us he can't talk.

All I can hear is background noise: a laugh, a kid shrieking, another door slam. Nothing from Zeke.

Finally, Zeke says, *"Adry, which direction are you parked on forty-first?"*

"Outside Finn's, facing west."

"Do a U-turn as fast as you can," he says.

As much as I want to, I know better than to ask him what's happening.

"OK," she says.

Silence.

Zeke's voice says, *"Oh, shit."*

I can't not ask. "What?"

"He was in the swimming pool. He came out carrying a purple gym bag."

I'm looking through the camera lens at the entrance to the community centre. No sign of Antonov. "Where is he now?"

"He went out a different entrance. The one on West Boulevard. There's a black SUV parked illegally at a bus stop on the other side of the street. Antonov's crossed over and he's getting into it. Some guy in a Hawaiian shirt is getting out." There's a brief pause and, *"They're driving off. Adry, have you made the turn?"*

"I can't. The traffic's blocked by the real housewives of Kerrisdale. I can't even pull out of my parking space."

"I'm on it," I say. I drop the camera onto the passenger

seat and pull out of the parking lot. As I drive down forty-second, I see a black SUV driving north on West Boulevard. "I see them."

Just as I pull up to the intersection an elderly man who looks like he's knock-knock-knocking on Heaven's door, presses the pedestrian button on the traffic lights and brings the West Boulevard traffic to a grinding halt in front of me. My left turn onto West Boulevard is blocked.

"CRAP!" I shout, banging on my steering wheel. With the frustration hissing out of me, I watch the man with his walker cross West Boulevard painfully slowly. The SUV crosses the lights at forty-first and accelerates away.

Finally, the man makes it across and the traffic starts to flow. In a very un-Vancouver move, I push my van forward into the traffic. It earns me a couple of honks and hard stares but gets me in pursuit. I can see the black SUV cross the lights at thirty-seventh just as the lights at forty-first turn red against me.

"Shit!"

Traffic lights change about every thirty seconds. That feels like an age when the scum bags you're pursuing vanish out of sight, down the hill six blocks ahead of you.

I wait out my time. The traffic going west on forty-first is heavy and when the lights finally go green for me, there are a bunch of cars stopped in the intersection. I use the swear-word I never use, then get washed in guilt. "Sorry, Adry," I add.

She gives a little laugh. *"No prob, Nick. I know how you feel."*

Without the intersection clearing, the lights go red again and I know that we've lost our tail on Mr. Yuri Antonov.

But maybe we've got something to work on.

Maybe.

35

CAL

L ucy is the only one in our makeshift office in Arnold's conference room. As I walk through the door, she leaps out of her chair and envelops me in a huge hug. It cheers my soul but sends a withdrawal pain through my bones. "I'm so glad you're OK, Cal," she says.

I'm not sure how OK I really am. I can feel the Beast stirring inside me. *It felt pretty good, didn't it Cal?* he whispers in my ear. *And it didn't kill you did it?* But I ignore him and just say, "Thanks, Luce. I guess I was lucky." She looks at me and I can see a question coming. I forestall it with, "Where is everyone?"

"Staking out Yuri Ant—"

Before she can finish, the door bursts open and Nick wheels in followed by Adry and Zeke. It's clear all three are surprised to see me.

Adry is the first to react by giving me a hug. She doesn't say anything. Her guy, Jason, works for Insite, Vancouver's safe injection site, so she probably knows enough about addiction not to waste energy on words but just to support me with the hug. I am truly grateful for the hug and avoid wincing at the physical effect.

"Great to see you, Cal," Nick says. The use of my first name tells me how much he really cares and I want to go over and give him a hug... but that's not his style.

I just say, "Thanks, man." Our eyes lock and he nods.

Zeke walks over and squeezes my shoulder and, in a way, that matters most to me; it's support without judgment from someone who has only known me for a couple of weeks.

"Tell me about the stakeout," I say.

The three of them tell me the details of the operation. It's odd. I ask Adry to describe the purple bag that Yuri Antonov took into the pool at Hillside. When she does, Zeke says, "Sounds exactly like the bag he brought out of the pool at Kerrisdale."

"Could it have been the same bag?" Lucy asks.

"Doubt it," Nick says.

My gut feel says Nick's right. But it's a good question. "Good thinking outside the box, Luce," I say. "I can't think why or how they would do that but maybe. Hold that thought."

Zeke says, "I can't work out why Antonov went to Oakridge and sat by the water fountains."

"Yeah," I agree, "go through that again."

Zeke repeats the story in detail. Nick is the first to speak. "It doesn't make sense. Maybe he just went there to take up time. What if Lucy's right? What if it was the same bag? Maybe the bag had money in it and maybe he handed it off to Micah or Melanie. They took the bag away, replaced the cash with drugs and then took it to the Kerrisdale pool to return it to him. He went to Oakridge to pass enough time while they did the transfer."

"I don't buy it," Zeke says. "Like I said before, drug

buyers don't pay upfront for drugs. It's a cash-and-carry business."

"Yeah, you're right," Nick says. "Stupid of me."

We lapse into silence. I agree Zeke's right. I've learned enough about drug gangs to know—

"OMG!" Lucy breaks into my thoughts.

"What?" Nick asks his daughter.

She ignores his question. "Zeke, you said Antonov put his hand in the water. What did he do immediately before that?"

Zeke looks up and thinks. "He walked up to the fountain and looked at it for a moment. Then he put his hand into his pocket and sat down."

"You said he waggled his fingers in the water. Was it his other hand?"

He processes this for a moment. "No. He put his hand into his pocket but he took it out as he sat down, *then* he put his fingers in the water."

"How deeply did he put his hand in?" Lucy asks.

"Where are you going with this, Luce?" Nick asks but she waves him off.

"I couldn't see," Zeke says. "I was standing in this jewellery store and the woman who worked there kept distracting me trying to sell me a watch. She was pretty persistent." He looks up again and thinks about it. Nick is about to say something but again Lucy waves him to silence. "When I pulled myself away from her, Antonov was standing up again. He shook the water off his hand and then put his hand back in his pocket."

"Yes!" she says. "It was a dead-letter drop."

"What?" Nick says.

"Oakridge. It was a dead-letter drop." She looks at our faces and giggles. "Don't you guys ever read spy novels?"

During the confused silence her brow creases as she thinks.

"I was wrong. It wasn't the same bag," she says.

"How do you know?" Adry asks.

"What do swimming pools all have?" she asks.

"Water."

"Chlorine."

"Pee."

"No. Lockers. They all have lockers," she says.

I can feel her hypothesis getting through to my somewhat addled brain.

"Micah and Melanie sell crystal meth to Yuri Antonov, right?"

We all nod.

"But maybe they're a bit scared of him or they don't one hundred percent trust him."

Again with the nods.

"So they devise this scheme that will keep them safe and assure Antonov that he's not going to get ripped off." She looks at each of us. I smile and nod at her. I think she's worked it out better than any of us. "Antonov fills a purple gym bag with money," she continues. "He takes it to Hillcrest and puts it in one of the lockers in the swimming pool. He takes the key with him. Previously Melanie and/or Micah, took the drugs, in an identical bag, to the Kerrisdale pool. They put them in a locker there and take the key. They drive to Oakridge and drop the key in the water fountain. Antonov goes to Oakridge, drops his Hillcrest key and picks up the Kerrisdale key. He goes to Kerrisdale and gets the drugs, Micah or Melanie retrieve the Hillcrest key and go pick up the cash."

I look at the stunned faces.

"That's brilliant, Luce," Adry says.

"Of course it is. Look whose daughter she is." Nick says with a proud look on his face.

I feel like a flash of lightning has illuminated Lucy's hypothesis, showing me every detail.

"The woman who worked in the jewellery store," I ask, "can you describe her?"

"Sure," Zeke says. "She was stunning. Quite tall, about five-ten, slim, blond and she had a small v-shaped scar on her chin."

"Melanie Weston!" I say.

"Holy crap," says Nick and the others just shake their heads.

"Zeke," I ask, "do you think she spotted that you were surveilling Antonov?"

"Oh yeah," he sighs. "No doubt about that."

"And *that*," Nick says, "explains the sudden change of vehicles at the Kerrisdale Pool. She must have tipped Antonov that he was under surveillance."

"I am so sorry, you guys," Zeke says. "I shouldn't have chosen that jewellery store to keep a watch on Antonov. If I'd have watched from anywhere else, she wouldn't have known."

"Don't blame yourself," Nick says. "It was the best place to watch from; that's why she chose it."

"The good news," I say, "is that we know how Melanie and Micah sell drugs to Antonov. The bad news is that now Melanie knows we know. They are never going to use that method again."

Silence reigns for a long moment.

Lucy breaks it. "I've got a question," she says. "A dead-letter drop is a Cold-War spy technique. Why go to all that trouble? It's twenty-twenty-one, for heaven's sake. Why not use Bitcoin?"

"That's a damn good question, Luce," Nick says.

Another silence as we all ponder. Bitcoin is a boon to criminals everywhere. Why *would* they go to all that trouble?

"We may never know. But the question is: where do we go from here?" Adry asks.

I wish I knew.

But there is one thing I have to do.

———

I walk into the store. The lone shop assistant walks over. He gives me an appraising look and I guess I pass muster. "Hi, I'm Justin. How can I help you, sir?" he asks, his tonality announcing that he's a proud, gay man.

"I was in here earlier," I lie, "and Melanie was showing me some watches. Is she here?"

"Melanie?" he says, his eyes narrowing. "We don't have anyone by that name."

"Tall, blonde, beautiful," I say, "with a small v-shaped scar on her chin."

A slightly theatrical frown wrinkles his brow. "Huh," he grunts. "*Melanie...*" he says the name with some vitriol. "Is that what she was calling herself? We knew her as Rachel. Can you believe, she walked out of the store today and left it unattended? Unattended! I was on my lunch break but did she wait for me to get back? Oh, no. She just left. *Anyone* could have walked into the store and stolen *everything*. And then she didn't come *back*. I *told* Mr. Fredericks not to hire her in the first place. I *knew* there was something about her that just wasn't right."

"How long had she worked here?"

"Today was her second day!" He looks like he's going to

explode with exasperation. "I was given the responsibility of training her but she took *no* interest in what I was trying to teach her. Absolutely... no... interest."

"Mr. Fredericks is the manager?"

"Yes and he's also one of the owners. He's a wonderful boss but Rachel, or Melanie, or whatever her name is, completely fooled him. I told him. I said—"

"How could I get hold of Mr. Fredericks," I interrupt, to stem the lava flow of his ire.

"He's in the back. I called him as soon as I got back from lunch and found her gone. We were worried that she might have stolen something so he came in immediately and he's checking the inventory to see if anything's missing. I wouldn't put it past her. I could tell from the get-go that she wasn't the sort of person we should—"

While he rants, I take out my security licence and hold it in his line of sight. "Would you tell Mr. Fredericks that I have some information that would be helpful to him?"

He looks at my licence. It looks pretty much the same as a BC driver's licence but I see the moment he spots the difference. "A private investigator," he says, giving me another appraising look. "Well, you certainly look the part. Come with me."

He turns and walks to the back of the shop. There is a door subtly built into the wood panelling. He knocks and pops his head through the door. "Davis," he says. "There's a private investigator here. He has some information about Rachel."

I hear a reply and Justin opens the door wide and ushers me in.

Davis Fredericks is about five-ten, not only in feet and inches but also in pounds. He pushes himself up from a tiny desk, struggles to his feet and offers a giant hand. I take it, introduce myself and give him my card. He indicates for me to sit. Justin cannot resist staying in the doorway to hear the juicy tidbits I might have to offer. He divides his attention between the office and the showroom and I'm guessing he's praying a customer doesn't walk in and drag him away.

"What can you tell me, Mr. Rogan?" he asks. His accent is decidedly Scottish.

"The real name of the woman you know as Rachel is Ruth Weston but she goes by the name Melanie. She's a drug dealer and a con artist. I'm trying to track down her and her brother, Micah."

Justin gives a little "huh" that screams, 'I told you.'

I continue, "She took the job here so that she could complete a drug transaction using the store as cover."

Davis' face is mortified.

"Don't worry," I say. "She didn't do the transaction *in* the store so you're not exposed to any legal issues. But I need to find her. When she applied for the job, did she give you any personal details like an address or a phone number?"

He pulls open a drawer from under his desktop, revealing a computer keyboard. A few taps of the keyboard and he says, "Rachel Shepherd. She gave me a cell phone number but after Justin told me what happened, I called it and got one of those annoying 'This phone is either not on the network or is turned off' messages."

"It was almost certainly a burner phone," I say. "Did she give you an address?"

He turns back to his screen, "She gave an address in Langley," he says. He reads it off the screen and I recognize it as the address of her parents, whom Adry visited.

"Any other information? Social insurance number, driver's licence?"

"When I hired her yesterday she said she would bring

them in today but when she arrived this morning, she said she had forgotten them."

"You sell very high-value merchandise here. Didn't you do a criminal records check before you hired her?"

Davis Fredericks looks more than a little embarrassed and I'm guessing I know why. "Normally we would do that before someone started but we're really short-staffed at the moment so I needed someone fast and Rachel seemed a good fit. The plan was to have her go down to the Cambie police station this afternoon for the criminal record check."

"I sympathize," I say. "She used her amazing looks to con me."

He shifts uncomfortably in his seat. "Yes... well... she did rather charm me, I have to admit." He looks at the ceiling for a moment. "Ah, who am I kidding," he says. "She gave me every indication that she was interested in me... you know... romantically. At some level, I knew I was being conned, but hope springs eternal, as they say."

A disapproving grunt emanates from Justin.

"I understand you were checking the inventory?" I ask. "Is anything missing?"

"Aye," he says, his Scottish accent very noticeable. "A thirty-thousand dollar tennis bracelet. I'm praying the insurance company will cover the loss."

"When I find her, I'll do everything I can to get it back to you," I tell him.

It's a promise I have every intention of keeping.

Because I *will* find Melanie Weston and her killer brother, Micah.

———

"I KNOW YOU'RE SUPERMAN AND BATMAN AND ALBERT Einstein all rolled into one, but how *are* you going to find them?" Tina's question is the one I've been contemplating for the last several hours and I think I'm closing in on an answer.

I take a drink of my Tsingtao beer. It's remarkably good for a beer from a huge brewing company.

"It's tricky. Melanie is cautious. I'm betting she designed that whole process for the transfer of the drugs and the money. She charmed her way into the job at the jewellery store and then chose the water feature as the place to do the exchange of the keys. It was our hard luck that Zeke chose the store as a good place to observe what Antonov was doing. Now she won't use Oakridge as the dead-letter drop again. Poor Zeke thinks he blew it."

Tina and Ellie simultaneously take pieces of lemon chicken with their chopsticks and bite into them.

"Tell him he didn't," Tina says around her mouthful of chicken. "Melanie wasn't ever going to use that location again anyway."

"How do you know that?" Ellie asks between bites. She beat me to it; that's exactly what I was going to ask.

"I don't know how long it takes to cook up a batch of crystal meth, but they aren't going to be doing deliveries every day. Let's say they do deliveries once a week. Is a girl like Melanie Weston going to go and work in that store every day for a week just so she can watch that one spot? Not a chance. She's going to change the hand-off place every time."

"Yes, and now they know we've blown their cover, they won't be using the pools anymore either," I say.

"They probably weren't going to anyway," Tina says. "You said you thought Melanie was using the whole process because she was scared of the Russian gang. I'll bet she is planning to use different places for every batch she sells to them. And the gang will go along with it because she and Micah are their best source for the meth."

"You're right," I say. "Zeke's going to feel a whole lot better."

"Gee, Tina," Ellie says. "Maybe Dad should hire you to work for them, you'd be a great detective."

"Oh, no," comes the reply. "I'll stick with journalism. I don't want to deal with gangs. I'm as frightened of them as Melanie is."

Her words stir up feelings of guilt in me. We are having to stay in hotels and nearby restaurants because I poked this particular hornet's nest. "That's why Nick and I are trying to work out a way to take down this gang so we don't have to hide from them anymore."

Ellie looks a little afraid. She asks, "Are you going to just keep watching the hotel until you can follow that Yuri guy again?"

"He's too smart to stay living at the Hyatt. He knows we were staking him out there."

"Do you think he will have moved to another hotel already?"

Her question fires up some neurons that were sitting idly in my brain. They excite some other neurons and, in a chain reaction, the answers come pouring into my head. My mind races and I hear Tina saying "Cal?" but I have to finish my train of thought. I hold my finger up for quiet as, one after the other, the pieces fall into place.

I stand up from the table. "I've gotta go," I say. Pulling out my phone I head out of the restaurant.

"Siri, call Nick Stammo."

I tell him what I need and where to meet me. He can

hear the tone and timbre of my voice. He doesn't waste time asking why; he just says, "On it."

I hope we're not too late.

––––––

As I walk towards the ramp that leads down to the Hyatt car park, I spot the black SUV. It's parked by the entrance door to the hotel. The licence plate is the same as the licence plate Tommy saw in the alley. The door of the hotel opens and a bellhop pushes out a cart laden with bags. Then I see him. The man who pumped me full of heroin. He points the bellhop towards the SUV.

A host of conflicting emotions struggle inside me. Prime among them is the almost overwhelming desire to run over and beat the son of a bitch to death. I push it down. The mission comes first. I let the relief rise to the surface. Tina was right. It's taken Yuri Antonov some time to organize his move out of the Hyatt. His sidekick is supervising the loading of Yuri's luggage into the SUV. I speed my pace, praying that he doesn't turn and recognize me behind my mask.

As I descend the ramp, I move out of his line of sight and break into a run. I need to move fast even if every step triggers a stab of pain. If his stuff is being loaded into the SUV, Yuri himself will be leaving soon. I have to get to his Lexus before that happens.

At the bottom of the ramp, I look across the expanse of high-end cars. The white Lexus LC500 is immediately apparent because it's moving. It pulls out of its stall and turns towards me. Frustration explodes inside me. I'm two minutes too late, damn it! Then a new emotion bubbles up: fear. If Antonov recognizes me...

But he doesn't. Because it isn't him behind the wheel. It's a uniformed parking valet. A double reprieve.

I pull the magnetic GPS tracker out of my pocket with my right hand and wave frantically at the valet with my left. I run in front of the car, still waving at him. The tires offer a small protest as he hits the brake. I run to the driver's door and crouch down, bringing myself face-to-face with him. As the window comes down, I say the first thing that comes into my mind.

"Can you help me?"

I slide my right hand below the door, wondering what to say next.

He looks at me like I might be a crazy person. A pause. "What's the problem, sir?"

My right shoulder moves down as I reach underneath.

"I think someone has stolen my car," I improvise, as I press the tracker up towards the underside of the doorframe.

"Are you a guest of the hotel, sir?" There is suspicion in his voice.

"Yes, I'm in room ten-oh-five." Ellie's birthday, October the fifth.

I feel the tracker jump out of my hand as its rare-earth magnet grabs onto the car.

He buys it. Pointing towards my left, he says, "The valet desk is over there, sir. Wait there. I'll just deliver this car and then I'll bring security down to talk with you."

"Thanks so much," I say. The relief in my voice is genuine.

I stand and as I walk in the direction he indicated, I hear the Lexus accelerate up the ramp.

I run past the valet desk and into the hotel, then grab an elevator to the conference level. The elevator seems unbearably slow. Standing still I feel the pains from my recent exertion. One hit of heroin and they would all be banished. Thankfully, it stops and the doors open onto the conference floor. I stride across the floor and sink into a plush beige couch, pull out my phone and fire up the app Nick installed. "Yes," I breathe as the red dot blinks on the map. Thank heavens for relativity and quantum physics which brought us GPS, cellular technology and batteries which should last for a month.

36

ADRY

Friday

Frustration. It has been eight long days. Days when Nick, Zeke and Lucy have been working double-time to keep up on all our paying cases, while Cal and I have been spending boring, sixteen-hour days following Yuri Antonov. In an abundance of caution, we have both been driving average-looking rental cars and changing them daily. We have also upped our photography skills by taking thousands of pictures of Mr. Antonov, many of his colleagues, and their activities—most were pretty mundane but some were definitely criminal. When this is over, VPD will enjoy going through them.

Antonov moved from the Hyatt to Hotel Blu on Robson. The rooms start at four-sixty a night—must be nice. According to the tracker, his car's in the car park. I'm parked on Robson, kitty-corner to the hotel, where I can keep an eye on the front door, in case Antonov decides to walk somewhere. Cal is around the corner on Beatty.

Stakeouts are long periods of boring inactivity with

interesting bits in between. As I stare at the hotel I'm thinking about the new, steamy romance by my favourite author. The sun is streaming through my windshield and my mind wanders to thoughts of Jason. The long hours of surveillance have sure put a dent into our time together. My thoughts slip into a delicious fantasy; it's based on the novel but with Jason in the lead role. Maybe—

The damned app on my phone beeps. I tap the screen. The red dot of Antonov's car is moving. I look up. The Lexus is pulling out of the hotel car park. He turns left and drives south on Cambie, crossing the lights right in front of me. I can see him in the driver's seat. I pull out of my parking spot and let two cars and a bus pass in front of me before I turn right. This GPS tracker is great. You don't need eyes on the vehicle you're following.

Cal's voice comes out of my phone. *"You got him, Adry?"*

"Yup."

"OK. I'll follow a few blocks behind."

Antonov has turned right onto Smithe. I wait for the lights to change and follow him, about six cars behind. He doesn't turn off at any of the usual intersections but continues to the end of Smithe. Most of the cars between us have turned off and I am just one car back. He turns south on Thurlow. Maybe he's going to head down Nelson for somewhere in the west end. He's been for dinner in the west end a couple of times in the last week.

But he doesn't. He continues down Thurlow. I drop back and let another car get between us. When he crosses Davie, I get a tingle in my spine.

"This is it," I say. "I think I know where he's going."

"I think you're right." Cal knows it too. *"If he crosses Pacific, pull over and park."*

He does and I do.

37

CAL

I have been driving down Howe, keeping parallel with Antonov. I take the off-ramp just before the Granville bridge and head down towards Pacific. By some miracle the lights are green. I accelerate down Howe and find a parking spot on Beach in plenty of time to have eyes on Antonov's Lexus as he pulls into the car park of the Aquatic Centre.

"We were right," I tell Adry as I adjust the telephoto lens of the camera.

I hear the electronic simulation of a shutter as I take each picture: Antonov getting out of his car; looking around the car park; opening his trunk; taking out the purple bag; walking to the door of the Aquatic Centre; going inside.

When I conference Nick into the call, all I say is, "It's a go."

"About friggin' time," he says. *"I'm on it."* He hangs up.

Four minutes later, I take pictures of an empty-handed Antonov: leaving the Aquatic Centre; scanning the car park; getting into his car.

"He's out," I tell Adry.

"I'm ready." I can hear the grin in her voice.

Neither Antonov nor Melanie has ever seen Adry, so she needs to be the one to surveil the dead-letter drop.

As Antonov pulls out of the car park, I get ready to duck below the dashboard in case he turns towards me.

He doesn't.

"Going west," I say. "He's all yours."

"10-4." She giggles. *"I love saying that."*

I take a deep breath. Over the last eight days, the withdrawal pains from my massive overdose have finally abated to be replaced by a more insidious longing. It comes on strongly when I'm inactive. It's fine at home because Tina's there to get me through it but during the stakeout times, I have been haunted by the thoughts of a fix. When Mr. Well-Dressed shot me up it was so intense that it almost equalled the bliss of that very first hit of heroin that I took all those years ago. The Beast who will always live inside me, and is so much a part of me, wants that shot so very, very badly.

I rail against having to just sit here but... *I am to wait, though waiting so be hell.*

38

ADRY

I watch the red dot of Antonov's car move west. I bet he's going to exchange the keys in Stanley Park. I let a few other cars pass then pull onto Beach Avenue and follow him. But I was wrong. He doesn't go more than a couple of hundred metres before pulling into a car park overlooking the beach. I have no alternative but to follow him. The car park is fairly crowded but I find a spot three cars away from him.

He strolls over to the pay parking machine and feeds it. I use the parking app to pay. I sit on the hood of the car and pretend to text but watch him out of the corner of my eye. He walks down the path to the beach and I follow about twenty metres behind him.

With a big smile like I'm chatting to a friend, I say to Cal, "I'm going down to the beach."

"You're following him?"

"Of course," I say.

"Be careful."

When Antonov reaches the footpath, he turns left and walks to a concession stand. He stands behind the only person being served.

I feel an adrenaline high as I catch up and stand a couple of metres behind him.

"Yes, it's lovely down by the beach," I say. "I'm just lining up to buy an ice cream."

"If you're so close to him that you have to talk in code, you shouldn't be," he says. *"Remember, this man's dangerous."* Cal's so protective, bless him.

The man at the front of the line walks away biting into a soft-serve, ice-cream cone covered in chocolate and Antonov steps up. He takes something out of his back pocket. It's a folded white envelope and what looks like a hundred-dollar bill. Without a word, he hands the envelope and the money to the vendor, who takes it, and with a glance towards the beach—which looks like a guilty glance to me—he reaches under the counter and hands a lilac envelope to Antonov.

"Yes," I say, like I'm chatting with an old friend, "everything is working out just as we thought it would. I couldn't be happier."

"Score."

Antonov pulls out his phone and walks back the way he came, speaking to someone in what is probably Russian. I don't let my eyes follow him. I might be watched. He's Cal's problem now.

"Do you have a creamsicle?" I ask.

"Sure," the vendor says with a smile, "what flavour?"

I snatch a glance at his name badge. "Orange please, Mark." I return his smile. We will probably need his evidence at some point.

He dives his hand down into the cooler and pulls out the treat, which was invented by an eleven-year-old, over one hundred and fifteen years ago, and is my personal favourite ice cream. I pay him and, with a final big smile, I wander over to a picnic table which is on the sand right beside the footpath. It gives me a good view of the beach and the concession stand. I tell Cal exactly what just happened.

"Way to go!" he says. *"Can you still see Antonov?"*

I move my head left and right, like I'm stretching my neck muscles, so that I can see Antonov. He's no longer on his phone. "He's almost at his car."

"Great. Hang in there."

I don't think I'll have long to wait. I sit on the bench and lean back against the table, enjoying the sun on my face. I've lived in Vancouver my entire life and I never remember it being so warm at this time of year.

I look around like a tourist enjoying one of the most beautiful cities in the world. Even though it's a workday, the beach is full of people. Joggers and walkers use the footpath which is part of Vancouver's twenty-eight-kilometre seawall.

My eye catches someone who looks out of place. He's sitting on a picnic table on the other side of the concession stand and he's wearing a three-piece suit with shiny, black shoes which probably cost him more than any shoes I've ever owned... and I *love* shoes. What's odd is that he's watching the concession stand like a hawk. Two skateboarders are purchasing hot dogs and potato chips. When they complete their purchases and skate away, Mr. Three-Piece is still watching the stand. Or is he watching Mark, the vendor?

Or is he just a businessman, enjoying the sun during a break between meetings.

I bite into my creamsicle and wait.

But not for long.

She's hard to miss. Melanie Weston/Ruth Weston/Rachel Shepherd walks up from the beach towards the concession stand. She's tall and the pictures I've seen of her don't do her justice. She is *stunning*. And I'm jealous. Not only that, she's wearing a Lise Charmel one-piece navy swimsuit that I have been lusting after but can't justify paying three hundred and fifty bucks for. Her lower half is covered by a colourful wraparound and the outfit is complete with a pair of strappy sandals and a matching Hermès mini pouch. If that's not a knock-off—and I'm betting it isn't—it's worth a month of my salary, or more.

She walks up to the concession stand. I sneak a peek at Mr. Three-Piece. His eyes are riveted on her and he's talking into his cellphone, which reminds me. "I have eyes on her," I say. "She's at the concession stand."

"Atta girl. Friend Yuri is on the move too. He's heading east."

I capture it on my phone as Melanie takes a couple of fifties out of her pouch and hands then to Mark. He hands her the folded white envelope.

"She's done the exchange," I say.

"Good. Don't let her out of your sight but be careful."

She slips the white envelope into her Hermès and turns away from the concession stand. I can't follow her with my phone, it would be too obvious. I see Mr. Three-Piece stand up. Melanie makes her way to the path that leads up to the car park, but instead of taking it, she cuts diagonally across the grass in the direction of the Aquatic Centre. Mr. Three-Piece heads up to the car park but keeps glancing across at her.

I relay this to Cal and, after a moment of silence, he says, *"Describe him."*

I don't get halfway through my description when he says, *"That's the guy who pumped me full of drugs."* I feel a tingle of fear. After a much longer moment of silence, he says, *"Adry. I want you to abort."*

"But Cal—"

"No buts. It's waaay too dangerous."

I can tell from his tone that he's absolutely not going to change his mind. "OK," I say, the disappointment heavy in my voice. "I'll go back to the office then."

I hang up, stand up, take the last bite of my creamsicle and drop the wooden stick into the compost bin beside the picnic table. I hurry up the path to my car. To my right, Melanie's long legs have taken her about a third of the way to the Aquatic Centre; up ahead Mr. Three-Piece is getting into a black Chevy SUV. As he pulls out of the car park, I get into my rent-a-car.

I think I know what's happening here. The gang's fed up with this dead-letter drop process Melanie has devised. Mr. Three-Piece has been tasked with following her in order to find out where she and Micah are manufacturing the crystal meth. Then they're going to 'negotiate' a different arrangement.

As I pull out of the car park, my phone rings. I ignore it. I can see the black SUV. It's parking on the street, half a block past the Aquatic Centre. I drive in the same direction but turn left onto the short block of Thurlow between Beach and Pacific. I hang a U-ie and park where I can see the Aquatic Centre. I get my camera in position just as Melanie steps towards the entrance. Perfect timing. I take four pictures of her before she vanishes inside.

My phone rings again. It's Cal. I let it go to voicemail.

Sorry, Cal. You should meet my mom and dad sometime. They'd tell you I never was that good at doing what I'm told.

39

CAL

When Adry hangs up, I call Nick and give him an update. He's definitely not supportive of my decision to have Adry abort her surveillance of Melanie Weston. *"Shit Rogan,"* he says. *"What were you thinking? We need to find Melanie and that murderous brother of hers and hand them over to VPD. If things go according to Hoyle today, she and Micah are going to be in the wind if we don't know where they are. We'll forever be the PIs who got a murderer set free."*

"Didn't you hear me, Nick? That well-dressed gangbanger, who tried to kill me, is also following Melanie. It's just too dangerous."

"I'm gonna conference Adry into this call. The three of us need to talk." He's gone for thirty seconds. *"She didn't pick up. She's probably mad."*

"No, Adry's a team player. Let me try." I try to get hold of her... "Voicemail," I say.

"You should have talked to me first before aborting," he grunts.

He's right. It's just that Adry is a great detective and she's becoming kind of a role model for Ellie. Sometimes I think of Adry as a grown-up Ellie, which makes me feel protective of her.

Time for a change of subject. "Is everything organized at your end?"

"*Ab-so-lutely,*" he says. "*Where are you right now?*"

I glance at the app on my phone, which is stuck on the rent-a-car dashboard. The red dot of Antonov's car is flashing on the map. "I'm about two blocks behind him. The traffic's pretty busy, so there are a bunch of cars between us."

"*Where do you think he's going?*"

"I assumed he would head for a swimming pool, but he's going north on Hornby. There aren't any public pools downtown."

"*Maybe it's not a pool. Where else would have lockers?*"

"Waterfront Station?"

"*No. They used to have, years ago, but they took 'em out.*"

"He just turned East onto Georgia."

"*I see that.*"

"There's a post office on Georgia and Richards. Maybe they're using a PO box."

"*No, PO boxes are too small and there are too many cameras.*"

Nick's right again. I rack my brain as to where Antonov might be heading. Somewhere where there's a locker.

"*He just crossed Richards. Maybe he's going over the Georgia Viaduct.*"

Where is he going?

I can almost hear Nick's brain trying to grind out the answer.

Then I know.

"The bus station!" "*The bus station!*"

"*Hang on,*" he says and the line goes dead. I use the time to accelerate down Georgia. I just catch a couple of lights and I can see Yuri's Lexus a block ahead stopped at the lights on Beatty. After thirty seconds, Nick comes back on. *"It's still a go."*

The lights change and I accelerate past the Lexus, turning my head left so that there's no chance of him looking over and recognizing me.

In a few minutes, we are going to take down Yuri Antonov. I want to be at the bus station ahead of him.

The thrill of that thought is blunted by the decision to have Adry abort her pursuit of Melanie Weston.

40

ADRY

Maybe I should call Nick. I can't decide. If I do, will he agree with Cal and tell me to abort? As I struggle to decide, the door of the Aquatic Centre opens. I snatch up my camera and focus the telephoto lens on Melanie. She has the purple bag in her hand. It looks like it's heavy. As I video her, Lucy's question flickers across my mind again: why are they using bags of cash and not doing the financial transaction with Bitcoin? Is it just because Micah and Melanie are scared to meet face-to-face with the gang?

She opens the door of a Tesla, throws the bag onto the passenger seat and climbs in. She turns in her seat and it seems like she's checking out the bag. After a moment, she straightens up and looks down for about fifteen seconds. She's texting. Probably telling Micah that she's got the money. OMG, I know why they're not using Bitcoin.

I have to tell Nick right now. Keeping the camera focused on her, I grab my phone and tell Siri to call Nick.

"Adry, where are you?"

I ignore his question. "Nick, listen to me!" It comes out

like an order. It feels strange giving orders to my boss. "She's picked up the money, she checked it out and I'm sure she's texting Micah."

"Good work. I'm glad you ignored Ro—"

"Nick, *listen*. Do you know yet where Antonov is heading to pick up the drugs?"

"Yeah, the bus terminal. We just worked it out."

"If you want to grab up Micah, he's there. He waits until he gets the call from Melanie. She tells him she's got the cash, *then* he puts the drugs in the locker for Antonov to pick up."

He thinks this through for a moment. *"That doesn't make sense, Antonov's already got the key to the locker. How can Micah open it and put the drugs inside."*

He's right.

It doesn't matter. I know I'm right too. "Just tell Cal to be on the lookout for Micah. I'm *sure* he's there. Please, Nick, trust me on this."

He hesitates for a second. *"OK. I'll tell Rogan."* He hangs up.

Melanie is pulling out of the Aquatic Centre car park. I drop the camera on the passenger seat and press the record button on the camera duct-taped to the rent-a-car's dashboard.

She turns right and drives along Beach. I pull out of my parking spot and follow. There is a silver Honda between us.

As she passes the black Chevy, he pulls out behind her.

I'm hoping that he is so intent on tailing her, that he doesn't spot me tailing him.

41

CAL

I park at a meter in front of the bus station. As I get out of the car I look around for any sign of police. There's a white Ford Transit van parked about twenty metres in front of me. It could be the command vehicle but I doubt they would have got here so fast. I look at my watch. It was less than forty minutes ago that Nick called Domenic Dixon at the drug squad. Nick planned this whole operation with him a week ago and he has had a team ready to spring into action on short notice.

My phone burbles. Nick.

He tells me Adry's theory that Micah's here and a big grin spreads across my face. I so want to see him taken down here! Nick adds that he's just spoken to Dom. The arrest team is still a few minutes out. It's cutting it fine.

I cross the street and walk into the station. Now called Pacific Central, it is an impressive stone building that used to be the terminus for the Canadian National Railway. Although it's still used for passenger trains, its main function is for long-distance buses. It was built in the Beaux-Arts style, over a hundred years ago. I don't have time to take in the wonderful interior; I just head across the granite floor towards the lockers. There are two banks of them. I look around and see a perfect place on a wooden bench that's far enough away from the lockers that I will be able to observe without being observed. As I walk over, I take a Vancouver Canadians baseball cap out of my pocket and put it on, pulling the peak down to conceal my face as much as possible.

Looking around, I don't see anyone who might be a cop but I do see Yuri Antonov. His eyes are focused on the left-hand bank of lockers. As he reaches them, his back to me, I cast my eyes around again looking for some sign of Domenic Dixon's team. Nothing.

I tap my phone's camera app and point it toward the lockers. I start the video and zoom in.

Antonov pulls a lilac-coloured envelope from his pocket and takes a key out of the envelope. He squints at it then scans the lockers until he finds the matching number. He opens it and reaches in. He doesn't take out the purple gym bag full of crystal meth that I was expecting to see. Have we got this wrong? I feel a wave of embarrassment. Have we got a team from the VPD drug unit out on a wild goose chase?

Although it's not what I was hoping for, Antonov does take something out of the locker. It's too small for me to see from here. He looks closely at it and again scans the lockers. He walks over to the right-hand bank and opens a locker in the middle of the bottom row. It was a key in the first locker! I breathe a sigh of relief as he pulls out the purple bag.

Nick picks up immediately. "Where are the cavalry?" I ask.

Antonov is making his way back towards the station entrance. I pull the peak of my cap down a bit further and follow him. If the VPD doesn't get here in time, I'm going to have to tail him.

"Hang on I'm going to conference you in with Dom."

After a moment, there's a beep and Dom says, *"Hi Cal, we're literally a minute out. What's the status."*

"Antonov has picked up the drugs and is heading back to his car. I'm following him about thirty metres back."

"Good. Keep eyes on him."

Just as he says the words, Antonov walks through the doors and turns left out of my line of sight. I hurry towards the doors. As I approach them, I can see my rent-a-car parked across the street. Yuri's Lexus is parked right behind it. He's not making for his car. I run through the doors and look left along the sidewalk. It's empty.

What the—

As I look desperately around, I see him. He has crossed the road and is just disappearing behind the white van I thought might be a VPD command vehicle.

"He's leaving on foot." As I walk towards the van, I see a Skytrain pull into the elevated Main Street station. "He's going to take the Skytrain."

"Follow him. We're nearly there." Dom says.

I jog across the road and pass between an olive-green Subaru Outback and the white Transit. I have an unobstructed view of the Skytrain station across Thornton Park. There are several people crossing the park but Yuri Antonov is not one of them.

"I've lost him."

Nick's *"Shit, Rogan! How can you lose him?"* is partially drowned out by the Transit's starter motor.

I spin round. Although I can only see his ear and a three-quarter view of his face, I know it's Antonov in the passenger seat.

The van pulls away from the curb.

"He's in a white Ford Transit heading south on Station Street."

"We'll get him." Dom's voice is remarkably calm. *"We're on Terminal just crossing Main."*

I look over towards the Skytrain station and can see the flashing red and blue lights on the VPD trucks. I look along Station Street. The white Transit is pulling up to the lights at Terminal.

"It's the white van at the lights."

As he says, *"Got it,"* I hear the sirens turn on. One of the VPD trucks does a U-turn and blocks the front of the Transit. The other pulls up beside the driver's door.

The passenger door flies open and Antonov jumps out. The purple bag swinging in his hand, he runs back down Station Street. He's heading for his car and he's fast. The VPD truck blocking the front of the Transit can't move and the one parked on the driver's side probably hasn't yet seen that Antonov is escaping. He has a small window of opportunity. I'll bet he's thinking that if he can get to his Lexus he can U-turn his way out of here. I take one step off the sidewalk onto the grass, like I'm a scared bystander who needs to get out of his way. If he has seen me he doesn't recognize me. I try to keep the grin off my face.

He's five metres away. I tense my muscles and take two steps forward. In his eyes, I can see he knows what's going to happen but he's running just too fast to do anything about it. I slam my shoulder into him. He stumbles off the sidewalk, trips over his own feet and his momentum carries him headfirst into the grill of the Subaru. Antonov flops onto the pavement and I wonder how the owner of the Outback is going to explain the damage to a skeptical insurance adjuster.

I tell Dom and, sixty seconds later, Antonov is trying to struggle to his feet as a police cruiser pulls up beside him. As they cuff him and read him his rights, I walk up the street. I recognize the giant standing, cuffed, beside the white Transit. He's the size of a house and he's the thug I watched kill our informer, Henry.

A uniformed officer has opened the rear doors of the van. There's a skinny kid curled up on the floor. He's bound with duct tape. "Don't worry sir," the officer says. "We'll have you free in no time."

"Excuse me, Constable," I say. "You might want to check with Inspector Dixon before you do anything other than cuff him and read him his rights."

He gives me a confused look.

I smile at the skinny kid.

"Hi there Micah. Nice to see you again." My smile broadens until it hurts my cheeks. "When you get back to Kent Institution, I have a feeling your former friend Blackbird will be very happy to see you."

I know I shouldn't, but I really do relish the unadulterated fear in his eyes.

42

ADRY

Nick taught me that tailing a target is always easier on busier streets. You can stay undetected by keeping other cars between you and the target. On empty streets, that's not something you can do. It's even worse at night, but thank heavens it's still afternoon.

I'm staying at least a hundred metres behind the black SUV. I'm hoping the well-dressed driver is too intent on Melanie's red Tesla to check his mirror and notice me following him up Union Street in my anonymous grey rent-a-car. He pulls left and I see why. Melanie is parallel parking. He continues along Union and turns right. He's probably going to park, get out of his car and watch her from cover. I see a spot up ahead about six cars back from Melanie. I park, grab the camera from the passenger seat and wait.

She doesn't get out of the car. Did she spot that the black SUV was following her? If she did, surely she would have done a U-turn and headed back in the other direction. I need to get Nick's advice. I call him but he doesn't reply.

I point the camera and start recording.

Then I see her. She's getting out of the car and she has her phone to her ear; she's listening, not talking. She hoists the purple bag out of the car and puts it on the roof while she locks the doors with her key fob. She takes the phone from her ear and jabs once at the screen then returns to listening. Maybe she's calling Micah to confirm that he's put the drugs in the locker.

Still listening, she grabs the purple bag from the Tesla's roof and strides across the road. I keep the camera on her. She pushes through the gate to a house and walks up the steps to the grey front door. She puts down the bag and rummages in that wonderful Hermès pouch. I can feel the excitement building. She pulls out a key and opens the door. Yes! This *is* where she lives. I zoom in on the door and can see the house number clearly.

When she walks inside, I stop the recording.

I grab my phone. Still no reply from Nick. Maybe I should call Cal. He won't care that I ignored his instructions if I've got a good result. I call but Cal doesn't reply either. Maybe he's in the middle of watching Yuri Antonov and Micah get arrested.

The words of a Clash song wander through my head. *Should I stay or should I go?* If Micah was at the bus station when Melanie called from the Aquatic Centre parking lot and, if he left before Cal arrived, he could be here at any minute. I could stay and get a video of him going into the house. On the other hand, there's the well-dressed guy from the SUV. Has he observed Melanie going into the house? I don't really want to run into him.

I jump out of my skin as, simultaneously, I catch a movement in my side mirror and hear a knock on my window. My head snaps left and all I can see is the gun. I hate guns. Up until now, the worst thing I've had pointed at me since I started this job is a belligerent finger. It has an extended barrel. I don't know a lot about guns but just enough to know that's a silencer

I look up into his face and swallow hard. It's the face of a handsome reptile. Zero emotion.

He waggles the gun in a signal for me to get out of the car.

My mind races.

"Should I stay or should I go?" the Clash sing in my ear.

I had to parallel park to get into this spot. I can't just start the engine and drive off. There is no 'go' option.

I open the door and get out of the car.

"Camera," he says.

I take it off the dashboard.

"Door."

I close the car's door.

He grabs my bicep and jabs my ribs with the gun. I know what I should do but the gun is paralyzing me. I allow him to lead me across the street and up the steps to the grey door. The door is flush with the walls on either side; there are no glass panels. There is a peephole in the door. He sees it too. He moves to the side and says, "Ring the doorbell."

I do as I'm told, trying hard to control the tremble in my hand. Four chimes ring out. Almost immediately, the door sweeps open. The excited grin slides off her face as she sees me. Irritation. "Who are y—" Then she sees Mr. Three-Piece. Frown. Then she sees his gun pointed at her chest. Fear.

As much as I dislike Melanie, I can't try anything while that gun is pointed at her chest.

"Back up," he says.

She does.

"Step inside," he says.

I do.

Melanie recovers from the shock in double-quick time. "What the hell do you think you're doing?" she spits out at him. "My brother and I are making a fortune for you. Without us, where the hell are you guys going to get an unlimited supply of high-quality meth like—?"

The silenced gun cracks.

Melanie staggers back, a shocked look on her face.

I'm next.

Before her body hits the floor, I barrel into the shooter.

He reacts and pushes back. Good boy! Pull, twist, trip. As he falls over my leg, I follow him down and add my weight to his as he slams onto the floor. The crack of his head and the whoosh of air from his lungs are a symphony to my ears. I hear the gun skittering across the hardwood. Perfect! I spring to my feet and stamp my foot down with every ounce I can muster. As it connects with his groin, he screams. That should hold him for a moment, but not long enough for me to help Melanie.

Forcing down my revulsion, I scoop up his gun and step over to his whimpering body. I press the gun to his knee and try not to close my eyes as I pull the trigger. This time his scream is louder than the considerable crack of the gun. I had no idea silenced guns were so loud. Or men's screams for that matter.

Melanie's on her back, a jagged circle of blood blossoming across her chest. She's making a sound between a rasp and a gurgle. 911. Damn, my phone's in the car. She's still wearing the Hermès pouch. I open it and take out her phone. When I get the passcode screen, I jab my finger at the emergency button and give the operator the details.

My first aid training didn't cover gunshot wounds. All I

can think to do is apply pressure to the wound until the paramedics arrive.

I take off my jacket, bunch it up and press down on the wound.

I feel the reaction settle in and I start to tremble.

Melanie looks so helpless, like a child. As much as I despise what she has done, I feel so, so sorry for her. Nobody deserves this. I think of her rather stern mother in Langley. Despite the rift between them, she will be devastated if she loses her daughter permanently.

I can't take my hands away to wipe my eyes.

I press harder and pray I'm doing the right thing.

43

CAL

A dry is the last to arrive, Jason by her side, his arm protectively encircling her shoulder. We all shuffle around the table so they can squeeze in. Adry gets a big hug from Lucy who is sitting next to her. She gives a pixie smile to Nick. "I'm putting in an expense report for a new jacket," she says.

"You've earned it," he says.

"You did amazing work, Adry," Zeke says.

She smiles and shrugs while Jason beams proudly.

"How did you know Micah was going to be at the station when the gang picked up the drugs?" he asks.

"Bitcoin," she says and sweeps her gaze at all of us. "Criminals love using Bitcoin to buy and sell their stuff. I couldn't stop wondering why Melanie and the Russians were using cash. It was really bugging me. Normally when doing a drug deal, the two parties meet, the buyer inspects the merchandise and sends the bitcoin payment on his phone. They wait a minute or two for the transaction to get added to the blockchain and then the seller hands over the drugs and they all disappear into the woodwork. When I saw her texting, it came to me. Who was she texting? It had to be Micah. They were frightened of the Russians and didn't want to meet them face-to-face. Plus she didn't trust them not to rip her off. So she devised the dead-drop plan. She arranged for the dead-drop location to be where she could observe it. As soon as Antonov exchanged the keys, she grabbed her key and went to pick up the money. If it was all there, she texted Micah and he put the drugs in the locker."

"Yes but how?" Zeke says. "Those lockers only have one key and Antonov had it. How could Micah open the locker to put the drugs in?"

"That's what I said," Nick echoes.

"I have no idea," she says.

The server comes over and takes Adry's and Jason's drink orders. I order another Flagship IPA and several plates of various appys for us to nibble

When she leaves, I say, "I know how he did it."

They all look at me.

"How?" Nick says.

I grin at him and paraphrase one of his favourite lines, "Listen and learn." I wait for his grunt before I continue. "I watched Yuri Antonov pick up the drugs at the station today. He opened a locker and there was a key inside which he used to open a second locker which held the drugs. I figure when Micah got the go-ahead from his sister, he put the drugs in the second locker. He then took the key from that locker and slipped it through the front of the locker for which Antonov had the key. After the arrests had been made, I checked the lockers at the station. They have air slats in the doors and they are just wide enough to slip a key through. I'm guessing the Kerrisdale pool is the same."

"Now that's clever," Lucy says.

"A bit too clever," I say. "It was their undoing."

"How do you figure?" she asks.

"The first time, at the Kerrisdale pool, when Antonov opened the first locker and found a key to the second locker, he must have worked out what they were doing. He realized that they could rip him off at any time. So the second time, he had his lieutenants wait at the dead-drop point and the pick-up point, with instructions to follow and kill Melanie—who was the brains behind the whole thing—and kidnap Micah so that he could be forced to manufacture the drugs under the gang's control. Micah and Melanie may be smart in lots of ways but they couldn't match wits with Antonov and his gang."

"Why do you think Antonov agreed to do the dead-drop thing in the first place?" Lucy asks. "He couldn't have really trusted Micah and Melanie."

"I can guess the answer to that," Nick says. "With Micah out of prison, he wanted to get his hands on all the crystal meth that Micah could manufacture. He went along with Melanie's plan the first time because he didn't have an option."

The server brings our food and drinks.

"Does anyone know how Melanie is doing?" Adry asks.

"Yeah," Nick says. "I had a debrief with Dom Dixon an hour or so ago. She's out of surgery and in the ICU. They have an officer posted outside. When she is well enough to understand, the officer will read her her rights, place her under arrest and handcuff her to her bed."

I think I'll take the time to visit her in VGH. Not just to gloat but also to see if she's wearing the tennis bracelet she stole from the jewellery store in Oakridge. I would love to return it to Davis Fredericks, the owner-manager.

"Also, they've got Micah, Yuri Antonov, and his house-sized sidekick in the cells at Cambie. The assassin, who Adry took down, is handcuffed to a bed in the Orthopaedic ward at VGH."

"Do you think Micah will go back to jail for murdering Kitana?" Adry asks around a honey-garlic chicken wing.

"Unfortunately not," I say. "Eric Street's membership in the Rasul Brigade has forever tarnished the DNA evidence."

"I don't think it matters," Nick says. "Dom told me that in the house on Union Street, where Micah and Melanie were living, there was a well-equipped meth lab in the basement. It had Micah's fingerprints all over it. He'll be going back to Kent for a good few years."

"He's in for a tough time if they send him to Kent. His buddy Drozdov a.k.a. Blackbird won't be protecting him this time around. If they send him to Millhaven instead, he'll be no better off." I almost feel sorry for him. Almost.

We sit in silence for a while, enjoying the fine food and drink at the Kingston.

A question springs into my mind.

"Nick, you said you had some other business with Steve. What was that?"

Nick takes a deep breath. "He offered me a job."

"Doing what?"

"It's kind of a management position. They call it a case manager. I'd be managing and mentoring the newer detectives. It's all the excitement of the job with none of the dangers."

Adry breaks the shocked silence. "You're not going to take it are you?"

We all hold our breath as he looks at each of us in turn.

His face is deadly serious. "It's a no-brainer," he says. "It's good money *and* I keep my pension."

None of us has Nick's management skills. The firm without him won't last a year.

"So you accepted Steve's offer?" I ask.

Five long seconds pass.

He grins. "Hell no. I figured that if he thought he had a chance of hiring me, it might make it easier for me to get information from him on the Micah Weston case. And it did."

His grin turns into laughter. "You guys! You didn't actually think I'd quit did you?"

A collective sigh envelops the table.

"I can't believe you fell for it. Look what we've just done. We handed a terrorist group over to CSIS and the RCMP. We took a pretty evil drug gang off the streets. We thought we righted a wrong, but when we discovered we were wrong, we re-righted it. Not too bad for a few weeks' work." He lifts his glass of bourbon. "Cheers."

"Cheers," everybody echoes.

And like a floodgate has opened, we all start chatting and laughing about everything under the sun except our work. As I look around the group, the thought of going back to SFU doesn't feel right anymore.

This is where I belong.

AFTERWORD

Thank you for reading *Jailed*. Reviews are the life blood of an independent author. If you have a minute to do a review on Amazon, it would be *really* appreciated. Also, a review at Goodreads or Bookbub is always appreciated.

If this is your first Cal Rogan book and you would like to read more, the other books in the series are:
Junkie (Cal Rogan Mysteries Book 1)
Oboe (Cal Rogan Mysteries Book 2)
Lockstep (Cal Rogan Mysteries Book 3)
Three (Cal Rogan Mysteries Book 4)
Cabal (Cal Rogan Mysteries Book 5)
Captive (Cal Rogan Mysteries Book 6)

All are available in paperback and large-print paperback from Amazon.

ABOUT THE AUTHOR

Hi. I am a former software developer, turned actor, turned author. The Cal Rogan mysteries are set in Vancouver Canada and, I hope, reflect the best and worst of the city. If you would like to know more about my views on the drug scene, publishing and writing, or would like to contact me:

My website: robertpfrench.com.

Facebook: facebook.com/robertpfrenchauthor